PATH

OF

THUNDER

Mike Green

Peacemaker Productions, LLC

Peacemaker Productions, LLC
Post Office Box 2722
Ponte Vedra Beach, FL 32204-2722

Visit our web site at www.peaceproduct.net

Manufactured in the United States of America.

ISBN: 978 – 0 – 692 – 00162 - 2

On the cover is an Armenian Katchkar. These symbols are commonly found on ancient headstones and they represent, among other things, the vitality of the Armenian people.

To my fellow peacemakers
who have endured the heat at
'the tip of the spear' –
this book is for you.

Thanks for your service.

PATH
OF
THUNDER

CHAPTER

1

"Father, wait!"

Aria Palestinio flew down the brick steps of her apartment building and into the dark, empty streets of Baku, hurrying to catch up before her father got too far along on his walk home. What she intended to be a quiet dinner had turned into a disagreeable exchange, and he had rushed out the door after only a quick kiss on the cheek and a terse "I'll see you soon." As soon as she was alone, she felt miserable about being so difficult.

Of course she understood why he insisted on staying in Baku. But she still worried. Azerbaijan's capital city had become so dangerous with the recent rise of Islamic militancy and the violence that went with it. Her father loved Baku as much as he loved his native Italy. Yet, when she had asked for equal understanding, he demanded she leave the city: if not for Italy, at least for her uncle's place in the mountains. She turned both options down. She would not leave him now, not when his mind seemed so troubled. World-renowned archeologist or not, he was still her beloved father. She would leave, but not without him.

The occasional streetlights gave only enough light to keep her from stumbling on the roughly paved street. She looked ahead, squinting at silhouettes that resembled his tall, slender form. Each time, she walked on.

Soon, she came to an intersection. Not seeing him there,

she quickened her step and turned the corner. What she saw stunned her. Three men were attacking him!

Frozen, she watched his frantic efforts to fight them off. When she saw one of the men make a stabbing motion into his chest, terror unlocked her vocal chords, and she opened her mouth.

Her cry caught in her throat when a black-clad man sprang from the shadows. In one graceful and deadly move, the mysterious figure reached behind his head, unsheathed a sword he carried along the length of his back, leaped forward, and drove it into the man with the knife. Then he crouched and spun, wheeling the blade into the chest of a second man who, like the first, shuddered and fell lifeless. Aria could see the streetlight glint off steel with each swift motion, and she could now hear the third attacker, who was backing up while he stammered out, "Allah be merciful!" Those were his last words.

Unaware that she'd begun a shaky stumble toward the scene, she fought for breath, trying to scream at the shadowy figure that knelt next to her father.

The man suddenly threw his head to the dark sky with a shouted curse. When his head lowered, then snapped toward her trembling form, she locked eyes with taut Asian features visible to her for the first time. His stern look gave way to recognition, and he spoke to her in accented English, "Go! Quickly! You are not safe here…. They would have killed you too!"

Out of breath, Aria watched the man recede into the shadows. Then she turned and raced away, desperately trying to numb her mind to the unthinkable.

CHAPTER

2

James Marshall sank his teeth into another succulent orange wedge. His lunchtime workout in the CIA's basement gym was invigorating, but always drained his lean frame of fluids. Now, in the quiet refuge of his cubicle, he relished the natural sugars coursing through his system while he hastily worked through the favorites list on his computer. He raced through geopolitical headlines and the score at Wrigley Field, then checked out the latest car designs until his side vision was distracted by someone at the cubicle's entrance.

"Been working out, James?" Bill Schoffner was leaning against the cubicle wall, one hand on his hip.

Schoffner's greeting was friendly, but James felt his stomach sour when he looked through the man's plastic Cheshire smile and vacant eyes. The two were both in their mid-thirties, yet Schoffner was decidedly on the CIA fast track. He *managed up* better than most and never stuck out his neck for anyone, unlike James, who never turned his back on a friend and never met a rule he didn't want to break. Three years earlier, James had asked to be moved over into the analytical side of the business. But Schoffner had recently *moved up* to the seventh floor, the domain of the CIA's most senior executives and where at least a minimal level of ring kissing was required; something James would never do.

"Hey, Bill, how've you been?" James offered a hand and forced smile.

"Your Cubs doing okay this year?" Schoffner asked, noting James' lucky baseball cap on top of a nearby file cabinet.

"Best team in the league. What brings you trolling around these parts?"

Schoffner paused, as if to make note of James' lack of deference. He then leaned over and whispered, "DDO wants to talk to you. Something's up." The DDO was Deputy Director of Operations, the senior man directly responsible for all CIA undertakings around the world.

James kept his face a blank. Inside, his gut twisted, something that hadn't happened since his active duty as a Naval Reserve Intelligence Officer in the wake of 9/11. Two years roaming around between wars in the Middle East had been enough for him. He had lost some good friends there, and paid his own share of dues. These things were quietly acknowledged around the building. But the only reason the head of operations could possibly want to speak to him was to get him back into the field.

"P.R. wants me?" he said. "Now?" Schoffner nodded a response that James interpreted as a summons. "Well, I guess I'd better get properly dressed if I'm going *upstairs*."

Schoffner nodded to James' gym bag on the floor next to his chair. "I'll wait."

Minutes later, the two headed to the elevator while James put on his coat and straightened his tie. And as the doors closed on the small space, that little steel box became even smaller.

* * *

The briefing room door adjacent to the DDO's office opened, and the man himself entered. "Come on in, James, have a seat," he said with a friendly wave. Schoffner left them alone with a salutatory nod to their boss, ignoring James' own call of goodbye.

James lowered himself into an overstuffed leather chair, his eyes scanning the souvenirs placed neatly around the room. A visitor could readily see that P.R. Nicholson was a die-hard operations guy who had traveled the world and made his mark on it. James respected P.R.'s thirty-plus years of experience, but his admiration stemmed more from the man's earthy, gritty personality. Both of them had that edge, something that could only be earned in a tough get-it-done environment, and it garnered their mutual respect.

P.R. settled into his seat, pulled two cigars from his humidor, and held one out, an offer James politely declined. P.R. lit up his stogie. The smoke wafted up into an air-conditioning vent as he continued to work the lighter. The ceiling unit actually worked quite well; there was no evidence of 'cigar' in the outer offices, so only a few people knew about his misdemeanor violation of federal law. Those who did would say nothing. Political correctness had its limits.

"You've been with us now, what, eight years?" P.R. asked.

"Yes, sir, eight years in March."

"I've got a job I want you to do."

James shifted his weight in his seat, exhaling softly as he strained to be polite. "Sir, … what can I do for you?"

"You have a Naval Academy classmate … Steve Kranzer. Served with you in VFA-81, right?"

P.R.'s voice now held a somber tone that put James on alert. "Yes, sir," he said, straightening in his chair. "We were roommates on the carrier. And we've kept in loose touch over the past several years. He's currently our naval attaché in Morocco."

P.R. nodded and took a pull on his cigar, watching the smoke trail rise to the ceiling to be sucked into the air-conditioning vent. "No easy way to say this. Kranzer was killed a few days ago in Tangier. His body was found in the surf a few miles south of the city limits."

James winced, trying to absorb the shock of the news, and instinctively rubbed a hairline scar above his eyebrow.

Noting his silence, P.R. continued. "A shame. It was supposed to have been his twilight tour. Only had two months to go. Rotten luck. I know you and he were friends." He leveled dark eyes on James. "I'd like you to pick this up. You knew Kranzer better than anybody here in this building, and … he was on to something."

James leaned forward, his hazel eyes smoldering coals. "Sir, how do you know that?"

"First, it appears to have been a contract hit. A sniper." James nodded but then looked at the floor, unable to hold P.R.'s gaze, fury welling up inside him."

"Second," P.R. went on, "Kranzer had been having an escalating dialogue with a guy in Baku … Azerbaijan."

The country of Azerbaijan was little known to most, but the region was familiar, especially to the CIA and U.S. military. Bordered by the Caspian Sea, Azerbaijan was a crossroads for Eastern Europe and Southwest Asia. With Russia on its northern border and Iran to the south, the nation of mostly cultural Muslims was struggling with democracy. And like any emerging democracy, Azerbaijan suffered serious growing pains—deadly growing pains.

"We've taken a preliminary look at Kranzer's cell phone and email records, and there was definitely something there," P.R. was saying. "The couple of weeks before he was killed, he traded a number of phone calls with one Davide Palestinio, an Italian archeologist who was apparently working on a site in a cave somewhere in Azerbaijan."

James was still leaning forward, trying not to let his fury erupt before P.R. His earlier trepidation about fieldwork was gone. He didn't want to lose the chance to get to the *who* and *why*. Particularly the *who* of Kranzer's death. "Have we spoken to him, sir?" he asked. "Palestinio?"

"Unfortunately, he's also been killed. Separate incident, but …," P.R. sighed. "I'll let you have a look at the file: police reports, some interesting observations from the FBI teams sent to both sites. We're getting some background on him as we speak, along with forensics on Kranzer's computer … We should know more this afternoon."

James' head jerked up. "So we don't know yet what this is about?"

"No. But my gut tells me it's something major." P.R. leaned

back and took another long pull. "That's why I want you to pick this up where the good Commander Kranzer left off."

He tapped ashes into a nearly empty soda can, and now it was his turn to lean forward, eyebrows lifting. "But I will say this. I don't think Kranzer's death had anything to do with Morocco. The real story has to be in Azerbaijan. Based on what we've put together so far, we think that archeologist stumbled into something big, and he was calling Kranzer for advice. But that's it."

P.R.'s expression then went blank, as if to invite James to speak. James shook his head, sighed, and leaned back in his chair. "It doesn't matter where this trail takes me," he said at last. "I'm on it. What else is there, sir?"

"Nothing more I can tell you about the investigation … you'll see what else we have in the file." P.R. picked up a folder on his desk and began scanning through it. "This will take you to Azerbaijan. We'll use your Naval Reserve status as a cover, put you in the Embassy in Baku as a defense attaché."

"I can do that. But why involve the Defense Intelligence Agency at all? I'd be more effective if no one knows I'm in the country."

"Actually, it's also because they need the warm body. The regular guy rolled out last week, and DIA hasn't found a replacement for him yet because of … demands for people in the Middle East. So you might have another small assignment or two while you're there. As a reservist, you can go in with diplomatic credentials without making a lot of waves."

P.R.'s expression changed to uncharacteristic worry. "Please don't make too many waves over there."

James grinned and gave an understanding nod. P.R. waited for a yes, didn't get one, and gave a nod of his own before continuing. "I've been trying to beef up our presence in Baku lately, anyway. We're actually pretty thin. The station chief job is vacant, and we just moved a capable midgrade case officer over from Cairo to help out. Name's Raffi Rahman. And here's where it gets really interesting. We're also tracking what appears to be an insurgent build-up in the area. And *that's* what's captured my attention."

James looked away. P.R. noticed, leaned back, and studied him. "I know that's a cold thing to say. But they—whoever *they* are—wouldn't whack a diplomat unless they had a good reason. If we're going to find out what happened to your friend, we have to follow *all* the leads. That buildup could very well be one."

James didn't answer, and with a sigh, P.R. continued. "I'll say it again. Based on a few clues we have so far, there's probably a connection between these two murders and the insurgency. And because of that, I'm personally running this operation. You'll be reporting directly to me."

"When do I start?" The question came out neutral, the force roiling behind it anything but.

"Soon." P.R. tossed a manila envelope across the desk. "Tuesday afternoon."

James grabbed the envelope and glanced through its contents. Among other things, a black diplomatic passport and an airline ticket. He caught himself and forced a faint smile as he got up to leave. "Tuesday? Not soon enough."

The two men shook hands but didn't need to speak further. They both knew the drill. The good news for James was that he had a guy behind him who would move heaven and earth to support him and his mission, and who didn't care much about the rules either, as long as the job was done.

CHAPTER

3

"The girl has disappeared."

Chairman Sun stopped pacing his exquisitely furnished office, and his stocky, five-foot-eight-inch frame stood tensely motionless, waiting for his oil minister's explanation. He and Wan Chang were alone now, but he had just heard other bad news from a gathering of China's top oil executives, who all said the same thing: China's demand for oil would continue to leap ahead of supply over the foreseeable future, in spite of the global economic downturn.

And now this news. He didn't turn to look at the cringing man who had braced for a response. Instead he looked out over Tiananmen Square, watching the gaggle of international oilmen exit the building and begin their march back to their offices around Beijing.

"China's future may depend on this plan...." He turned slowly toward the cowering minister. "And you would risk its failure?"

Chang bowed his head.

"How did this happen?"

"Some unexpected events," Chang said, his head still lowered. "Dr. Palestinio left early, as our team was approaching his daughter's home."

"Our team?"

Chang corrected himself. "The Iranians. They killed him on the street shortly after he left her."

"Sloppy." Sun shook his head in disapproval. "And the girl? How could the Iranian's have possibly *lost* her?"

"The Iranians were attacked by another group before they could get to her."

"Who?"

"We don't know. Perhaps the Japanese. Based on the … ferocity of the attack, the Iranians were killed by a team of expert swordsmen."

"Swordsmen? Swords?" Sun said, his tone sharper now. "Do we automatically equate swords with the Japanese? And didn't the Iranians have *guns*?"

"Yes, but they must have been caught off guard in the dark. A group of Japanese businessmen arrived in Baku three weeks ago. We found no business reason why they should be in Baku. Therefore, we believe they are with the Japanese Special Forces."

Now more than ever, Chairman Sun felt the weight of all China on his shoulders as he began pacing again. He wore a western business suit, a not-so-new departure from the ways of his Mao-jacketed predecessors, the original communists who came to power in a war-weary China on a platform of ideology and a promise to end corruption. Today, he was both sustained and threatened by China's growing capitalism and the new brand of corruption that went with it.

Chang misjudged the chairman's restlessness for a desire for more information and said, "That was yesterday, and we have not seen the girl since."

"Why wasn't I told about this sooner?" Sun recognized the agitation in his voice, but didn't care.

"I learned of this myself only an hour ago, Mr. Chairman."

"Find her and take care of her. We must not draw any unwanted attention. Let me see the file again."

Chang fumbled with his briefcase and produced a folder that was snatched from his hands. Sun pulled out his bifocals as he seated himself at a small conference table, mentally trying to get past his annoyance and move on to other parts of the plan. He paged through until he plucked out a formal photograph of an odious-looking man.

"Ivan Mitrofanov?"

"Yes, Mr. Chairman."

The answer brought a sigh. He didn't need to see the photograph to be certain of one thing: This man clearly was not one to be trusted; an honorable man would not sell out his own people. But honor and expediency were sometimes incompatible. If Sun had his way, this rogue would soon be the first president of a new country. "We can control Mitrofanov? You're certain of this?"

Chang could finally give a positive answer. "He is ours. Once he is president, his country's oil is assuredly ours as well."

Sun continued through the file and then looked up at the minister with another photograph in his hand. "I have great confidence in General Lu's ability to carry out this operation. Tell him, and the general staff, that I want a close eye on Mr. Mitrofanov, and that we need to move with great care in our next steps. We have coached this scoundrel extensively for his upcoming United Nations address, and we are too close to success to have any more foolish mistakes."

He tapped the picture of Mitrofanov in thought. "And you … you must keep me better informed of *any* major developments! That is all."

When dismissed, Chang retreated with a final bow. The chairman ignored his leaving. Already, he was contemplating his circumstances. China's growth in industrial might was like that of Japan's in the early 20th century. But one key difference was China's subtle approach to wresting control of resources. Unlike the militaristic Japan of eighty years ago, China was much more effective, if silent—like a giant walking in the night.

He reflected on the panic he had just seen in the oil executives' faces, and their suggestion that oil was quickly becoming *the* limiting factor on the new China. China's large landmass allowed them to mine for coal: dirty, but abundant. But mining accidents cost thousands more lives each year. That did not concern him, but so many deaths brought unwanted attention from the rest of the world. Natural gas was to have been the remedy, but market prices caused their contracts with Australia, Iran, and Indonesia to fall through. And the Siberian gas pipeline from Russia was years away from completion. The major oil setback had come when the Americans invaded Iraq in 2003, ending China's negotiations to develop two of Iraq's promising oilfields. And now he was told that the current low demand for oil was but a moment in time compared to how long it took to develop new fields. The current recession would be over in a year or two, and demand would come back almost as quickly as it had abated.

But there was fresh hope. He picked up the folder again and flipped through it. No one suspected that the key to so much could be held by a small, nearly forgotten area like Nagorno Karabakh, which by anyone's account had no oil at all. At least until that archeologist had stumbled across an ancient scientific discovery and made the fatal mistake of talking to the Americans. And thanks to the incompetence of the Iranians, the man's daughter was free to talk to anyone she wished. He couldn't discount the possibility that her father had confided in her, so she had to be found and stopped from ever talking again.

He caught himself looking out over Tiananmen Square once again, thinking of the plan that he and his inner circle were now putting into motion. It was actually quite brilliant. China, using its seat on the United Nations Security Council to push for a free and completely independent Nagorno Karabakh, could not be reasonably opposed. This would highlight China's stature as an emergent global leader: yet another example of its expanding influence. At the same time, as an independent nation, Karabakh could make energy agreements with any nation it chose.

It must be done quietly, he reminded himself, *a giant*

of stealth.

A light rain again distracted his thoughts. Out on the Square, throngs of people, some on foot, some on bicycles, rushed to escape the weather. He quickly abandoned their capricious plight when he recalled that the United States alone held enough power to foil the plan. The United States—a country that continued to destroy and then steadily reinvent itself politically—a maze of constant and bewildering change that often puzzled him.

No matter. America was a country resigned to reactive planning, and to fighting political battles against itself, while its enemies lurked at its door. One day, when Americans found themselves in a weakened and confused state of anarchy, all China would have to do would be to let the United States collapse under the weight of its own decadent bureaucracy, something that may already be close at hand. Then, an unopposed China would quietly fill the vacuum. And if this plan succeeded, China would soon control all the oil it needed to become the world's dominant superpower.

But, in spite of this sound reasoning, the chairman could not escape a vague, shapeless doubt that nagged at his consciousness and haunted him. To work, his plan required two things. One, he must confirm the presence of oil under the Caspian Sea. Two, he must be certain of complete secrecy. To ensure this, the girl must be found and silenced.

CHAPTER

4

Aria welcomed her uncle's comforting embrace, yet her heart still screamed for justice. The night before, the news of her father's murder had sent shockwaves throughout the countryside around their family home. Now, friends and relatives mourned with her. Her brother, Themieux, had sent word he would be there the following day. If the man who had tried to save her father was right, his killers were now looking for her.

But for the moment, in this tiny, isolated enclave nestled in Karabakh's Caucasus Mountains, she was safe. The afternoon was sunny, carrying the heavy scents of fresh earth, hay, and wildflowers that mingled with aromas from the luncheon that had been served on the front porch. Some of the village elders lingered there in quiet conversation. Aria and her Uncle Lev had moved inside for privacy. Now, they stood in his expansive living room, trying to comprehend. He had mourned the loss of Aria's mother, his only sister, not long ago. And now, the man she had loved … a man he also had grown to love as a brother … was gone.

"Uncle Lev, *why*?" She asked the question rhetorically; it had gone unanswered last night, when she spat the words at his hard, worn features in misdirected anger. And there would be no answer now. She pulled at her long dark hair, blinking back fresh tears from eyes red and swollen from a night of fitful sleep. She knew Uncle Lev could only offer comfort. Would there ever be an answer? His touch was clumsy holding her, but tenderness exuded from the swarthy middle-aged man's callused fingertips as he lovingly caressed her face, then her hair.

"Your mother's hair was so much like yours," Lev said, his voice breaking. "When we were small, your grandmother would plait it. 'Too wild!' she would say. And now, I look at your hair and remember how your mother would undo the plaits the moment she was out of our mother's sight."

Aria tried to listen, tried to appreciate his attempt to distract her, but desperation pushed her sorrow toward anger again, and her mind launched into an examination of recent events, from scene to scene, conversation to conversation, searching for clues that would unveil her father's killers.

In spite of his mild tone, she knew Lev's thoughts were also full of unsettling events—not just this tragedy, but also events in the Karabakh parliament, where he was an elected member.

He gently pushed her away from his shoulder, holding her at arm's length so he could meet her eyes with his own. "My dearest niece, there are forces in motion that we don't understand, but I still don't think Davide's murder is connected to them."

Aria wasn't so sure. Karabakh was a tiny country where few things happened, including murder, that didn't have something to do with politics. When she'd visited her father on various digs, even her very presence had caused her to run afoul of those politics. Protests that she, a young woman, was present among the mostly male crews often forced her father to cut her visits short. Her turbulent mind now assessed her Uncle Lev. She had often listened to his impassioned speeches about why this upstart, Mitrofanov, a Russian who had married into a southern community of Karabakh, had suddenly become a powerful man. Father's murder *must* somehow be a part of all of the confusion right now!

Allah be merciful! The last words of Father's attacker floated through her head, and she tried again to convince Uncle Lev that the senseless religious killings that had troubled nearby Baku, Azerbaijan's capital, must be related to it. Islamic militancy had been on the rise since last year's elections, but more so in the past couple of months.

In reply, her uncle said the same thing he'd said before: "The corruption of man has always been with us, and it will always be so. And again, your father abhorred politics, dear. You know that. Just as much as your own brother lives and breathes for politics…" He sighed. "Albeit in his own way. I don't know why Davide was killed so horribly. I am just grateful that the killers never saw you."

"Then what about the Asian man who tried to help?" she blurted. "How did he *know* we were in danger? Why would someone who clearly isn't a local be involved at all?"

This time, Lev had no answer.

The more she struggled to understand, the more questions arose in her tortured mind. She leaned into his side. In response, he stroked her shoulder and stared sadly through the window, fixing his eyes on the distant Caucasus Mountains, which had stood sentry over his family for countless generations. "As when your dear mother left us," he whispered, "justice, as always, must rest with God."

Aria wasn't so certain of that, either. And her mind continued toiling.

* * *

Outside on the porch, four octogenarians, all village elders, were deeply concerned with not only Davide's murder, but also the spate of similarly violent events going on all around them. Kasim was especially bothered; while he hadn't been as close to Aria's father as Lev had been, Lev was his nephew, who had now lost both his sister and his beloved brother-in-law. There was little Kasim could do about that, except try to keep the situation around their grieving as normal as possible.

And now, this group has had enough serious talk, he decided. It was time to break it up a little. He had just finished a delicious meal, capped off with a final piece of *jingala* bread made by his niece, finer than any you would find at any of

Karabakh's *shukas*. Yes, it was time to talk of other things while their food happily digested.

He slid his stool away from the table and pulled out his pipe. The others noticed, and with nods of understanding, did the same as they settled into chairs away from most of the small crowd. These four proud veterans of the Great Patriotic War, known to westerners as World War II, governed this small village in the northern mountains of Karabakh, on the northwestern edge of Azerbaijan. With only one hundred and sixty villagers, the people didn't need much by way of governance. Even so, every Tuesday at lunch they conducted their most important business: a little gossip mixed with some grand tales, and grand disagreement, about the war against the Nazis. Consensus was unthinkable in this forum, yet their gentle chiding of each another never stepped out of unwritten bounds. Lately though, the dark topic of recent local politics was usually where they ended up, in a state of mixed emotions with frustration, sadness, and anger topping the list.

When the conversation became a little more heated than he cared for, Kasim chimed in, knowing the subject was serious but still thinking it was time for some levity. "Would you muddy the toes of your boots to carry Boris' dirty argument, Vigen?"

Vigen snorted. "What would you know, Kasim? You still believe that Alexander was a Turk in disguise."

"One of your relatives, Vigen?" Kasim said, adding a knowing nod that always baited the man more. "Was your uncle not from Istanbul?"

"Yes, but … you old goat, you know well that he was Armenian!"

Kasim smiled as he drew on his pipe, satisfied that he had edged them away from their morose mood.

Boris began adjusting his belt as a prelude to his tirade. "The Azeris never should have invaded this place. Our own neighbors turned into betrayers at the first opportunity. The massacres that followed are their fault!"

"Ahh, no, no, no," Kasim said, continuing his struggle for

comic relief. "You cannot find a face to give tribute to that story. The Azeris only invaded because of your wife's cooking."

Boris' eyes popped open. "She has been dead for years!"

Kasim grinned, then looked at Vigen. "See what I mean? They must have *really* not liked her cooking."

"You are an old goat, Vigen," he said, drawing out the words. "You know, we *all* know, the Russians started all of this. Or …" He turned his head to the side and frowned. "Or *was* it the Russians? Didn't they once send you a gift from Moscow, Vigen?"

Vigen stared at Kasim's face, which was colored with feigned innocence. "You are a sly one, Kasim," he said. "You have always been sly. I think that you lie awake at night rehearsing these conversations. I bought something from a catalogue at the GUM Department Store. Once. That's all!"

Kasim maintained his innocence. "After your family's Turkish brandy, Vigen, those are the nights that I lie awake."

At that moment, a jet could be seen flying high over the area. "Look, another one of those Turkish fighter planes," Boris said

Kasim peered upward. "No, Boris. Iranian."

"The Iranians don't have such jets, you Cossack!"

He lowered his gaze to meet his friend's. "You son of a peasant, if you weren't such an old man, I would beat you."

"And if you weren't my Christian brother, I would smash your pipe."

Chuckling, Boris and Vigen slowly got up, made a few parting comments to adjourn their meeting, left their outdoor office on the porch and went their separate ways for a nap.

Sattar, who'd been quiet this afternoon, looked over at his younger brother as soon as they were alone. He had a look on his face that Kasim knew well, but hadn't seen for many years. Well over sixty, in fact. It had been that many since the Great Patriotic War.

"The path of thunder," Sattar said suddenly. "Do you feel it too, Kasim?"

Sattar referred to an old play on words they had bantered about in their difficult, wartime-ravaged youth. An Azeri composer named Karayev had written a ballet named "The Path of Thunder." But to Sattar and Kasim, growing up in an era where a single bomb or bullet could end one's life in an instant, the title had become the place where cultures collided like clouds, leaving a thunderous wake of turbulence and misery. And they decided that to know the *sound* of that thunder, and the signs that precede it well before that happens, was to survive a coming storm.

To survive…

The brothers continued their eye contact until Kasim voiced his thought. "Yes, I do feel the thunder, my brother. Yes, I do. I fear we are headed into some very troubled times."

CHAPTER

5

"Definitely a professional hit. Your friend never knew what was coming."

James nodded in agreement with the FBI agent, who was giving him a tour of Kranzer's murder site, an isolated spot just south of Tangier. No traces of the killer remained, if there ever were any. The location the sniper had chosen was obvious, though, by the smoothed-over sand. No other place in the tree line was completely smooth like this.

"Handheld compressed air," the agent said with a grim smile. "Just like the ones used to make noise at a football game. Only this can of air was much quieter. We've gone over this site with a fine-toothed comb, and nothing—no spent shell casings, gum wrappers, hair, cigarette butts, spit. Nothing. Not even an eyelash."

He shook his head and, for the first time, met James' eyes. "When a guy goes to this kind of trouble to wipe the trail clean, especially in such a desolate area with no witnesses, we really have a hard time chasing it down. No bullet for ballistics. It went clean through with a modest amount of tumbling, but it's somewhere out there." He pointed out to sea, then dug deep into a bag of potato chips.

As he had in P.R.'s office, James rubbed the scar above his eyebrow, remembering the bar fight where he and Steve had stood together against four drunk Dutch sailors. Steve had saved his butt that night. "So what's the next step?" he said. The question was merely a courtesy. He knew the only thing left was following the paper trail.

"The Moroccans are cooperating. Lots of good information there. Possible suspects, recent large-dollar cash transactions, who recently came and went out of the country. Unfortunately, the only person of interest profiled around the date of the murder is a Chinese diplomat. He showed up around ten days ago, left yesterday morning. We're digging into that."

"You do that," he said. "What about the email trail?"

"Kranzer's hard drive is toast. Best we can tell, someone sent him a Trojan horse, activated right around the time of his murder. Pretty slick stuff. Got through our firewalls undetected. Fortunately, certain emails, because of their keyword content, were automatically archived on a backup server. And get this … practically every other word was *oil*."

James had been looking at the view, but now his head jerked toward the agent's "Really?"

"Yep. About six months ago this archeologist, Davide Palestinio, came across some on one of his digs in Azerbaijan. Anyway, Commander Kranzer knew this Palestinio guy because Kranzer was an amateur archeologist. They met on a dig a few years ago while he was stationed in Sicily. He advised Palestinio to send a sample to London to be tested. More out of curiosity than anything else. Time went by, and I guess they sort of forgot about it."

The archeologist's name, James instantly recalled from P.R.'s briefing. But not one word had been mentioned about oil, or about Kranzer's interest in archeology. Something Kranzer had never shared with him, either. He felt a finger of guilt creep into his gut. "Does my DDO have this information?"

"It was on his desk this morning, along with others on our usual distribution."

"So what's the rest of the story on the oil sample?"

The agent stopped walking, crumpled his now empty bag, and looked around. He turned back to James, embarrassed. "Guess I was thinking I was at Yellowstone. Trash cans everywhere there."

James nodded, fighting the urge to shout at the man to hurry. This might be the connection he and P.R. and the entire CIA had missed.

"Okay, here's where it gets really interesting. The sample went missing, *along with* the technician assigned to the project. Our London office was able to pull together some information on the oil, but the meat and potatoes of it are gone. Just gone. All we've got is in the files I gave your agency this morning."

"So what about the Chinese diplomat you mentioned," James said. "The one who disappeared. Is he a suspect?"

The agent smiled ruefully. "Closest we have right now. I mean, think about it. Here we are in Morocco, and a Chinese diplomat shows up and then scoots. Definitely of interest."

"How about the technician?" James said. "Is that person accounted for?"

"As much as she can be. A week after getting the sample, she suddenly had to fly home to Beijing to be with her sick mother. *And* she took all the test data with her."

"So if all this happened months ago, what's going on, and why now?"

"We think things heated up recently, when Palestinio and Kranzer brought it up again and started talking about going to another lab for more tests. The trail ends there."

The two men were approaching their vehicles, where they had left the three-man Moroccan police contingent. James noted that they all carried Heckler & Koch MP5 assault rifles. Since Moroccans spoke French as a second language, he dusted off his parlance with an obvious question. "*Que'sce que c' est ce ci? Pour quoi avez-vous des arms a repetition?* (What is this here? Why do you have these assault weapons?)"

"*Pour les sanglier.* (For wild boar.)"

The FBI agent looked at the officers, then at James. "What's that?"

James couldn't resist. He pointed to the weapons. "Al Qaeda. Never know when they'll show up."

The agent's eyes shifted, then widened, and then quickly

assumed an all-knowing look of false confidence. "Yeah, I ... uh ... I hear that there are several cells in Tangier and Casablanca."

The sergeant was the only one of the three Moroccans who spoke any English, and he and James shared a sly smile, which grew into restrained laughter when they realized that the FBI agent didn't know he'd been the target of some subtle humor.

James couldn't resist picking on an unseasoned agent, although this one did seem to have excellent crime scene and forensic skills. But, he lacked the *nose*, the instinctive feel for the scent of the trail. When James got around guys like him, he realized just how much fieldwork he had behind him.

"I've got to make a phone call," he said, and gave the agent a low wave. "Thanks for showing me around. See you back at the office."

"Are you sure you're okay out here alone?" the agent asked, opening the door of his vehicle and tossing in the potato chip bag. It bounced off the dashboard and landed in the passenger seat.

"I think I'll be okay." He gave the sergeant a friendly salute, which was returned with another smile.

Once the agent left, James walked down to where the surf rhythmically pounded the shore. He looked from side to side and as far he could see, but there was no trace of mankind. No condos, no sunbathers, no traffic, just nature at its best.

"I can see why you made a point to jog here, ole buddy," he whispered into the breeze coming off the Atlantic Ocean. "But that's the kind of predictability that got you killed, my friend."

He pulled out his cell phone. P.R. had been right. There was no story here. Kranzer's killer had to be in Azerbaijan, or linked to Azerbaijan, and that's where he was going next.

"James Marshall here, sir. Are you ready to go secure?"

"Hey, James, let's do it." P.R. initiated a scrambling sequence that ensured their conversation couldn't be monitored.

"I'm at the beach, but there's no bikini-clad women here."

P.R. chuckled. "I just read the FBI's report. Looks like a

quiet oil-play to me."

"That's the impression I've gotten too. It's a shame that Kranzer and Palestinio stumbled into this. But it did alert us that something rotten's going on."

"Exactly. Let's not lose sight of the silver lining here."

"I need to speak to someone who knows all about oil in Azerbaijan."

"One step ahead of you. I've got a guy in Cambridge who's expecting you."

James pulled the phone away, looked at it, then pressed it back to his ear. "Cambridge, *England*?"

"You got it. He's been on several scientific surveys of the area, and he's worked with us before. He can answer any question you come up with." A pause, then, "And I know you'll come up with all of them."

"Yes, sir. Send me his contact info and I'll meet with him in the morning."

"Roger that. Just one more thing." Another pause, this one longer. "Once again, I'm sorry about your friend."

"Thanks. I mean, thanks for the opportunity to handle this. I couldn't have sat on the sidelines for this one."

"That's why I selected you. Good luck."

James put the phone away and scanned the horizon as the surf continued to pound the beautiful but desolate beach. When he was four years old, his family had taken him from their home in Raleigh, North Carolina to Virginia Beach. He remembered Ocean View Amusement Park, and seafood buffets, and sightseeing. But what stood out in his mind was that wondrous moment when he had looked out over the Atlantic Ocean for the first time. While his siblings tried to overcome their fear of the waves washing up on the sand, he could only think of one thing: what could possibly be on the other side of that great expanse. And now, as a man, he stood looking back across from the other side.

Back then, he never could have foreseen that someone would kill one of his friends for a secret, right here, in the very spot his young imagination had struggled to see. Unfathomable for a child, but painfully easy for the man he'd become to envision. Kranzer was shot in the back with a high-caliber rifle. The shot missed his heart by millimeters, most likely because of an unexpected gust of wind, allowing him a few extra steps to stumble into the surf and die. He would have had only a vague sense of falling forward into the water, and would have seen the world turning murky and cold as he sank into the ocean, continuing a hopeless struggle for breath.

Whoever they were, they would kill him too, and anyone else who represented a threat to whatever secret was tied to this oil.

"I'm going to avenge you, my friend," he whispered, then returned to his car.

* * *

That Wednesday morning, James ambled down a long, oak-paneled corridor, feeling like he'd walked into a mausoleum, and each of his noisy footsteps was a desecration of the dead. From what P.R. had told James, Professor Alex Denton preferred the academic purity of Cambridge, considered it a refuge from the visceral distractions of humanity, and the epicenter of pure intellectual thought. Thinking was what Denton did best, and, in his opinion, Cambridge was unquestionably the best place on Earth for it. P.R. had also mentioned that, as a petroleum geochemist, Denton really had no business being there; the curriculum afforded him no meaningful opportunity to teach.

"Funny thing is," P.R. had said with a chuckle, "Denton chose Cambridge because they still use chalkboards. You know—the kind that can be rolled aside with fresh slates underneath? The guy has to be in his mid-seventies, so he's definitely of the old school. When you see him, don't even get him started on calculators or personal computers."

When James entered Denton's office, the man barely noticed that the heavy wooden doors of the large, richly paneled classroom had opened. He was scrawling on the chalkboard in solitude. Yellow chalk dust drifted, and occasionally even flew in chunks, as his hand attempted to keep up with his soaring mind.

Slowly, he became aware of his guest, and peered over his thick glasses. "May I help you, young man?"

"Good afternoon, Professor Denton. My name is James Marshall."

Denton leaned toward him and squinted. "Ahh, yes, I've been expecting you." His voice changed from polite inquiry to excitement. "I spoke with your Mr. Nicholson again this morning, a delightful man. Please do come in."

James approached the chalkboard full of mathematical equations.

"He ran me through the purpose of your visit." Denton motioned with the chalk still in his hand. "I was just working through a problem involving the Carnot Cycle. Did you ever take thermodynamics in school?"

He had, but when he gave Denton a look that was a dramatic *Don't go there*, Denton actually laughed. "I can see that I'd be wise not to attempt to entertain you with numbers."

He smiled and shrugged. "I wouldn't know a Wenz curve from a Ouija board."

"Then you *have* applied yourself in your studies," exclaimed Denton at the mention of the Wenz curve, an engineer's tool for calculating, among other things, enthalpy in steam.

"To a degree, yes … and that would be one degree. Bachelor of Science. Actually, I had to dig deep for the Wenz curve. I nearly flunked thermodynamics at Annapolis."

Denton laughed again. "Mr. Nicholson said you were witty, and he was right. Please do sit down, young man."

They took chairs across from each other at the office's mahogany conference table. Denton's motions caused a small cloud of yellow dust to rise from his hands.

James produced a short stack of folders from a leather briefcase, folders created by the FBI. He had reviewed them on the flight to London, finding them enough to provide outline information on the samples, but not enough to reveal their secrets. "I have some data I'll leave with you to look over, Professor. Essentially, it's associated with testing conducted at the Emerson Labs in London. Oil type, viscosity measurements, those sorts of things. They were conducted on a sample from Azerbaijan."

Denton's eyes widened with interest. "No need to just leave them if you have time to hang around, as the young folks say."

At James' nod, he began leafing through the files, taking his time, peering through the lower lenses of his bifocals, silent except for occasional, sporadic grunts and mutterings. Finally, he put the last folder down. "What you have here is a fraction of the total story, my friend."

As he spoke the words, the elderly man's face held wonder … and something else that surprised James, a nearly palpable longing.

"A few months ago," Denton continued, "I had a lengthy conversation with a colleague about this very information."

Now, the professor's voice held hesitation. James decided to tread lightly. "My trip here has the potential to do a lot of good. Please, tell me about the conversation."

"These samples were sent back for testing as part of a geological expedition, one I was never made familiar with. Seems that the samples were slightly radioactive. That came to light during the testing. Just trace amounts, just enough to leave a signature."

James tried to make sense of it, but couldn't. Denton's somber face revealed nothing to help him. Finally, he asked, "Is it unusual to find such radiation in the oil from this area?"

"Yes, and no." Denton stood and walked over to a globe of the Earth nearly half his height. He slowly spun to the Caspian Sea area and tapped a yellow-chalk-stained finger on that spot. "In the late sixties, I was part of a geological survey team that studied the geophysics of the Caspian seabed. Setting the stage for future oil exploration, you see. We found radiation. Lots of it. Finding the radiation set off all sorts of red flags. For one thing, the Soviet Union was an ecological disaster."

Denton began pacing and shaking his head. "They scattered bomb-grade tritium all over the region. Tritium!"

"Why? *How* would they do something like that?" James asked.

"Through bomb tests, careless disposal. *In spite* of what was already known back then about the dangers. They even believed that nuclear explosions would increase the productivity of oilfields. Can you believe that?"

Denton's voice roiled with incredulity, and he looked at James through his thick glasses; he gazed into the distance, as if recalling vivid memories of his experiences. "Most of the members of my team developed leukemia. All dead. I expect that it was my taste for brandy that warded off any bad reaction to the radiation." He reached up to adjust his glasses and stopped speaking, as if his attempt at humor couldn't totally shake the pain of his loss.

"Professor, was there any evidence of tritium in this report?"

"No, and this is the interesting part. I said yes *and* no about whether radiation was in the sample. This is the *no* part. The Caspian Sea is actually a lake, the largest in the world. Radionuclides *naturally* abound in the region. They're collected by drainage and runoff into the lake itself. The stuff's been collected and concentrated for millions of years in the sediment of that seabed."

He went over to the globe again and located the Caspian area, his index finger trembling slightly as it traced the routes. "In our core sampling, we found mollusk fossils that were millions of years old. But they had significantly *higher* uranium levels in them than modern mollusks. It's curious, and it's certainly something that isn't talked about, but it's all very natural."

There was no stopping the professor's effusive discourse, but James was taking some good mental notes. He asked, "So these samples in question came from the seabed then, based on the radiation signature?"

"Most likely, or possibly from a site on the coast. But here's the main point. Wherever the samples came from, it seems that the people who took them had stumbled across an oilfield. Yet that wasn't the part that had me scratching my head. Oil samples are tested for lots of things. First and foremost are viscosity and gravity … to determine the quality of the oil itself. The one most intriguing to me, and to my visiting colleague as well, was the genetic fingerprint."

"You mean you can tell, just by testing, where a sample came from?"

Denton nodded. "In a similar way that testing the DNA from a skeleton's bones can reveal the race and sex of the, ah, previous owner. The genetic fingerprint of that oil sample somewhat matched that of the Dagestan area, but with some differences."

James leaned forward. "Dagestan? Where's that?"

"Oh, yes. Dagestan is one of the largest oilfields at the bottom of the Caspian seabed. But … there were three elements found with the samples, elements suggesting they had originated farther inland, up in the mountains." His head cocked to the side. "Possible, I suppose, but very unlikely. That would suggest a natural vein of seabed oil running for almost a hundred miles. It would have to be a staggering amount of oil to make a run like that!"

Enough to kill for. James winced at the thought. "You say nearly a hundred miles. Do you know where the samples themselves were found?"

"No, and not knowing has cost me many hours of sleep. Based on the elemental composition, you could identify a general area, say about fifty kilometers by fifty kilometers. That's assuming the sample did come from the mountains in the first place, not from the seabed. Strange, though …"

"Sir?"

"The man I spoke to about this … he made a point, more than once, of saying he didn't know where the samples were from."

"Tell me about this guy."

"A fellow alum from London's own Birbeck. Dr. Patrick Ho. Chinese, you see. And he did know his geochemistry. He also had a great deal of knowledge about oil. And of the Caspian Sea region, too. Especially Azerbaijan."

"What did Dr. Ho want from you … specifically?"

Denton shrugged. "What most people want from me these days. My opinion. You see, each of the three major fields of the Caspian seabed has unique characteristics. He wanted my opinion on whether it was possible that the three fields came from one source, deep beneath them."

"And your opinion is?"

"Yes indeed! Not only possible, quite likely based on the genetic signatures of the samples." The professor was visibly excited now. His eyebrows moved up and down in an odd rhythm with each impassioned sentence, punctuated by repeated use of his chalk-yellowed index finger, as if to accentuate the importance of his message. "Most intriguing thing I've come across in years. A blockbuster if you can find the source of the samples. I've been tempted to pack my bags and go looking, but I'm just too old."

"But are you willing to help us, to the degree you're able?"

Denton left the globe spinning and lowered himself back into his chair. "At your service, on one condition. It's always burned my soul that I couldn't ever get Dr. Ho to reveal where he found the sample. But I'm an old man. My expedition days are over. If I help you, and your agency does find the sample's source, you'll tell me?"

Steve Kranzer's image jumped into James' mind. Would sharing information with anyone else put them at risk? Was Dr. Denton already in danger?

"If I can," he finally said, "I will." That was as far as he was willing to go.

* * *

Later, as he cruised along the English Midlands countryside—on the left side of the road, something that he frequently had to remind himself about—James couldn't stop thinking about the oil sample. Denton's mission had become his own, if for different reasons. If they could make the connection between the oilfields based on genetics, this all might start to make sense. And maybe they'd finally have some idea of which country or entity wanted oil so badly, they'd kill to get it.

He studied his odometer, then turned down a nondescript country road and drove for another few kilometers into a thick forest. A few minutes later, he broke out of the forest and there, in front of him, was a gate with heavily armed fatigue-clad sentries wearing berets. The seven-meter-high fence that surrounded the former RAF base was topped with concertina wire, hinting at a secure location, one of only a few sites in England where James could engage in a video teleconference using a top-secret encrypted system.

Upon review of his credentials, the British guards snapped to attention.

"Will you need a map of the base, Commander?"

"No thanks, I've been here before. Carry on."

The men rendered a stiff salute, with the sergeant of the guard adding a crisp "Sahh."

Minutes later, he was ushered into a briefing room that had a wide-screen video teleconference system on the wall. They were setting up at the CIA for the briefing that P.R. had hastily arranged before James left for Azerbaijan. These briefings were invariably boring, but necessary; more than one agent's life had been saved by a random bit of briefing information.

The face of the senior analyst appeared on the screen, followed by an attractive woman with short blonde hair pushed behind her ears in a no-nonsense way.

After a short greeting, the man jumped right in. "Good afternoon sir, I'm Bob Perkins, and I'll be giving the historical background portion of the briefs...."

James drifted in and out as Perkins described the history of Azerbaijan, which Perkins called by its acronym, AZ. He glanced at the woman from time to time, but she only sat, hands primly folded on top of a thick folder.

James digested Perkins' words, noting that the people of the region were forcibly converted to Islam from Christianity in the seventh century. Much later, the Soviets tore down all of the mosques and imposed their brand of atheism.

"The Azeris are still a little confused today with regard to religion," Perkins said, and stopped to take a breath. James grabbed the bottle of water on the table next to him. He wished it were a cold beer, but he gulped it down. The way Perkins described it, over the last six centuries, Christians, Russians, and Muslim Iranians had been in something of a shoving match in the region. When the Soviet empire was finally gone as of 1991, it was Iran's turn to push harder, although Russia's recent invasion to the north in Georgia was another story altogether. Oil revenues had re-cast things in a big way for Russia."

When Perkins began again, James' interest was piqued for the first time when he said, "The capital, Baku, is considered the birthplace of the modern oil industry. That's how Alfred Nobel and his brothers made a chunk of their fortune. Today it's still a tough region. Lots of infighting and other countries vying to take over. Once AZ gained independence from the Soviets, things started to get difficult in Karabakh, which also wanted independence. Actually, it declared it *was* independent in 1992, and they elected a guy named Artur Mkrtchian as president. He was dead a couple of months later."

"How did he die?" James asked.

Perkins looked up and shrugged. "Some kind of weapons malfunction or something." He looked down and continued scanning his notes as he spoke. "The worst fighting was between AZ's army and the so-called 'Karabakh Defense Forces,' a.k.a. the Armenian Army. Continued until the Azerbaijan army was driven from the region in May of '94. But things are still, ah, *tense* over there. Over sixteen thousand dead in the war and nearly a million refugees, almost evenly split between Azeris and Armenians. Several massacres, pogroms as they call them, since '94."

When Perkins invited final questions. James gave a smile and a thumbs-up. "Sounds like you covered just about everything, Bob. Thanks, great brief."

It now seemed the woman's turn to speak. "Good afternoon, Commander Marshall, my name is Kathy Bartowski. I'll be briefing the religious culture of Azerbaijan. This portion of the brief is classified as secret."

She waited to make sure he understood, and he gave her a nod.

"To build on Perkins' comments, just a bit of history—…"

James stifled a groan. Kathy saw it, but her face showed no change as she continued. "As Perkins mentioned, Islam was forcibly imposed on the Azeris by the Persians. Today, because of the Soviets forcing atheism, most Azeris feel more of a *cultural* Islamic identity than a religious one. Many couldn't tell you if their ancestors were Sunni or Shia Muslims, and no longer observe the customs one would expect to find in Muslim behavior."

"Like?"

She consulted her notes, and he could swear he saw her blush when she said, "Many Azeris drink alcohol, and in the summer months, clothing is … anything but modest on the women."

"I see." No doubt she had photographs in the file to prove those things, but he decided she wouldn't see the humor if he asked to see them.

At his answer, she continued. "The following are things you'll especially need to know. Lately, there's been a rise of what some consider as Iran's efforts to foment Islamic revolution. The 1,400 Azerbaijan mosques the Russians closed have been reopened, and Iran's pumping lots of cash into the poorest neighborhoods through them. To help recruit the faithful, according to most public reports. Iran is appalled by the so-called poor state of Islam in AZ, and they're sending its mullahs to Tehran and other sites, where they can get, quote, the highest quality religious training, unquote. There are reports of sporadic riots by militant fundamentalists, and acts of resistance to the Baku government's authority. Several Islamic groups now provoke unrest in Azerbaijan: some legal, some not so legal. Most advocate the peaceful establishment of a Central Asian caliphate."

Memory prompted James to say, "That was one of Osama Bin Laden's dreams, wasn't it?"

"Yes, sir, I was getting to that."

"Sorry, didn't mean to get so far ahead." He leaned back in his chair.

"One final point, and then I'll answer any questions you have. The thing I find ironic is that Tehran's current theocracy tilts slightly in favor of an independent Karabakh. This doesn't make much surface sense. Karabakh is mostly ethnic Armenian Christian. But Tehran might see this as an advantage. Those refugees aren't happy, making them fertile ground for extremist recruitment."

She looked up at him, and her eyes were hard. "If you don't take away anything else from this brief, remember this: The *people* of Iran are generally not hostile to the West. But Iran's theocracy is. Sir, you know they don't like us at all. And they're all about spreading Islam through any means necessary—including the sponsorship of terrorism. Now, any questions?"

The obvious one—what all this had to do with finding Steve Kranzer's killer—he left unsaid. That was for him to answer. "No. Thanks, Kathy."

The next brief was the latest intelligence estimate from Perkins, which was classified top secret. A few minutes in, James understood why.

"Our sources in Beijing tell our friends in Japan that something really big's going on in the oil patch, and it involves Azerbaijan. As I'm sure you know, China's consumption of oil has been going through the roof, and they're hungry for more. They've spent tens of billions on exploration, and they're negotiating new contracts all over the world. Everywhere you go these days, where there's oil, you see more and more

Chinese."

"So where's the Azerbaijan connection?" James asked.

"Well, Baku *is* an oil center. A lot of oil-related business is conducted there. But we think it's more than that. Azerbaijan's teeming with Iranian agents. And the Chinese have gotten really cozy with the Iranians there. *Really* cozy. To the point of helping the Iranians indirectly help militarize Karabakh. They're delivering arms to Iran, which the Iranians are sending through Armenia and into Karabakh." As he spoke, he cycled through some annotated satellite imagery showing trains loaded with tanks, trucks, and armored personnel carriers.

"Yeah, I'd say they're helping out with the big guns," James said. "I had no idea."

"What's more troubling, and harder to pin down, is that Armenia, which has a lot of influence in Karabakh, seems to be laying down for this shifting balance of power, and we don't know why yet. There's no oil in Karabakh, which would be an obvious motive for all this activity. But as Kathy suggested a minute ago, the Iranians might be making a play on Azerbaijan's instability, maybe setting up for a run at Baku itself. That would give both Iran *and* China power there. We're all scratching our heads here. But one thing is certain … something's about to happen."

James gave in to the urge to get up and begin pacing, causing Perkins to have to move his head to keep him in visual range.

"So *none* of us have a good idea what's going on over there," James said. "Is that what I'm hearing you say? Something's going to happen soon, but we haven't got any idea what?"

"Correct. But we might know more before long. Ivan Mitrofanov—he's an influential member of Karabakh's Parliament—is scheduled to address the United Nations tomorrow. And he's been 'on the rise,' so to speak. And China's been pushing hard to advance him up the proverbial ladder."

James stopped pacing. "So?"

"So … I don't know. Nobody knows, just that this is all tied together somehow, and Mitrofanov's speech tomorrow might give us a few more clues."

With a sigh, Perkins added, "The only thing we're sure of is that from the minute you land in AZ, you'd better start watching your back … and any other body part you care about."

James quelled his annoyance and began pacing again. These guys were only trying to help; it was up to him to figure out how to best use what they were telling him. Which, so far, sounded more like a warning than anything useful. *Except about the oil connection. I'll definitely follow that thread as soon as I get there.*

He stopped pacing when a third person entered and sat in front of the camera. He felt a knot twist its way around his stomach when he recognized Bill Schoffner.

Schoffner's artificial smile sent his imagination flashing to a vision of Schoffner whispering who-knows-what into P.R.'s ear, edging Schoffner into the periphery of this mission: Schoffner's standard ploy. If there was any glory to be had that would advance his career, he'd jump in with both feet, welcome or not. And if Bill Schoffner was involved, James' life might be in the hands of someone he'd never been able to trust. Someone he knew too much about to ever trust.

"Hey bud, I just talked to P.R., and I've got a lot of items to discuss with you before you head off to Azerbaijan."

James lowered himself back into his chair. "Such as?"

"Rules of engagement, backup—"

James recognized Schoffner's boilerplate mission briefing starting up, and decided to take the offensive. "Stay out of this, Schoffner."

"Whoa. We can help each other out here, friend." That plastic smile was all over the screen.

"I don't need your kind of help."

"Look, tomorrow we'll go through some really good information together—"

"Sorry. You must have missed *your* briefing. Tomorrow morning, first thing, I'm on a plane to Baku. Save your *helpful* boilerplate lecture for someone who needs it."

"Hey, listen, I'm here on P.R.'s direct orders. Don't you get insubordinate—"

"Yeah, and I bet you badgered him into those *direct orders*. Go feather your nest somewhere else, Schoffner. You're not in charge here, so butt out." James leveled his eyes at Schoffner's image. "And if you do anything to slow me down or get in my way, God help you."

He reached out and turned off the monitor while Schoffner was still winding up for his reply.

CHAPTER

6

The placard read "United States," and the man seated behind it was Charles Purvis, U.S. Ambassador to the United Nations. It was an unseasonably cool day in New York, but this meeting of the General Assembly left Purvis even colder.

The man at the podium was passionately laying out his vision for a free Karabakh, while bashing America and heralding his embrace of China as the new rising superpower. The thing that rang hollow to Purvis, aside from the obvious, was that the man was an outcast in his own parliament. His parents were from Russia, not from Karabakh, two cultures that were light-years apart. But there was much more. The clout the man seemed to carry was recent; he wore his rivals and grudges on his sleeve; his closest buddies were of questionable integrity at best.

If Purvis believed the media hype, and even his own briefers, Karabakh's hope rested in the hollow of Ivan Mitrofanov's hands. The man painted a grand picture of the future. But Purvis wasn't buying it. He knew Mitrofanov was being propped up by a slew of third-world front men who'd somehow floated to the surface of their pecking order and now wanted to curry favor and get aid, much of which would find its way into their own pockets. Purvis counted China high among that number of questionable supporters; the country was writing some very big checks, and word was they had sponsored Mitrofanov's meteoric rise to *savior* status. No nation would support such a dark horse unless they expected something big in return.

Wondering how long Mitrofanov could possibly go on, Purvis yawned and glanced over at China's stoic representative, who listened politely.

Perhaps China was in the dark, but Charles Purvis was privy to one thing that gave him comic relief, yet made him wonder. A brief from the State Department's envoy to Karabakh detailed Mitrofanov's pariah status in his very own parliament. Why even the U.S. press ignored that, he couldn't comprehend. State had, however, quietly penned a nickname for him: Ivan the Terrible, after the fallen angel, one of the more infamous of the Muscovites who whipped the Mongols in 1552.

Charming.

As soon as Mitrofanov closed and left the podium, Purvis made a mental note to call P.R. Nicholson. Not only an old friend, but on the same page about Mr. Mitrofanov.

* * *

Congratulating himself, Mitrofanov left the podium to deafening applause and was ushered into a car, nearly blinded by flashes from the press, who were desperate to learn more about this charismatic new leader.

"Let us toast to our success!" he said once seated in the refuge of his limousine. The speech had gone so well, he had difficulty containing his joy. He bathed his Chinese companions in an exhilarated smile while he popped open a bottle of champagne. They accepted crystal glasses from him as the car roared off towards their destination in the Hamptons.

"I was magnificent, wasn't I?" he said, expecting agreement so not really paying attention to see if it was there. It wasn't.

The car continued on toward a secluded estate, rented for this occasion. The evening was resplendent with flowing champagne and scripted lines that gushed almost as freely. Ambassadors, senators, and wealthy contributors all pandered and bowed and raved over a shared sense of the ideological masterpiece unfolding before them, which, without their enlightened guidance and support, of course would succumb to the forces of those *less* enlightened.

But as the evening wore on, each drink whittled away at Mitrofanov's wit and charm, and, once depleted of his litany of apropos sound bites, he was advised by his Chinese friends to bid his guests good evening. Obligingly, bowed them out the door, after which his Chinese friends left too.

Later, very much alone in the now too quiet house, he studied his wine glass as he slowly rotated it. His head lay on one arm, which was stretched out across the elegant dining room table, and the remnants of a fine Hungarian wine slipped up and down the sides of the crystal goblet. It was late. The housekeeping staff had adjourned, at his request, not far behind the Chinese contingent. Soft candlelight still warmed the room.

Out of the corner of his eye, he leered at the scantily clad woman entering the doorway of the dining room. A gift from his benefactors. Her sheer negligee and silky body language revealed sumptuous curves and cleavage that was presented in an overabundance of invitation. She smiled, then pouted teasingly.

"You have great legs. Oh yes you do!" He slurred the words as he returned to his study of the wine's movement in the glass. "The legs of a strong horse!"

"What?" she asked softly, confused.

Chuckling at his little joke, he rolled his head on his arm, and whispered. "Not you, my sweet, dear, whore. The wine! It has great legs!" He continued to watch the remnants of the wine slip up and down the sides of the goblet. "This leg here, this one is the Chinese. They want someone who will make sure they get their oil. Someone just … like … me!"

Belching softly, he reached for a nearby vodka bottle and shot glass. "Funny how a little discovery will change things so much. This leg here … who is it? Oh, yes … sshhhh! The Iranians. But don't tell anyone. It's a secret." He held his extended index finger over his mouth, looked from side to side and giggled to himself, ignoring the woman. "They want someone who will let Muslims be happy here. And that is easy! Everyone will be happy. Everyone!"

He downed a sloppily poured shot of vodka, stood up laboriously, and steadied himself on a chair back with one hand as he picked up the wine goblet.

"Because that is what *you* want too.... Where did you go?"

The woman misunderstood, started walking toward him, but he waved at her to stop and studied the goblet further. "Oh. There you are. You have been hiding from me. My horse's third leg, the United Nations."

He laughed again, deeper this time. "Everybody will be happy!"

He stood tall, as if addressing a large audience. "Ladies and gentlemen, may I introduce to you the advocate of the little guys out there … the United Nations." He paused, as if responding to massive applause. "I like those guys, because they are always trying to stand up to the big bad wolf United States." He stumbled but caught himself. "Big bad wolf...."

He swayed and caught himself again, decided it was time to finish this performance and bed his eager wench.

"And then there is the last leg of the beautiful horse that I now ride." He sloppily waved his hand in the air. "My little friends, who, like me, have been scorned by Parliament. My little friends have been good to me, done me many favors. Some very dirty favors." He smiled as he hung on to the chair. "They will help me to deal with those bad boys of Parliament."

In sudden rage, he hurled the goblet across the room. As it smashed into the corner he screamed like a madman, spittle swinging from his chin. "We will deal with those bad boys of Parliament! We will deal with them!" The drunken haze left his eyes and he spoke with teeth clenched, his eyes fixated on his tight, trembling fist.

He turned to the woman, knowing her attentions would give little relief from the emotions swirling in him. And as she backed up in fear, he resolved to stop thinking of his plan and now gave *her* his undivided attention....

"You bitch!"

CHAPTER

7

Pain seared up James' right arm, rousting him from deep but turbulent slumber. He struggled to collect himself, releasing the tightly wadded, sweat-soaked bedsheets from his right hand. The dream had been dreadfully familiar, pitching him headlong deep into the bowels of the United States Central Command in Tampa, Florida.

The building was known as 540, also the "Death Star." As a mobilized Naval Reserve Intelligence Officer, he had directed the team that guided smart bombs and other long-range weapons onto targets in Afghanistan—a first in warfare history, where targets were not only selected but executed from the other side of the earth. As the missiles bore down on final impact, James had watched men die on the other side of the world. It all seemed surreal, then and now, fighting the sense of distasteful but necessary madness that manifested itself as a new kind of "air-conditioned combat," a virtual expedition into a place known euphemistically as the "tip of the spear," where the military faced whatever challenger the world brought on. For James, that had been his first time facing off with such a challenger, after the then-recent events of 9/11 had taken him away from all he'd thought safe.

As always, touching that place left him with a vacant numbness. But now, the lack of feeling was replaced by the anger he had endured since learning of Steve Kranzer's death. The smell of the bedsheets was fresh and familiar, the room was clean, but the sense of death was old. James wasn't afraid to die, nor did he want to. He just didn't want to go back to that place of the demons and experience the revulsion of mixing with them.

And the killing that went with it.

He shook off the dream and caught himself wishing that the ugliness and the emptiness of it all would just leave him. It did, but with aching slowness, replaced by the memory of last night's call to P.R. Nicholson, which had been dominated by his potent denunciation of Bill Schoffner's involvement. He hoped P.R.'s ears were still burning, because even now, thinking of having to depend on that devious slime made him burn all over again. In the end, P.R. had convinced him that Schoffner's involvement as the top analyst was necessary. *"Go with me on this one, James,"* he'd said. *"Please. Just trust me."* P.R.'s words didn't make any sense, but James' respect for him made him relent.

Street noises came to him, the downtown evening rush hour of Baku five stories below, and he remembered promising to meet Raffi Rahman, Baku's station chief and his liaison, for dinner. As the noisy bustling below him seemed to reach its peak, he pulled himself from the bed and stumbled toward the shower.

The hot water helped relax his stiff body, and he reflected on his arrival just hours earlier. The U.S. Embassy had arranged his quarters, and it had been about two p.m. Baku time when he arrived in front of the upscale midrise apartment building. He'd tuned out the talkative cabby's recounting of Islamic extremists' most recent violence. At the hotel, he strode into the building's lobby, hanging his carryon bag over one shoulder, taking note of the surveillance cameras and foot patrols around the building, as secure a place as he would find in such a dangerous city. The last thing he recalled was a grateful collapse onto his bed after winding through six time zones in two days to get here.

The shower was reviving him, washing away the soils that cluttered his mind, save one question that never seemed to find an answer: *Why?* What secret was so important, Kranzer had to die for it? It didn't make sense to him, nor did it seem real, not yet.

He knew he'd have to mix with the devil to see his agenda, and suspected the opportunity would find him soon.

Thirty minutes later, he leaned against the back wall of the elevator trying to decide which he needed more, a cup of coffee or a cold beer. Halfway to the ground floor, the elevator stopped and one of the building's porters entered.

"You have just checked in to Room 626, yes?"

"Yes." James narrowed eyes at him. "Did I meet you when I checked in?"

"No, sir." The man's face held a slight smirk.

James wondered how this man knew who he was. Not many porters knew guests by sight prior to meeting them. This guy had a key to his room, could have killed him just now while he slept, but he hadn't. James decided to play with him a bit. The elevator's doors slid apart at the ground floor, and the porter held them open and politely invited him through.

"*Masaa al-khair*. (Good evening.)" James spoke in Arabic, an attempt to catch him off guard.

"*Masaa an-noor,* Commander Marshall."

James smiled and continued through the lobby and out onto the sidewalk. Whoever the guy was, he had balls.

The brisk spring evening air had revived him, and he mused over the man as he walked to where Raffi would pick him up. He didn't feel threatened. Sure, the man could have been an assassin waiting to make a positive ID before the kill. But he was likely a "friendly"—an agent of Azerbaijan or another country, keeping an eye on things. Spies bumped into each other more than most people would expect.

He chuckled at the memory of a time in the U.S. Embassy in Moscow. By all accounts, the maid didn't speak a word of English. But even though he only said, "Ma'am, you have a spider on your shoulder," she screamed and tried to brush it off. Turned out she was the kind of operative who simply watch and then download a laundry list of details to their handlers. The ones who really got into their job were the ones who showed panache, like the porter. They were the fun ones, but also the most dangerous. Next time, for a laugh, he'd try out his Farsi on the man.

At a street corner two blocks away, he hopped into a black Suburban when it pulled up at the prearranged location. It still had the new-car smell, and, in spite of its size, James sensed that it was an Embassy vehicle.

"Welcome to Baku, I'm Raffi Rahman." As they shook hands, James immediately noted youthful Egyptian features that the file photograph didn't do justice. Raffi was in his late twenties, and in their short phone call, James had learned that he'd become a father for the first time three months ago.

"James Marshall. Nice to meet you, Raffi. How's your wife and daughter?"

"Both doing very well in Cairo, thanks. I miss them terribly. How was your trip?"

"Long." James held up his cell phone, which he'd discreetly used to take a picture of the porter. "Hey, who is this joker?"

Raffi laughed. "He's with the Azeri police detail assigned to protect your building. He knew you were coming." Still chuckling, Raffi steered the big Suburban into the traffic flow. "The guy thinks of himself as a high-powered secret agent. Harmless. An okay guy."

He then looked over at James, his face appraising. "So you've got quite the reputation. At least, you did. I heard that you used to like jumping into hornets' nests like this, but not now. Not since the war."

James looked out his window. "Hornets' nests are still my specialty. But first, I need something to eat. Where are we going?"

"A place you're gonna like if what they say about you is true. *A Taste of Persia*. Beer and belly dancers."

James swiveled his head back and smiled. "You've been talking to the right people."

"Actually, this is a business call as well. The owners are an Iranian couple who moved here a couple of years ago from Los Angeles to be closer to relatives. They've worked with us before, but … they're really scared this time."

"How so?"

Raffi shrugged. "The situation's so tense here. Those who don't love Iranians hate Iranians. I stopped by yesterday hoping to talk to Maharani. She's the wife. But she's lying low. Wasn't there."

Outside the car, the traffic continued to wheel by, and James couldn't help but notice the wild nature of Azeri drivers: dangerous, if not as bad as the Italians. Nobody drove worse than Italians.

"She's our primary contact for the couple?" he asked.

"Yep. And I've learned that she's good friends with Aria Palestinio, the dead guy's daughter. Apparently, the daughter sometimes dances there."

James glanced at him in surprise, and he said quickly, "As a hobby to stay in shape, I guess. But she's not there anymore. She vanished after her father's murder. I asked the maître d' to tell Maharani we'd be there tonight. Hopefully, she'll show up at least. If not, we'll just eat and enjoy the show."

"Have we got a photo of Aria Palestinio?"

Raffi shook his head and swerved to avoid a pothole. "Getting her father's was easy, but she's tough, and we don't know why. We've got a lot of good background on her though. Good grades at Stanford, majored in business administration, returned to the area to help boost small businesses in the region. Here, she lives on a cash basis, doesn't own a car, apparently hates cell phones. It's hard to track someone like that. My guess? She's hiding up in the mountains somewhere with her mother's family. An uncle, a brother. Her mother died a while back."

James processed this, and allowed himself a grin. *Dislikes being noticed. Doesn't want to stand out. Kinda like me.* "Stanford, huh? Wouldn't have guessed that about an Azeri mountain girl. No yearbook photo?"

"Nope. And no student ID from Stanford either. Unusual. She's got a passport, but that photo was taken before these guys went digital over here. But about Stanford? Remember, her father was a big-time archeologist. She would've been expected to get the best education possible."

"And she's the only one who has any idea where her father was working."

"Correct. And that makes it much more difficult. No one has any idea who was working on his crew. He didn't always file for permits to dig, something the Azeri government didn't like. This was one of those times he didn't."

"Then we definitely need to get in touch with her."

"Agreed."

Raffi parked his car and they took in the evening air for the last couple of blocks, noticing the swelling nighttime foot traffic. James was surprised that the architecture was mostly European, with lots of midrise buildings, many with ornate stone facades. Vendors sold flowers, couples strolled, a variety of music drifted in and out of the shops and restaurants. Sometimes it was *mugams*, local folk songs, sometimes Persian music or Western rock and roll, all of these underscoring the richness of Baku's secular diversity. But he cringed each time he caught the more commonly heard Russian pop rock and roll, something he found particularly annoying. He noted that Raffi was frequently checking their perimeter as they walked along. He smiled to himself. Situational awareness was ninety percent of staying out of trouble on assignment: in other words, just paying attention. Unlike the FBI agent in Morocco, Raffi possessed the *nose*.

The two men came up behind a group of seven girls in their late teens, dressed in light summer attire and speaking Russian. Both James and Raffi spoke Russian fluently and quickly realized they were ballerinas on tour from St. Petersburg. The young girls laughed and joked among themselves while they strolled along, enjoying the spring evening. That is, until the two men were jolted by a loud voice.

"Hey, you boys lost?" A middle-aged man wearing a cowboy hat leaned out from behind the wheel of a pickup truck as he slowly paced the two men. The old truck was full of dents, but purred as if its owner knew the art of keeping an engine at peak performance. The owner's unmistakable Texas accent was incongruous on the streets of Baku. While he showed some softening around the jowls, the developed muscles and leathery skin told the story of a hard physical life.

Raffi smiled and motioned toward the girls. "Just checking out the scenery. How's it going, Roger?"

"Just ducky. Who's the new fellah?" Roger's amicable question seemed part Texas, part paternal to James.

"Our new deputy defense attaché. Meet Commander James Marshall."

Hearing that, Roger pulled the truck next to the curb and parked.

"Howdy, Commander." He nodded in greeting and cocked his cowboy hat back with panache. "I'm the go-to guy 'round the Embassy. You need anything …" he patted the truck's dash, "you name it, me and Betsy'll get it for ya. And if you're lookin' for barbeque, there's only one place in this part of the world: Roger's kitchen." He put emphasis on this point by motioning with his half-full beer bottle. "So where you from, Commander?"

James smiled at him. "North Carolina."

"North Cackalaki … they make good moonshine there." He took a hearty gulp of his beer and continued. "Raffi here knows where to find me, but you'll see me around. Y'all have fun tonight, ya'hear?"

He muscled his way back into the slow-moving traffic, which was impeded by pedestrians chatting in the street. As he roared off, James heard him yell, "Get out of the way, you gawking mall zombies! Move your sorry ass or it'll have Ford written all over it!"

James grinned at that. He always got a kick out of the variety of U.S. expatriates who wound their way round the globe. He could also see why the waterfront area was the most crowded and popular part of downtown Baku. As he took in the sights, he could now see the restaurant's sign. Recalling Raffi's description of the food there—traditional Iranian dishes, as well as local favorites like *dolma* and *plov*, both a mix of minced mutton, rice, and assorted spices or grape leaves—his stomach growled in anticipation. Fresh air flowed off the Caspian Sea, and he almost hated the thought of leaving it, but *A Taste of Persia* called to him.

Raffi led the way inside, and James immediately warmed up to the relaxed blend of Persian and Middle Eastern décor that also captured the city's mix of Soviet and European influences. The composite of cultures seasoned this hideaway's distant, almost mystical atmosphere, whisking its patrons abruptly into the parlor of the exotic and long forgotten.

A husky Persian maître d' greeted them, as did a delicious blend of aromas. After a polite bow, he seated them on wide pillows surrounding a brass table in a corner near what appeared to be a dance floor. Both men complied with custom and took off their shoes. As they did, James caught himself thinking, *Ahhh, to be in an ex-Soviet, secular-Muslim country. Life could be worse*.

He surveyed the menu's offering of a wide range of beers and wines, but kept one eye scanning the room. The restaurant wasn't overcrowded, but it certainly had a full house, including four swarthy Iranian men whose uneasy presence reminded him that they weren't here to have a good time. When the waiter brought pita bread, Raffi offered. "Let me order for both of us. I'll get a little bit of everything and you can sample what you like. Next time we come here, you're on your own, okay?"

"Sounds like a plan!"

"I see that you've also noticed our Iranian friends over there."

James nodded. "They're hard to miss."

They split a bottle of good red wine and indulged themselves with dishes like *ghormeh sabzi*, a delicious lamb dish, and *sesenjan*, a chicken-and-pomegranate concoction. The food wasn't as spicy as he expected, and he noticed that herbs and fruit were used in both dishes. They each savored the hints of plum, quince, and raisins, and some things James didn't recognize. The red wine complemented everything, though.

A four-piece Middle Eastern band stood up, and after a few warm-up tunes, a belly dancer took the stage. She was a good dancer … a bit heavy, not a fresh young face, yet a capable performer … but James quickly lost interest and turned his attention back to his meal. Soon, he and Raffi were sharing competing stories about their separate trips around the Mediterranean. As their jousting efforts to outdo each other peaked, their attention was drawn by a middle-aged woman approaching.

"*Khosh amadid!* Welcome! Are you two enjoying yourselves?"

The woman was dressed in Persian garb. Her fine linen robes were sequined and colorful, uncommon for day-to-day wear. Usually, women in Islamic countries wore the customary black. But this, again, wasn't Persia … or Iran for that matter.

"*Salam, Salam aleikom!* (Hello! Peace be upon you!)" Raffi replied, then bowed his head slightly and gestured an invitation with his hands. The woman seated herself with them with an infectious smile. "Maharani," Raffi said, "I would like you to meet my good friend James Marshall."

"*Hal-e shoma chetor ast?* (How do you do?)" James replied in his best Farsi.

She gave him an admiring smile. "So … you've been around a bit, like your friend here? You must try the kabob, oh, it's awesome!" The waiter had just brought more food, and she picked up a piece with a fork and playfully offered it to him. He accepted to be polite, but was truly appreciative after a few bites.

After a moment, she glanced side to side and lowered her voice. "There are *muhajadeen* here. There has always been a presence, a few who stood out. But lately, they are everywhere. Most of them do not speak Azeri, and they travel in groups. Gangs. Not only in the mosques, but all over. Sometimes they come in here, and they are rude."

She gave a grateful glance at Raffi, whom she knew to be Egyptian but didn't take offense at her comments, then glanced quickly over at the Iranian men. She continued, her voice so low now, James and Raffi had to lean forward to hear her.

"They resent the fact that I am a liberated woman, and that we serve liquor here." Then, laughing, she added, "But, now, I am an American. They can all, as you say, kiss my butt!"

Despite her mirthful demeanor, James could tell she was putting on a front to hide her fear of the *muhajadeen*, proponents of a holy war against infidels, which included anyone who wasn't Muslim, and to some, even Muslims who didn't agree with their particular platform. He suspected she would be the kind of friend you sometimes wished you had when you needed one.

The band started up again, and a second dancer took the floor. This one was a profound improvement over the first. He felt his heartbeat pick up as he watched her graceful and elegant movements. The music and the dancer flowed together, and her whole body seemed to move in exhilarated celebration of the moment. She leaned back with her full, firm breasts swaying while her hips undulated in an unabashed, almost bawdy offering of her sensuality. Her eager male audience clapped in rapt unison, and in the distant background, he could hear Maharani speaking about her use of Persian rice, which was twice as good, and twice as expensive, as anything from the Orient.

"So, you like her?" Maharani had asked him the question with the lighthearted curiosity of a matchmaker, but he could see she was actually making a polite attempt to recapture his attention.

"Oh, yes I do." He sipped his wine and attempted to refocus on his work. "I like everything about your place. You've done a good job with it."

"Thank you." She leaned over to him. "Raffi tells me that you've come here to help Aria Palestinio, yes?"

When he nodded, Maharani laughed, reached out and put her arm around his shoulder. "You silly boy," she said loudly, and then, under her breath, "We cannot speak of this here. Meet me atop the Maiden's Tower at dawn tomorrow morning. But you must be careful." Then her serious look melted and she pinched his cheek. "You both enjoy yourselves, okay?" She moved on to another table under the watchful eye of the Iranian men.

* * *

"Do you always have a following like this?" James asked as he and Raffi left the restaurant, referring to the four Iranians, who were now walking twenty careful paces behind them.

"For the past several weeks. It's part of the big mystery around here. At first those guys were low-key. Over the past five or six days, they've really started to piss me off. I had them picked up Tuesday, but they hadn't broken any laws and were back on the street a few hours later."

James looked at Raffi incredulously. "Is *that* your biggest problem here? Let's take care of these bozos, and then first thing in the morning, I'm headed off to meet Maharani."

He explained his plan and finished with, "And this is only the fun warm-up."

Raffi smiled. "It's always fun opening a hornet's nest. That's why we do this."

They walked a few blocks along the waterfront. The streets had a fair amount of foot traffic this time of night, and the bars were full of roughnecks in town for a break from the oil platforms. Roughnecks were pretty much the same all over the world. They worked like dogs and were paid well. A roughneck with a fat wallet was headed for good food, women, alcohol, and maybe even a good bar fight. A roughneck with a thin wallet was headed back to the rigs.

At James' direction they ducked into a bar, the busiest and most raucous one they could find. The smoke from heavy Russian tobacco was thick inside, and the mostly male crowd wandered the noisy space, drinking and laughing. The crowd spoke a host of languages, Russian being dominant.

Raffi and James sidled up to the bar and ordered beers. Soon they noticed a group of men gathered around a table where two very large men were engaged in an arm-wrestling contest. Both contestants grimaced in their struggle, and the men surrounding them shouted for their favorite. James bet $100 worth of *manat*, the Azeri currency, on the bald-headed one named Victor, who sported a handlebar mustache and gold teeth. James noticed one of the cheering spectators had an emblem on his shirt—that of a Russian oil company called Itochu. He and Raffi struck up a conversation with another large man named Boris, who was trying to distract Victor by periodically sticking his tongue in his ear. Victor's response each time was to jerk his head in the direction of the tongue in an effort to whack his skull against the man's face.

The few women in the bar appeared to be regulars, some who looked as tough as the men, including some who were clearly available for the right price. James appraised their wispy long blonde hair, busty torsos and hiked skirts, reflecting on how different Russian women in Baku were from the western impression of the short, frumpy, and featureless babushka in heavy coat and headscarf.

Victor had finally won his contest, knocking a few empty shot glasses off the end of the table as his opponent's hand touched its surface. He stood, revealing his nearly seven-foot stature and broad shoulders, and raised his arms in the air to a chorus of cheers. He downed the shot of vodka Boris handed him, certainly not his first of the evening, and slammed the glass, upside down, on the table.

Raffi by now had Boris convinced that he and James were midlevel executives with Itochu, and had been on their rig a few days ago. He had also convinced Boris that he was going to complain, loudly, at the home offices about the poor quality of the food and the stench on the rig. Boris was beginning to warm up to these new guys.

James now had roughly $200 in *manat* in his hand. He looked at the men who had begun to gather around him and Raffi, and slapped some of the money on the bar. "Bartender!" he shouted. "Pour these men your best Kazakh vodka! And keep it coming."

He looked at the man next to him, who was visibly curious

about the man buying him a drink. "I have seen your work, and we just don't pay you enough!"

The man was a little wary, but didn't argue, just took his drink with a calloused hand from a line of shot glasses the bartender continued to set up.

James held up his glass; the other men followed suit. "*Do kontsah!* (To the bottom of the glass!)" At his exuberant shout, the others repeated it in a drunken chorus.

"*Do kontsah!*" shouted Raffi, they all drank, and in a loud series of slams, the shot glasses were left on the bar upside down amidst small bowls of pickles.

A couple more rounds followed, and they took turns making bawdy toasts in Russian. Stories were told, backs slapped, insults hurled, and best of all, the four Iranians were still loitering outside the bar.

Then, the right moment came.

"We have to go back out to the rigs in a few hours, guys, but this has been great," James said. "Just one last thing … those four guys outside?" He pointed with his thumb over his shoulder. "You might want to know, on our way in here, we overheard them talking about you. They were going on and on about what a bunch of drunken infidels you all are."

Victor's eyes grew wide. "Those four?"

Raffi nodded in support of James' allegation.

Boris started laughing, picked up two shots of vodka from the bar, and handed them both to Victor. Raffi and James could easily see that Boris' adrenaline was flowing; he seemed almost giddy.

"Whoa," Raffi whispered, "it's like they're about to do something they've done before."

"And something they're eager to do again," James finished.

Hiding grins, they watched as Victor led the way, the two drinks he held dwarfed in his huge hands. One of the men opened the door for him, and the tall Russian had to duck slightly to get his giant frame through it.

Through the bar's plate-glass window, James watched the Iranians as Victor approached. They were essentially cornered; a hedge blocked their exit. Two of them now sat on a bench placed against the building. The other two, standing in front of them, turned to see what had blanched their comrades' faces. James and Raffi sidled to the door of the bar, mingling with the crowd gathered there.

As Victor approached the men he bellowed, "I understand that you do not want me to enjoy my vodka. Is this true?"

The largest of the Iranians, who seemed to be their leader, addressed him. "We do not want trouble with you, sir." He opened his arms in a conciliatory gesture. "Please …"

"Then share a drink with me, then."

"Sir, I do not drink—"

"Am I not good enough to drink with?"

"Ah … Mohammed forbids it."

"Mohammed said you could not drink wine. Your prophet said nothing about vodka. Drink!"

The crowd of drunken Russians pressed in around them.

"Please, I do not wish to—"

"Should I pour it out then?"

"Yes."

"That would be a sacrilege. Here … I'll do this instead."

Keeping his eyes locked with the man's, Victor drank both shots, then to James' amazement, bit the top off one of the glasses and chewed on it as he moved toward the largest Iranian. He grabbed him by the throat with the hand that had held the half-eaten glass, and leftover shards cut the man's neck as he was lifted off the ground.

One of the Iranians went to reach for something in his windbreaker. Boris stopped him with a viselike grip, pried a cell phone from the man's hand, and threw it across the street into some bushes. The Iranian men looked terrified as the burly Russians pressed closer.

"You think I am an infidel, yes?"

The Iranian's eyes bulged out as he choked.

"You think I should bow to Mecca every day, yes?"

Again, only gasps for breath as the Iranian's feet dangled in the air. The glass had cut Victor's mouth. Blood dripped from the sides of his mouth as he spoke, and his gold teeth looked even more formidable against the red blood.

The rest of the Russians from inside the bar were now gathering around, so no one noticed James and Raffi slip back into the bar and through the back door. They were soon in Raffi's car.

Raffi turned the ignition, but James said, "Hang on a sec," rolled down his window and motioned to two young boys walking along the sidewalk. He offered them cash to retrieve the cell phone in the bushes across the street from the bar. Once the trade was made, Raffi and James left the scene of the melee, letting it come to its own conclusion. At his hotel, as he climbed out of the car, James handed the SIM card from the cell phone to Raffi. "Send what's on this to Alexis Brown in my office at Langley. She'll know what to do with it."

Raffi took the SIM card and slipped it into his jacket pocket. "Consider it done."

* * *

Later that night, his cell phone rang, drawing him from the deep slumber brought about by one too many shots of vodka. He sat up, struggling to get his head clear from the lingering alcohol haze, and answered the call.

"James, it's Alexis."

"Uhhh, what time is it?"

"Sorry. The phone that you got the SIM card from—"

"Can we do this in the morning?"

"James! One of the phone numbers in that phone was to a conference room here at Langley!"

He dropped back on the pillow. "Whoa. Does P.R. know?"

"I just came from his office."

"Good for you …, thanks."

"James …, P.R. said to tell you to stay the course and stick with the game plan. He also said, quote, you need to trust him now more than ever."

"Like I don't already? And oh ..., Alexis? Keep this to yourself. Anything else?"

"One more thing ..., please ... watch your back."

He hung up the phone. A face bearing a perpetually fake smile slipped into his mind like a snake.

CHAPTER

8

The stench met General Lu as he wound his way down into the safe house's crude basement. The tang of blood always aroused him, and he had never fought or suppressed his irregular sense of enjoyment. He often suspected that Chairman Sun was aware of his proclivity, but tolerated it to fulfill his need for the best staff around him ... something that gave Lu the sense of freedom to operate as he saw fit.

He pushed open the door at the bottom of the stairs, anticipating the odor's full impact, which he drew in deeply. Across the dim room, he could see the limp body of a man chained to the wall, his head splayed back as if to highlight the screwdriver's handle protruding from his forehead. A hammer, electric drill, chef's knife, and twisted wire coat hanger lay at his feet, as if in solemn affirmation of gruesome events that had brought him beyond anyone's mercy. A naked woman, little more than a girl, lay face down on the floor nearby, also in chains, unmoving. Lu's eyes scrolled across her contorted figure as a voice spoke reproachfully from a chair in the shadows.

"You're late. You've missed all the fun."

"I had important matters to tend to, Ivan—"

"More important than this?"

"To me."

"But not to me. This ... was a glorious afternoon."

"That, I can see for myself."

Mitrofanov sipped from a shot glass with bloodstained

hands. His silk bathrobe, like his hair, was matted with scarlet, already starting to dry. "Taking the girl was most pleasurable. But, with her father watching …" He gave a wicked smile and took another sip of vodka. "The best part? When I watched this man's life slipping away. Until today, my most powerful rival. The look on his face at the end. The completeness of his despair. It was … delicious." Mitrofanov shuddered, reliving his orgy of depredation, then leaned back and drew a breath, eyes closed. "*Most* exquisite."

"What about the archeologist's daughter?"

With a sigh, Mitrofanov opened his eyes and reached for the vodka bottle, slick with blood now. "We will find her, stop worrying. And I will take care of her personally, right here in my little playroom. How is the militia coming, General?"

"Thirty-eight new men arrived this morning, mostly jihadists."

The last word, spoken with quiet distaste, brought a shrug. "I don't care why they fight, General, so long as they serve me well."

"They will. We're continuing with the gradual replacement of Armenian units."

"Good. You organize them, I will take care of the rest." Mitrofanov grinned. "Though your task should now be simpler. Now my enemies fear me, and with fear comes respect from all."

"You have definitely made big waves in this little pond. But on the world stage, you need to be careful about the image you cultivate. The West can be both a powerful ally and a potent enemy."

Lu was a man who chose his words carefully, and spoke to make a point, not just to make conversation. Something Mitrofanov often said he appreciated, but could never emulate.

"The West?" Mitrofanov said. "They only see me as a man of influence, a potential trading partner. They don't care about this sort of thing." He leaned over and patted the girl's ass, and let out a soft laugh as he grabbed at white skin.

There was no response from the girl, and Lu didn't expect one. Her lonely moment of fervent but futile objection had been dramatic, he imagined, and her energy had been exhausted in resisting Mitrofanov. Only submissive silence now greeted the capricious intrusions of his fingers.

Smiling, Mitrofanov said, "No, the West cares nothing about our … amusements. The West only cares about making profits."

"So long as you don't pretend that you have weapons of mass destruction, that is." Lu gently kicked the electric drill on the floor, and they both smirked.

"I've missed you, General. They say that you've been a bad boy in Morocco." Mitrofanov's smile became twisted, devilish.

"Yes." Lu opened and closed his right hand, a surgeon stretching his fingers before the operation. "I would never have delegated something with so much promise of pleasure. My best shot ever."

"Especially since it was an American naval officer, eh?"

Lu nodded, allowing himself to feel pride woven into the kindred spirit he felt in this man.

"Won't the Americans be upset with such a mean-spirited act?"

"Oh, of course they will. They will probably talk us to death."

Both men laughed again, and Lu said, "Or, they may actually send someone this time."

Mitrofanov reacted by peering through the hollow of his shot glass, then smiling at the dead man on the wall. "Then we will just have to kill him too, won't we?"

CHAPTER

9

Raffi's Suburban was waiting when James looked out of the sixth-story window of his apartment at 5:00 a.m. Right on time to get him to his predawn rendezvous with Maharani, *if* he could shake the vodka-induced haze in his head.

Showered and shaved, he went downstairs and hopped in, taking the cup of coffee Raffi held out to him with a chipper, "Morning!"

"Is it? I can't keep my days and nights straight anymore with all the traveling I've been doing. And those VTCs! Video teleconferences at all hours of the night haven't helped my body clock any."

Raffi nodded and edged into the early morning traffic. "Yes, those teleconferences are set up for the boss's convenience, no matter what time it is in our part of the world. A moment passed, and he said, "We're checking out the conference-room phone, but the log records aren't revealing anything. It's being looked over for fingerprints as we speak."

"What are the chances of finding anything that way?"

"Close to nil," Raffi admitted. "That whole idea is pretty scary."

"No kidding." He allowed his mind to recall a plastic smile on a video screen, an ingratiating, unwelcome presence in his assignment. But without solid data to back it up, what did he have to go to P.R. with? No, if Schoffner was having him followed by foreign agents, he'd have to let the man tie his own noose. And actually, the image of that seemed right somehow.

Raffi continued driving along the upscale street and headed toward the dark and ominous-looking building in the distance.

"You did pretty well last night," James said, referring to their instigation of the barroom brawl. "How'd you learn Russian while living in Cairo?"

"I went to a school that taught Russian, as well as classical Arabic."

"I forgot, the Russians were big in Egypt in the 1960s under Nasser."

Raffi slammed on his brakes to avoid a woman and child who'd suddenly decided to cross the busy street. "Hey, speaking of Russians, I've been thinking about getting some gold teeth, like that Victor-guy had. What do you think? Maybe it would enhance my image?"

James groaned. "Don't forget the extra two feet of height and 150 pounds more muscle that go with it. That guy was some piece of work."

Raffi laughed. "Well, at least no one's been following me this morning. First time in weeks!"

"Told you I could fix that. So tell me about this Maiden's Tower."

"Maharani picked a good place to meet you. Private, if a little creepy. Maiden's Tower is also known as Kyz Kalasy. It's ancient, some say built well before the time of Christ. And there are all sorts of legends about the place. A fire worshipers' temple, for one."

He looked over at James, who was struggling to wake up over his coffee. "Back then, pilgrims came from all over and kept on settling here. At first, the town was called Albana. At some point, the name changed to Albaku, and then finally to Baku. Means the capitol of sacred fires. Pretty cool, huh?"

James rubbed his neck and recalled the dancer at the restaurant, the one who had almost caused him to miss the four men following them. "No more history lessons. I've had so many lately, I'm starting to dream about 'em. Tell me more about this girl. About Aria." He grinned. "If she's a dancer at *A Taste of Persia*, then I'm going to have a heck of a time focusing on my work when I meet her. Wonder if she's single."

Raffi's smile was wicked, but his eyes remained on the busy street in front of them. "From all our reports, she is unattached. And you will do fine. I'm told she is actually very nice. And no doubt, *very* determined to find out why her father died and who killed him. If you get distracted by her body, she'll surely straighten you out."

They drove up to the eight-story tower's dark, still grounds, and Raffi stopped the Suburban. "For the sake of protecting the government's property," he swept a hand over the expensive SUV's dashboard, "I will let you go it alone. Follow that path, it leads to the entrance. It looks clear. Go ahead. I'll keep an eye on things down here."

With a nod, James slipped out of the car and went down the stone pathway to the oddly shaped tower. One side of it was a straight cylinder, but one side of it extended in a key shape, a design he couldn't recall ever seeing in his travels.

Trees lined part of the path, it was eerily quiet, and there was a breeze that put a slight chill into the air. Fighting a shiver, he found the entrance and saw that the gate had been left unlocked. It opened with a low, grinding squeak, and he went in.

The air was a bit musty inside, and shadows danced all around from the flames of torches James figured were permanent dedications to the fire gods. He walked along the side of the thick stone wall, then began a careful ascent up the stone staircase. As he climbed, the lights from the ground-floor torches faded. He patted his 9mm Beretta in his coat pocket for reassurance. It was illegal under Azeri law for him to have it, but he wasn't about to give up his protection to keep some bureaucrat happy. Besides, if he ran into the wrong people, the law would be the last of his concerns. If Maharani was being watched, she could have been followed here.

In his short time on the Internet this morning, he'd learned that Maiden's Tower was known for its unusual design, a main tower joined with a corresponding, narrower tower that yielded the shape of key from an aerial view. Sometime in the preceding centuries, narrow niches were cut on one side of the larger, cylindrical tower, about head high, which allowed the sun to light the inner chambers. As he continued to climb, the just-before-dawn light helped him see much better now, at least on one side of the spiral incline.

He rounded the top of the staircase and paused when he saw a woman on the roof, alone, in a dark hooded cape and boots. She stood next to a center post. From the top of it, he could hear a flag fluttering softly in the near darkness.

The woman turned. It was Maharani, who offered him the same warm smile as the night before. "Isn't it beautiful up here?"

"Yes it is," he said, walking to stand beside her. "Even a bit theatric."

"I'm sorry for this, but I no longer trust anyone."

"That's okay. This part of the world's beginning to make me look over my shoulder too."

They both turned to the sliver of sun that continued its rise over the horizon. After a moment, she spoke. "It is said that, long ago, a woman jumped from this tower to escape her father. But Aria comes here to remember hers."

She said the words as though she'd been holding them in, waiting for someone to relieve her of their pent-up pressure.

"He was infatuated with all of archeology, of course. But most of all, he loved this building he helped to restore. And whatever he loved, Aria also loved. That is why I wanted to meet you here. To show you the connection between father and daughter."

James looked down at the old city beneath, with its maze of narrow alleys and ancient buildings that seemed to glow with the color given them by the rising sun. "Does Aria have any other family here?"

"Not here. In Karabakh."

"Karabakh? Is that where her mother's from?"

She nodded. "Her father was Italian, but her mother was from there. Her mother passed away a few years ago from cancer."

"I'm sorry to hear that. Aria's had a tough few years, I guess."

"It has been hard for her. But she still has an older brother. His name is Themieux. And her uncle, Lev Wolf, is an important member of the Karabakh parliament." She gave him a warm smile. "And a great-uncle who is like a grandfather to her. His name is Kasim Beria. Also a good man. You will meet him, I'm sure."

"Is she with them now?"

"Yes." She reached under her cape and withdrew a folded piece of paper, then handed it to him. "Here is a map to Lev Wolf's home. You would never be able to find it otherwise. She will be there, or at her mother's home nearby. Where else would the poor girl go and be safe? Those who murdered her father surely know she was a witness. She is in danger as well."

She reached for James' other hand and placed an old skeleton key in his palm, then covered his palm with her own and squeezed. "She gave me this, the key to this tower, her greatest memento of her father. Give it to her, and tell her that I trust you with her father's memory. Then she will know to trust you."

She pulled her hand away and peered into his eyes. "James, you are American. I am also an American. And Aria is my friend. We have been praying that someone would do something about those … those *horrible* people—"

Ignoring her acid inference to the jihadists for the moment, he looked at the map, and then the key, feeling its age and heft, thinking this was getting a little too much like a Hardy Boys mystery for his taste. "Come on, Maharani, don't you think this is silly?" he said. "Just come with me to Karabakh and help me find her. Do it for Aria. No doubt she'll be glad to see you."

She sighed heavily and returned her gaze to the sun. "You don't understand yet, James. They watch me, too. And even if they didn't, the Karabakh border patrol won't let an Azeri pass. Or anyone that looks like an Azeri. But you're obviously an American. You won't have as much trouble…. Or at least, I hope not. But if I accompany you, you might be delayed. You might not get to Aria before those who killed her father do."

James shook his head, hating how these peoples' differences had set up not only ethnic boundaries, but hostile physical boundaries between two countries that should be depending on each other. "Don't worry about that," he said. "I'll figure something out. Just go pack an overnight bag and meet me—"

"Really, I can't."

James saw her fear of the night before return in her eyes. Questions bombarded his mind: *Has she already been approached by those looking for Aria? Maybe even been threatened?*

If so, she'd also likely been threatened not to tell. He should just be grateful that she trusted *him* with Aria's location.

"Okay," he said softly as he unfolded the map and began looking it over. A moment later he said, "This will work."

After giving her some reassurance and the contact information she asked for, he slipped back down the spiral stone staircase. When he got into the car and closed the door, he looked over at Raffi.

"What?" asked Raffi, seeing James' mind working but not knowing at what.

James stayed a few more seconds in silence, then said, "I'm gonna have to get creative here. Can you get me a small airplane, say, in about an hour?"

CHAPTER

10

P.R. gave a deep sigh as his body released a tourniquet of tension, and he continued walking from the front door of the White House and toward the armored black limousine waiting in the circular driveway. One of the two agents who served as his drivers noticed and said, "Rough meeting, sir?"

"No rougher than usual," P.R. replied and slipped into the vehicle, which pulled away silently moments later, on its way back to Langley. The Marine honor guard stood at attention and saluted as they passed, and P.R. gave a solemn nod to signal his appreciation, then leaned his head back on the plush leather.

Thank God the Secretary of Defense shared P.R.'s assessment of the situation, and his plan … and that the President trusted them both. State was dead against it. No surprise that the State Department kept harkening back to the CIA's missteps leading up to the invasion of Iraq. But no matter who sat behind the Secretary of State's desk, the office itself—*Hell, that entire department!*—had a "Let's get along" posture that set up a healthy check and balance within the Executive Branch, offset by the more muscular Department of Defense.

He couldn't help a smile, and muttered, "But then, Defense always holds the *ultimate* solution to problems, doesn't it?"

The agent in the passenger seat turned. "Did you say something, sir?"

He allowed his smile to widen. "No, no, just thinking out loud. Bad habit."

The agent grinned. "Usually, you're doing your thinking on your phone, sir."

"Not today," he replied with a shake of his head. "Today, it's a good day to just think."

Yes, the DOD could always be called on when all other options failed. Yet it was one mission of the CIA to prevent that ultimate solution from being needed. Even though it meant using the unknowing James to effect it. At least, he hoped James' mission would yield that result.

He reached into his suit's vest pocket and pulled out a small bag of licorice, popped a piece into his mouth and returned the bag to his pocket. As he chewed, he mused over the two departments' constant state of dynamic tension.

A few weeks ago, he had set things in motion to provide some firepower if James needed it. There was always a sense of crossing the Rubicon when it came to committing the military. Today, he had been able to gain sketchy agreement within the National Security Council.

Recalling the tense dialogue among everyone at the meeting, he was reminded of how tough it had been to convince the others. On the one hand, he struggled to unearth bad news before it happened anywhere in the world. Yet on the other, he always felt alone when he made a rare and bold prognostication. It was a no-win job.

"But," he muttered, "it's one you cherish anyway."

Another glance from the curious agent, and he committed to keeping the rest of his thoughts to himself. He was counting on James, his new man on the ground in Azerbaijan. And so was everyone else who supported him. If he were wrong, there would be a partisan field day inside the Beltway. If he were right, though, things would quietly move ahead without fanfare or fireworks. He allowed himself a prayer for the latter, reached for another piece of licorice, and forced himself to enjoy the view of the Potomac.

* * *

High above the oilrigs off Baku, the Cessna 172's engine

purred along, steadily plowing the open blue sky. The Caucasus Mountains loomed to the right, and at last, Iran marked the distant southern horizon. Fishing trawlers left wake trails in and amongst the thousands of oil and gas rigs that dotted the open sea here.

James banked the Cessna, and it shuddered at the steep turn back north, toward the uncontrolled airfield where he would close out his visual flight plan.

"Hey, Raffi, I think I've got the hang of this bird," he said when the wings leveled off. He spoke into the boom microphone of the headsets he and Raffi both wore. "Glad the Embassy had this for us to use."

The Sangachal oil terminal, the beginning of Azerbaijan's new Baku-Tbilisi-Ceyhan oil pipeline, bustled with activity. Raffi replied nervously as he gazed down at the oilrigs. "Yeah, you seem to have mastered it, my friend. Nice day for flying, too. GPS working okay?"

"Yep. Let's top off the tank, and I'll let you go pay our respects to our Ambassador's chief of staff while I take care of this little job."

Raffi smiled over at him. "He's not gonna like you hopping across the border."

"Too bad. We only have to advise him, not get his permission."

"He's gonna be pissed anyway. You sure you want to do this alone?"

James turned to him but didn't speak, just gave him a hard stare that showed a mix of determination and still-raw anger over Steve Kranzer's death. He appreciated Raffi's offer. But the guy had a family. And where he was going, the demons were at play.

"Okay, I get the picture," Raffi finally said. "But you know P.R. told me to help you if you need me. So call me if you open a hornet's nest you can't get out of."

With a slight grin, James nodded and returned his attention to the controls. The wheels touched down on the isolated runway, and the plane came to a full stop near a fuel pump. Eleven minutes later, he was lifting back off the runway, this time staying at a low altitude. He saw Raffi's lone figure watching, fading into the distance behind him. A turn to a northwesterly heading, and he prepared to dead reckon his way roughly one hundred eighty kilometers to an uncertain destination in the high reaches of the Caucasus.

He tried to stay focused on what he might encounter upon landing, or what he would do if he couldn't land when he got there; from all reports, the terrain was rough, with only a couple of options, both options in meadows mentioned by an old pilot he had spoken with about that area. But instead of the mental planning he should have been doing, his thoughts kept skipping back to his First Class summer at the Naval Academy. He and Steve Kranzer had been on the pistol detail at the range, teaching plebes how to shoot. But one hot Annapolis night, he and Kranzer both sat, drunk, on a ledge atop Bancroft Hall, the midshipmen's six-story dorm. The two foolhardy twenty-one-year-olds munched on pizza and sipped cold beers, something that was not only forbidden, but grounds for expulsion.

"We're training people how to launch these babies," Kranzer had said after a gulp of beer, studying a 9mm bullet he held in his free hand. He punctuated his statement with a belch.

"Yeah we are, Stevie, my boy," James had replied with a belch of his own. "That's because, every so often, some assholes come along and launch them at us first."

"*Exacilacily…*" Kranzer giggled. "*We* are the vanguard of freedom. And it all starts with these babies right here."

He continued to study the bullet in the moonlight. "Sometimes they're bigger, and go farther, but it all boils down to the same result."

Until now, James had forgotten other details of that evening, like burning the roof of his mouth with hot pizza and the terrific hangover the next morning. But he did remember the deep sense of common ground they had shared in their innocence that night.

Funny … our friendship started over a bullet, and ended over one, too.

When the irony hit him, he took a deep breath and forced his eyes to the instrument panel.

And just in time. The GPS revealed he was just a few kilometers from the coordinates on the map Maharani had given him.

He did a visual check of the area under him. *So far so good....* The small village of Vank was there, and he was relieved to find the landmark Maharani had labeled as Gandzaser Monastery.

"Probably just as well she didn't come," he muttered to himself. "She'd have been scared shitless flying around like this."

Crowning the summit of the grassy slope overlooking Vank, the Christian monastery had distinctive stone architecture. Maharani had told him it was very old, probably built around the twelfth or thirteenth century, but he could see monks strolling in the compound surrounding the church. A couple of them paused and appeared to look up, as though hearing the Cessna, but then continued walking as though the occasional airplane sighting was of no consequence.

He banked the aircraft and followed a poorly paved, tree-lined road for six kilometers before he spotted a place he might be able to land: a meadow surrounded by thick trees where he could keep the plane out of sight. From there, he'd be on foot.

His luck held; the meadow gave a smooth-enough landing. After a slow taxi into the trees, he locked the aircraft and turned toward the road. Only a herdsman and his dog guarded the horses he saw in the far-off meadows, with the snowcapped peaks of the Lesser Caucasus Mountains beyond them. Both seemed as tiny as toy soldiers at this distance. In such a remote area, there was a good chance no one had witnessed his landing.

The air was a bit thin, but crisp and clean, reminding him of his hometown in North Carolina at the foothills of the Smoky Mountains. And as that air had done to him so long ago, he began to feel hungry. He brought food with him, and considered it. But he could still see the monastery's rooftop in the distance. Probably friendly enough, but he didn't want to have to explain himself to anyone in territory he knew to be less-than-friendly to outsiders.

Muttering "Forget it," he reviewed the map and handheld GPS unit, discovered it was only a couple of kilometers to the home of Lev Wolf.

He grabbed his green helmet bag and shrugged it over one shoulder. "Well, Miss Aria Palestinio, ready or not, here I come."

CHAPTER

11

"I've got a full bag." The man strapped into the cockpit grinned; the radio's transmission crackled as always when he was so near a big hulk of metal like the refueling station. But that was just about to change. He keyed the mic again as he eased away from the in-flight refueling basket that floated behind the C-130 tanker. "You've got the lead, Major."

"Roger that. Did everyone go pee-pee?"

"Yes, Daddy. Are we there yet?"

Major Douglas "Sparky" Lester and his section of six A-10 Warthogs had finished topping off their tanks, and now began the breakaway sequence from the tanker. The Warthogs had been in a loose formation on this, the last leg of their flight from their home base in Texas. Now, one by one, they smartly peeled away from the lumbering C-130 and slipped along a jet route in the silky night sky. Radio silence had just become essential if they were to keep a low profile across the Black Sea and into Georgian air space. Their destination: Vaziani Air Base, not far from Tbilisi, Georgia's capitol city.

Sparky checked the next heading, which he'd earlier written on his kneeboard. Then, as he always did, he considered what the squadron would find at their destination. When Vaziani Air Base was abandoned by Russia in 2001 after Georgia won its independence, the United States deployed troops to it to help Georgia regain control of the area, which at the time was full of thousands of Chechens fleeing brutal Russian occupation.

But Georgia wasn't the Pentagon's top priority. Rather, the purpose was to have forces close to one of the world's largest oilfields. Because Georgia lay in the path of the 1600-kilometer Baku-Tbilisi-Ceyhan oil pipeline, one of three such pipelines originating in Baku that moved more than a million barrels a day of Caspian Sea oil to western markets, the U.S.-Georgian alliance meant less U.S. dependence on Middle Eastern oil. The problem was, Russia remained very touchy about this new U.S. presence, especially in light of friction between Moscow and Tbilisi over unrest in Abkhazia and South Ossetia…Russia's excuse to step in and make a power play there.

And that presence is just about to include Sparky and his gang, he thought, and grinned.

When they arrived an hour after sunset, the airfield runway lights were on, but there was no call for an approach, no direction from the tower whatsoever. Keeping their arrival quiet from Russian surveillance created some risks. But they had prepared for this. The six planes landed one after the other, and as they rounded the runway apron, an old gray Soviet truck with an illuminated sign that read "Follow Me" led the six venerable multimillion-dollar aircraft toward a row of hangars. As Sparky taxied past the first three hangars, he noted the crews inside, busily performing maintenance work on rows of Army Black Hawk and Apache helicopters in the first two buildings. In the third hangar, personnel from an Air Force Tactical Airlift Control Element (TALCE) serviced one of their Reaper drone surveillance aircraft.

The fourth hangar was reserved for the Hogs, where they'd be out of view from satellites and curious bystanders. Flashlight-wielding men directed them inside. After some routine maintenance and crew rest, Sparky and his gang would be ready for duty.

* * *

"Oh yeah, baby, I'm gonna *neeeed* you guys. If I have to go in, I want you watchin' over me."

The man stood on the edge of the runway, shrouded in darkness except for the glowing tip of his cigar, watching the last A-10 roll into the hangar. He punctuated his whispered greeting with a soft

"Ooh-rah," followed by "Yep. Something's up. Something big."

Lieutenant Colonel Rip Martin wasn't talking just to hear himself talk. Rip's Marine Expeditionary Unit had been in place for four weeks, and getting this kind of backup sent his warrior instincts into overdrive. Rip's nickname came honestly, from a jump he had made in Kuwait at the onset of the First Gulf War as a newly minted second lieutenant. His parachute had ripped two hundred feet into his descent. He had broken lots of bones on impact, even had to sit out the war. But Rip was a Marine's Marine, and his focus remained on two things: results on the battlefield, which he always delivered, and his men, who would follow him through the fires of hell. Four months later, he got up and put his uniform back on.

Now, he quietly watched the men in the hangars while reflecting on the phone call he had received from the Pentagon a week earlier. The general, the Commandant of the Marine Corps, had only one question: "Do you have everything you need?"

Rip's simple response was a request for more close air support, and here it was. For what, he still didn't know. But he didn't need to.

"Yep, something's up," he whispered, took another drag that sent his cigar tip into a red-hot shower of sparks, and considered what someone had said to him after a predeployment briefing.

"You'll probably end up tangling with an odd alliance of jihadists and Chinese advisors," that someone had warned.

To which he replied, "Any new weaponry or tactics?"

"Same ole."

"That, I can deal with." And after two combat tours in Iraq, Rip knew what he was talking about.

"This Islamo-Fascist business keeps popping up all over."

"And we will deal with it."

Rip now watched the Hogs shutting down inside the hangar. Yes, he had all he needed. He and his Marines were ready for a fight.

"And we *will* deal with it."

* * *

"It is with great pleasure that I welcome you to our new country."

The woman listening regarded the man behind the desk as she would a piece of gum on her stiletto-heeled shoe. "Try again," she said. "Except this time, pause after the word *you*. We want to place emphasis on the fact that this is a *new* country. Try to put some emotion into the tail end of that sentence, *sweetie*."

Ivan Mitrofanov, seated in the same spot where he'd fallen into a drunken stupor the night before, glared at her. For legions of his followers, the glare was enough to set them cowering. The woman only smiled at him.

"Don't like the *sweetie* part, eh?" She exhaled from a deep pull on her cigarette. "Sorry, but I'm here to build your image, not your ego. Now, let's try again.… Please," she added with a conciliatory smile.

Her years as a journalist had channeled her insatiable nosiness into an acceptable line of work. When her looks began fading and she was pushed out, bitterness fueled her to use her gifts to help up-and-coming political movers. And often, those gifts went to the highest bidder, even if they were unfriendly to the United States, yielding a comfortable lifestyle and a sense of purpose she hadn't felt since the day she got her first big news assignment.

Ivan's glare had receded, but didn't go away. He cleared his throat and repeated the sentence with the recommended emphasis.

"Better, much better," she said, nodding in approval. "You think I'm a big pain in the ass, I know. But these things make a big difference. Trust me." She flicked her ashes into a crystal ashtray and put one hand on her hip. "After twenty-two years at CBS News, I would know."

She examined his face, which wasn't glaring now, then gave him a slow smile. "Another thing. You're looking a little gaunt. Let's get you on a high-protein diet."

* * *

James kicked at some sod while he stepped onto the poorly surfaced road. The mountain air cooled his lungs as he walked along, but he allowed his anger to show itself in his brisk gait. He was in the middle of nowhere, on the other side of the planet, because someone had murdered his friend, and so far, only God and the murderer knew why.

And when he found out, he was going to kill the bastard who'd brought him here.

His agitation compounded with the realization that he landed too far away for an easy walk. He now wished he had parked that Cessna right in the backyard of Aria Palestinio's family farm. *Wherever it is.*

Sighing, he thought of Raffi standing at the edge of the runway as he took off, wished he had allowed him to come along.

After about three kilometers, he saw an old man smoking a pipe beneath an enormous shade tree. The bench he sat on seemed to have been carved from another tree, one that had fallen many years earlier. As James narrowed the distance between them, the man noticed him, but seemed unruffled by a stranger's approach. Still, James slipped one hand into the pocket of his heavy leather jacket.

When he judged himself within earshot, he said, "*Dobroje utro.* (Good morning.)"

"*Privet* (Hello)," the man answered back, also in Russian. From under his heavy fur hat, he surveyed James.

"Are you lost?" the man finally said, still speaking in Russian.

"Sort of. I'm looking for Lev Wolf. He lives not far from here?"

"You are not from here."

A statement, not a question. James noted the medals pinned on the man's dark wool overcoat, showing that he was a World War II veteran. Friendly chitchat wouldn't go anywhere with this guy. Only directness would work.

"Actually, I wanted to speak with his niece, Aria," he said. "I thought she might be with him."

The man studied James while he drew thoughtfully on his pipe. "Your Russian is very good, but you are not Russian."

"American. James Marshall." James extended his hand.

"Kasim Beria."

"Kasim?" James said as they shook hands. "This *is* my lucky day. Maharani sent me here. She mentioned your name."

Kasim responded with a nod and continued to work the pipe that protruded through his long white beard. At last, an avuncular smile came to his eyes. "She mentioned me? Favorably, I hope."

James chuckled and watched Kasim quietly muse over the answer to what was undoubtedly his biggest question: how James knew or suspected Aria was here. Attempting to draw him out, he smiled and said, "Favorably? No, not one kind word at all."

Kasim smiled back, this time with his whole face. "Lev Wolf's home is not far from here. You would have found it on your own, but I will take you there." He stood slowly, aided by a gnarled walking stick. Then, to James' surprise, he began walking with amazing speed for such an old man.

"Come," Kasim called over his shoulder. And the two men chatted as they walked toward what James hadn't seen before: a tiny cluster of houses just down the road.

* * *

P.R.'s desk was clean, except for the twelve folders neatly fanned down its left side. Across from him, Bill Schoffner was putting his notes back into a leather valise. They'd just finished a forty-five-minute budget discussion.

"Sorry so much got put off in this quarter's budget," Schoffner said conversationally. "But maybe it's for the best, considering James Marshall's unscheduled mission, huh?"

P.R. leaned back in his chair, knowing what was coming next, and tried not to wince. "We glossed over that, and we probably shouldn't have. He's not on the budget radar. But he will be. We need to set aside some contingency funding for what he's getting into. This is getting bigger by the day."

"Yes, I agree," Schoffner replied in his best Boy Scout voice. "And the longer he stays over there, the more I worry that he'll have a meltdown like he did when I tried to brief him. During the teleconference, remember?" Then, after a long silence that P.R. chose not to break, he said, "Have you happened to hear anything from him, sir?"

P.R. looked at his watch and decided to give him a quick summary. He had done his best to keep Schoffner out of the loop on this op, but with possible budget-juggling looming, which Schoffner would have to be involved with, he had no choice but to update him. "We think we know where the archeologist was digging, where the oil sample came from."

Schoffner sat, raptly attentive.

"There's a site in Azerbaijan called Gobustan, southwest of Baku, the capital. It's rife with Neolithic drawings. The archeologist was crawling around a cave not far from there."

P.R. leaned over and plucked out one of the files, handed it to Schoffner. "Maybe you could give me a second opinion that makes sense. Anyway, I see this getting much bigger, really quick. I need this back this afternoon."

Schoffner had stiffened at P.R.'s emphasis on "really quick." He took the top-secret folder and slipped it into his valise. "Yes, sir. You know I'll do my best."

After Schoffner made his goodbyes and nearly flew from the room, P.R. picked up his phone, dialed a two-digit internal extension, thinking about that conference room's phone number. Nothing concrete, not yet. But he trusted his instincts. They'd served him well over the years. Now he had to take action based on them.

He heard a click, and said, "He just left."

CHAPTER

12

Earlier that same day, as he did most mornings, Rip ran as if he were in pursuit of the enemy. The bones he broke on his ill-fated Gulf War jump still screamed at him whenever he pushed himself like this. But given the choice between death and admitting it, he would happily pick the six-feet-under option.

He had just finished a six-mile run that skirted the Vaziani airfield, a run that didn't get easier over time. But today, his mind needed the run as much as his body did; it offered him a rare moment of tranquility and a break for some clear thinking. He put his hands on his hips, mustered his best command face, and slowly turned around.

Coming up fast were one hundred and twenty Marines of the Sixth Marine Expeditionary Warfare Unit. The MEU stood in a sweaty loose formation, also catching their breath. Most were under twenty, in fantastic shape, and needed no cooling down. To glance at them in their PT gear, they didn't look like warriors at all. A bit closer, and the physical dimension of their abilities became clear, as well as their discipline and determination, a hardiness that one could describe as "presence." On the battlefield, no foe had ever stood before Marines like these without paying a very dear price. From different backgrounds, different towns, different religions, different ethnicities, they all marched to the same cadence, wore the same uniform, and would lay down their lives for each other. They were the essence of the U.S. Marine Corps. Just like Rip, twenty years removed.

"Who are you?" Rip bellowed.

"The United States Marine Corps, sir!" they chanted in unison, now at stiff attention.

"I didn't hear you?"

"The United States Marine Corps, sir!"

"That's better." He grunted, like an animal, "*Ooooraah!*"

"Ooooraah!"

"*Ooooraah!*" he repeated with primordial emphasis.

"Ooooraah!"

"When you fall out, stand tall because you are America's finest! Dismissed!"

There was a growl that roared, then didn't fade so much as dissipate while he and the men scattered. Rip moved his head from side to side, could hear the bones in his neck pop. But the adrenaline rush made his pain of moments ago a memory.

The group finished front and center of the four hangars. He saw some activity at the third hangar and headed over. Three Air Force enlisted men inside the open doors were working on an MQ-9 Reaper drone.

Rip surveyed the equipment, looked over the joysticks and other control items. "You know, I was a whiz at *Halo* … especially after a couple of beers. You videohounds are up early."

"Colonel, we were just about to go hit the rack." Tech Sergeant Benson punctuated his words with a laugh. "We've been up all night putting some enhancements into these units. All four drones are fully mission-capable on a turbo-version basis." He grinned at one of the other men. "Well, we *will* be, just as soon as Mr. Lukanski here finishes installing that new card."

Rip nodded. "You guys first used these in Bosnia, didn't you?"

"Yessir. Starting with the Predator version of this baby in Afghanistan, and then in Iraq. The Snoopy Team's always on the prowl."

The technicians looked at one another, sharing a confident smile.

Rip's gaze at the drones now showed grudging admiration. "I've benefited from these things in the field. Never had the chance to get up close and personal with one like this."

That was all Benson needed to show off his new baby. "Unmanned aerial vehicles have come a long way since they were introduced, Colonel. The newer UAVs have significantly better loiter time and electronics. The new ones are in service in priority-one theaters." He chuckled. "I guess we try harder as the number-two option. But these units have awesome surveillance capabilities."

He rubbed a rag across the back of his neck, then motioned to the drone's belly. "Check out the 955mm variable-zoom lens underneath. It's also got synthetic aperture radar that can see through cloud cover."

Rip accepted the invitation. While he was looking at the lens, he said, "How many of these things do we have military-wide?"

"Well, Sir, I, ah ... I can only speak for the 15th Reconnaissance Squadron—"

"Never mind. Here's a better question. How long can you stay on station with one of these things?"

This time, there was no hesitation. "That's the good news, Colonel. This is now an upgraded model—has a more powerful turbocharged engine and an improved relief on-station system. The exact time depends on the combat radius we need to accommodate. But we can rotate these in and out of your hot zone every twenty-four hours or so and never miss a beat."

Rip rose to a standing position, managing to make his grunt sound like appreciation, not pain, took a few steps back and surveyed the entire craft, noting its forty-six-foot wingspan and twenty-seven-foot overall length. "I've heard these puppies hit home a couple of times," he said, referring to the drone's fourteen Hellfire II antitank missiles. "Pretty neat to see the whole rig."

Benson continued, sounding more proud father than tech sergeant. "We can chat with you on secure voice, even help out with close air support if you get in a tough spot. This system gets better with every iteration."

Rip gave a slow nod. "So you guys can just lounge around in your air-conditioned trailer and fire missiles at bad guys?"

"You got it, sir."

"So, theoretically, you could link with some guy in Tampa, Florida, who drives this thing from a cubicle in Central Command's headquarters?"

"That's right. Except of course, not to correct the Colonel, but in this case it would be *European* Command." Benson referred to the fact that Azerbaijan and Georgia were countries assigned to the European Command, headquartered in Stuttgart, Germany.

"You got my drift," Rip said, fighting the urge to reach down and rub his sore knee. "My point was, warfare's changed."

Benson's face showed pride. "Yes, Colonel. One of these days, it'll be just a matter of who's got the best joystick dexterity."

"I beg to differ, Tech Sergeant. It'll always boil down to one thing, and that's boots on the ground. You'll never win a war without having to look your enemy in the eye and then kill him up close and personal."

He looked at the men, who were now silent, and finished his thought. "But in a way, I wish you were right. Thanks, guys."

With that, Rip turned to walk out of the hangar and head for the showers.

"Colonel, sir?"

He stopped at the call from a Marine just entering the hangar. "Good morning, Guns."

Guns stopped and rendered a salute. "Sir, there's been a VTC scheduled for 1730 this evening." Guns was a strapping, corn-fed Midwestern boy who was Rip's right hand. The driving force in the team's enlisted ranks, he had earned the respect of the grunts who were now in the showers—even the respect of the man who was showing him a thundercloud face right now. "A VTC? With who?"

Guns glanced at Benson's group, decided they were out of earshot. Still, he lowered his voice. "Several parties in Washington, sir. I recognize some of the addresses on the list from my tour in the Pentagon. Sir, this is big time."

Rip gave Guns a grim smile. "No, Master Gunnery Sergeant," he said, his voice gentle. "It's not big time. It's show time."

CHAPTER

13

Before James and Kasim reached Lev's house, James learned that Aria's father, Davide Palestinio, a simple man and an archeologist, had fallen in love with Mamkan, and that Mamkan was Lev's only sister. The two siblings were the heirs of an equestrian family long known for their breeding and training of the finest horses in the area. James strained for a peek while they walked, but the horse farm was barely visible from the road.

It had been a bit awkward at first, but the Italian Davide had quickly assimilated into the family. "Aria took Mamkan's beauty, but if you meet her older brother, Themieux, you will see her father's handsome features," Kasim told him. But then, he grinned. "Except, he has enough of his mother to have an … *impish* look, I believe you say in English."

"Sounds like an interesting fellow," James replied.

"Yes, and the girls *swoon* when Themieux enters the room," Kasim said with a chuckle. "But like his sister and parents, he has a good heart. And both brother and sister love this land." His face fell. "As their parents once did. So very sad, both of them gone."

"Yes, very sad," James murmured. He wanted to ask more questions about the brother and Aria, but later. Right now, it seemed more important to keep working on the camaraderie he had gained with Kasim. He still had no idea what kind of reception he'd get, or if Aria would even speak with him. An ally like Kasim could go miles toward helping him that way.

It surprised him that when they reached Lev Wolf's front door, the old man simply opened it and entered. But then he remembered this was a small village, where everyone knew everyone else. After a slight hesitation, James followed him, entering a foyer complete with fresh flowers on a table next to the door. The spacious living room held a rustic elegance that would fit any European country home. The kitchen, visible through an arched doorway to the right, had an abundance of fresh fruit and vegetables on both the huge center table and nearest counter. The savory scents of a pot roast wafted throughout. James' stomach began pleading, but he willed himself not to think about his hunger, just his mission.

Through the back window, he could see a few people seated on the corral fence, watching a lone rider in the main corral. Before he could ask about them, Kasim gestured toward one of the wooden chairs in the living room. "Wait here, I will bring Aria, if she will come."

Kasim disappeared through the arch while James lowered himself into the chair, and that's when he noticed the painting on the wall. It kept his thoughts occupied until he heard a noise coming from the direction of the kitchen. Minutes later, a woman with long dark hair stood in the archway, backlit by the sun-filled room.

Aria was alone when she entered. James was glad of that. Had the old man seen the look James couldn't hide quite fast enough, his walking stick might have become a weapon to defend his grandniece's honor. Aria didn't seem to notice, though. She was as beautiful as Kasim had described her, and her jeans and white cotton blouse flowed around her shapely breasts, shoulders, and hips as she walked up to greet him. He did his best to control his surprise as well. She was the dancer who'd captured his attention while Maharani visited his table.

"I'm Aria Palestinio," she said, offering him her hand.

"James Marshall. Nice to see you … again."

"You have a good memory," she replied coolly. "And

Kasim thinks highly of you."

Stanford University had lessened her accent, but it was there. He caught a whiff of cinnamon and a flower he couldn't identify. With reluctance, he let go of her hand. "Kasim and I hit it off, I guess."

Luscious brown eyes bored into his. "Maharani sent you to me?"

"Yes, she did. And she gave me something to give to you."

He retrieved the old key from his jacket pocket and held it out to her. "She was willing to take a chance on me. I was sorry to hear about your father."

At the sight of the key, Aria's face showed surprise, and something else, something ominous. "Did you know him?"

"No."

"Would I be rude to ask who you are and why you are here? Great-uncle Kasim sometimes trusts too much." Her mild tone held a threat.

"I'm sorry. Of course you couldn't know. I work for the government of the United States. I was sent here to investigate your father's murder."

"Why?"

He bit his lip, considering his words, then said, "Because we believe the same man who killed your father also killed our naval attaché in Morocco."

She was a good bit shorter than he, perhaps 5′4″. When she dipped her head, he had to resist the urge to bend his knees so he wouldn't lose sight of those brown eyes. But when she didn't reply, he had no choice but to break the awkward silence. "Your home is beautiful."

She looked back up, and he could breathe again. "Thanks. It's been in my family for many generations."

James indicated the painting on the wall with a small jerk of his chin. "An Armenian Khachkar?"

At last, she allowed him a smile. "So, you know your history." She moved over to the painting, followed its raised features with her fingertips. "Then you likely already know the cross represents the Armenian people's sufferings over the millennia, which my people share. The background, which is made up of plants, is symbolic of the vitality of my people, who have endured genocide, ferocious invaders, and other terrible means of death. But through it all, we kept our national pride, and our unity."

She looked at James. He was staring intently at the painting. While she waited, she pulled back her hair from her face.

He finally said, to himself as much as Aria, "How much longer will your people have to suffer?"

Her soft chuckle held rancor. "Is there an end to it?"

"Maybe there is…."

"But we haven't found it after centuries of searching."

James kept his eyes on the painting, but could sense her studying him. Picturing those eyes on him caused him to feel a passion that would certainly be unwelcome. Uncomfortable and abashed, he blurted, "I know how you feel."

Her gasp made him swivel his head just as she sputtered, "How could you *possibly*? Have you ever lost someone you loved to murder? Have you ever known that kind of pain?"

James turned his whole body away from the Khachkar to face her. "That's the reason I'm here."

Her face stilled, but he couldn't tell if she believed him. He weighed how much he could share with her. What if she already knew about the oil; what if she already knew that had led to her father's death? What if she was afraid to tell anyone, or had kept the oil quiet for reasons of her own? He had to trust her. But first, she had to trust him.

"The naval attaché who was killed … he was my best friend. Your father … I believe they were both killed over something your father found, or found out about. I think the people who killed them maybe didn't want anyone else to know, so they killed Steve. And your father. Maybe to keep them quiet."

She backed away from him and put her balled-up hand that held the key over her mouth. Her fist tightened around the key as she took in a deep breath.

"I'm going to find out what was so important to those people," he said, turned back to the Khachkar and dropped his head. "And then, I'm going to kill them." He spoke softly, but did nothing to obscure the determination in his voice.

She looked at him as his gaze drifted to the floor, and then studied the key in her hand. "Then we both want the same thing."

"Yes, I think we do."

She stood in deep reflection for a moment more, and she said, "What can I do?"

He looked up. "Show me where your father was working. His last dig. Perhaps your father left something there, some clue—"

"G'tichavank Mountain, south of here." Her eyes shifted away, then back to him. "There's a cave—"

"If you don't mind walking a few kilometers, my ride's just down the road."

She drew a deep expectant breath. "When do you want to leave?"

"Now," he replied with a shrug.

"Just like that?"

"Just like that."

She cautiously explored his expression for a moment. "I've just met you, and I have only your words and this," she held up the key, "to base any trust upon. And now, you want me to go away with you, alone."

"If you need to get your uncle's permission—"

"It isn't that," she said. "I'm a modern woman, I come and go as I please."

He nodded. "If you say no, I'll understand." *Just please don't say no—*

She pulled in a harsh breath, blew it out. "No. I mean yes. Let me leave Uncle Lev a note. Better that way." She smiled. "If I go outside and tell him, it will take us forever to leave."

He gave her a smile he hoped was reassuring. "Let's go, then."

The Iranian leader sniffed in disgust and sipped his green tea. He was surrounded by infidels who all had misplaced motives. Mitrofanov was a power-hungry pervert, tainted with Western ambitions for wealth and power. The Chinaman was no warrior for Allah, and therefore worthless. The two were allies of convenience, perhaps not even valuable ones. He reminded himself of an ancient Persian proverb: *Use your enemy's hand to catch a snake.*

Yes. Iran's hand will not be bitten by world opinion on this. Not that it mattered so much to him. After using Hezbollah to stop the unstoppable Israeli army in Lebanon, it did not matter. After disrupting democracy in Baghdad despite the crusading Americans and their Zionist supporters, it did not matter.

He said, "You will have your petroleum engineers share their findings with our engineers?"

General Lu nodded. "Yes, as soon as the testing is completed."

The dream of the Islamic caliphate moves steadily to reality, then. The meeting continued, but the Iranian barely listened. The Chinaman's answer gave him the final assurance he'd come for. Iran's nuclear program gained momentum in spite of the West's labors to contain it. In a few short years, Iran would wield the most powerful and terrible weapon known to mankind. *Then, the world will tremble.* In the interim, Iran was willing to accept the arms of China and this wretched Russian's assistance. Until they were no longer needed and could be swept aside. Then, there would be no need to go through middlemen for anything. Besides, neither man knew the French were giving him discreet information, facts that came directly from inside the American CIA itself. And why should he share any of that with them? He owed them nothing.

He forced himself to return to listening to the two men across the room, comfortably seated on low couches, not knowing that General Lu entertained similar private thoughts. Except that in Lu's vision, China was the victor. And that in Lu's vision, God under any name played no part in the victory.

* * *

Lu rubbed his chin. *'Oil for weapons.' 'Oil for power.' How much that sounds like the United States today…. And today, Iran exports Islam the way Europe once exported Christianity hundreds of years ago: exploiting, plundering and controlling. All in the name of God, or Allah, or whatever name these fools decided to call their fantasy father.*

No matter. China would get what it wanted, and if need be, would deal with this new form of fascism if and whenever necessary. But for now, he wanted to know who the Japanese agents were, and what steps were necessary to deal with them. Those agents, whoever they were, had stopped the Iranians from completing their mission in Baku. The only living person outside his government who knew of the oil under the Caspian Sea remained alive— alive to tell anyone she wished of the oil, including the Americans. For that, the Japanese would pay.

* * *

Ivan Mitrofanov walked out of the meeting, where he had sat quietly in turn, giving careful glances to both men as they spoke, his head swimming with roaring currents of rage and indignation. *They think I am their pawn. Soon, they will both see things very differently!*

Yes. Soon, the insignificant dog who had been kicked all his life would rise up against those who would oppress him, and he would show them no mercy.

His cell phone vibrated, but he waited to return the call until his bodyguards had escorted him to his car and were speeding away from the secret meeting-place. Grinning, he listened until the speaker's rantings slowed from a raging river to a trickle. Only then did he say, "So, you don't like the American, eh?" He let the words slip from his tongue with delicious deliberation.

"I would kill him if I had the chance," the gruff voice said.

"Oh, but you *did* have the chance."

Ivan listened for a rebuke, but heard only silence on the other end.

"I gave you the chance, but he and his little weak-kneed friend bested you," he continued, knowing the effect his taunt would have. "You let him turn a gang of drunken Russians on all four of you." Ivan chuckled aloud to further goad the man. "Admit it. You got your asses kicked."

"His blood will run in the gutter the next time I see him."

"Oh, so you would like another shot at this guy?"

"Name the time and the place." The man's Persian accent was overcome by his breathing, now heavy into the phone.

Tiring of the game, Ivan said, "Okay, tough man… I will give you another chance to show what you're made of. But if I do, and you fail, then it will be a heavy price for you to pay."

"He will perish, as if by the sting of the scorpion … painfully. Allah will guide me."

"You will hear from me in a few days, then." Ivan ended the call and laughed while he shifted his weight in his seat to expend the fresh rush of adrenaline. *Revenge is such a powerful motive… And stupidity just helps it along.*

CHAPTER

15

The silence had gotten heavy enough to be physically painful. Plus, it gave James too much time to think about his initial attraction to the woman he walked beside along the country road. "So, tell me about what's been going on around here," he said.

Aria shifted her backpack to the other shoulder and gave him a sideways glance, bemusement on her face. "There's *soooo* much to tell."

"No, not around the village. I mean in the country. How about when the war started?"

"I was just a girl in 1992, but it had a terrible impact on all of us. Everyone suffered, but the world didn't care. We had seventy-two horses here at our farm, but we loaned most of them to the army." She smiled and looked toward the mountains. "They still have most of them. They sometimes bring them in for special care."

"Things seem to be back to normal here now."

"It looks that way, but it will never be the same. Nothing is ever the same after war." .

James looked around him as they walked. "How are the other horse farms doing?"

She shrugged. "That's what I meant. Most of the Karabakh horse breeders were at Agdam, southeast of here. A big town of fifty thousand people. Now, it's abandoned, a ghost town. People only go there to get construction materials from the ruins."

"Oh, I didn't know. What happened to those horses?"

"They were sent to stables in Lenberan. Our farm is one of the few breeding farms left. That's one reason I chose the major I did at Stanford. My dream is to help this area become as prosperous as it once was. Before the war took so much away."

She spoke with a palpable sadness that James could almost reach out and touch, a melancholy that remained with her while they walked. They were almost at their destination. When near enough, hoping to distract her, James pointed toward the copse of trees. "There's our ride. See it in the shade?"

Her eyes flew wide, but she stepped off the road and into the trees to follow him. "You *flew* here? From where?"

"Not far from Baku. You okay with flying to G'tichavank?"

She didn't speak, but her face when she turned to him said, *Do I have a choice?*

"I'll take that as a yes," he said, opened the passenger door and held it for her. "Hop in."

She stared at him for a moment, and then climbed into the aircraft. Once inside, he handed her Raffi's headset. "Put this on. It's gonna get noisy for a while, and I need to hear your directions."

Eyes wider, Aria took the headset, placed it over her ears, and strapped herself in.

* * *

Minutes later and a hundred kilometers away, four tan-colored Range Rovers pulled over to the side of the dusty road. One man emerged from each, and one of the men motioned to the others. "*Viens ici.* (Come here.)"

Moments later, they stood over a map of the surrounding area that was spread out over the hood of the first vehicle. The SUV's radiator fans hummed underneath, working to keep the vehicles' engines cool in the midday heat.

A breeze lifted up one corner of the map. The second man smoothed it down while the first man unfolded wire-rimmed reading glasses and studied the ridgelines and notes on the ruffling paper beneath his searching fingertips. "Take half of the men and search this area," he said, his French accent heavy. "I will concentrate my search over here." He took off his cap and wiped his brow. As he did, his khaki vest opened slightly, revealing a shoulder holster.

"Are you sure they are here?" asked the second man, an Azeri.

"*Certainment*. Our information comes from the highest sources: the CIA itself. Marshall is here with the girl. I am sure of it."

"If we find the family's home, should we—?"

"*Non!* The family is too well known here. The uncle is too well connected politically. Only if we discover they are hiding the girl … If so …" The man smiled. "Then, we will do whatever we must."

* * *

"There." Aria was pointing to G'tichavank Mountain, which stood out for miles around, particularly from the air.

"When the snows cleared last spring, my father came across the entrance to the cave. No one had ever been inside before, he said. At least since the Ice Age."

"How big is it?"

"Big. I'll soon show you."

They were still fifteen minutes or so away. He looked over at her. She seemed to be enjoying the flight. He decided on some friendly banter. "So, Aria, tell me about your career as a belly dancer. Maharani says you're her best one."

She laughed, surprised by his lighthearted question. "I wouldn't exactly call it a career, nor am I her best dancer!"

"She did a good job of keeping you a secret last night."

"I had heard that you were looking for me, and I was too curious to sit on Uncle Lev's couch all night. Had you recognized me then, I would have left immediately. It wouldn't have been safe to talk there."

"So you *are* determined to get to the bottom of this…"

"Yes. Yes I am." Her expression became serious again.

"So, back to the belly dancing...tell me how you got started."

Her serious expression melted, and was replaced with a slight smile. "I met a woman at a class at Stanford. She and her husband own a restaurant called the Feast of the Balkans in Los Gatos, not far from the campus. She is Greek, and her husband ... Oh my God, he was a lot of fun. She would dance, and later, he would get into his table routine."

"Table routine?"

"He'd start out small. He'd pick up a chair with his teeth. Then he'd take a shot of ouzo, and then graduate on to picking up a *table* with his teeth. And then, after another shot of ouzo, he'd invite a pretty girl from the audience to sit on the table, and then he'd pick her *and* the table up with his teeth. Then, guess what? He'd have another shot of ouzo to celebrate!"

Aria now smiled broadly at the memory. "He brought the house down, he was lots of fun. Then we'd form a conga line that usually went all over the room, then through the kitchen, then out in the parking lot, then wherever...."

James grinned back at her, but had to keep his eyes on the controls now; they were close. "That place is on my list as a must-see."

"Anyway," she continued, "she and I got to be close friends, and one day she invited me to join her class. It's fun, and it keeps me in shape."

He began to slowly circle the mountain, looking for a suitable place to land. "The east is out," he muttered. "The face is too steep. Aha, the south side looks better."

He made a steep turn around this spot, noting that the tree cover was open along what appeared to be a dirt trail.

"That's the road to the abandoned monastery on top of the mountain," she said, following his gaze. "The one I told you about."

"You didn't tell me about a monastery."

"I didn't?"

"No, let's take a look."

After a couple of passes, he made up his mind to land right on the trail. The mountain's southern peak had an angled plateau. Thanks to the road, it would make a passable landing strip for the Cessna 172. The plateau was forested, but he estimated the clearing as big enough for the small aircraft. To leave, he need only turn the plane around and gain takeoff speed as he rolled down the plateau's slope.

But, landing that way might be downright scary to the uninitiated passenger. He glanced at Aria, decided it was probably better not to warn her, and said, "I'm going to land on top of the mountain."

"What? There's not enough room to land a plane! No way!"

"Way!" He set the flaps to full, swooped down on the trail's clearing, pulled back the throttle, and flared the aircraft for a soft landing.

Not understanding, Aria let out a muffled scream, tore off the headphones and put her hands flatly against both sides of her head …

"Are you crazy?" …

… then over her mouth …

"You are crazy, aren't you?"

… then back on her head as the plane touched down and she shrieked, "You are out of control!"

He didn't have time to laugh. The aircraft rumbled along as he pumped the brakes and slowed it to a near stop, stepped hard on the left brake and turned the aircraft, nestling it underneath a tree canopy.

"Ahh, nothing like a springtime stroll on a mountaintop," he said.

"You *are* completely nuts!"

And finally, he could let go of the laughter he'd been holding.

* * *

FBI Special Agent Jeffrey Miller knew the FBI pulled lots of threads together in fighting crime, but for this agent, who had walked a Moroccan beach chomping on potato chips just days ago, convinced this case was already cold, getting an odd lead on the sniper was a lucky long shot.

Maybe too lucky. Too easy.

Miller bit back his natural suspicion for now. He had only had time to scramble through the stack of paper his assistant had put on his chair so he wouldn't miss it. But there was no time for a leisurely review: not then, and not yet. If what he'd just read was true, he had to move on it.

He put the stack down, picked up the phone, and dialed the contact in a small township in upper New York State. Soon, the person who answered was saying, "It weren't pretty. According to the doc who treated her, he beat that poor girl all to hell."

"Sheriff Bingham, I've read your report, but do you have any guess as to why she offered the tape in the first place?"

"Well, she said she had the recorder hidden in her purse, I'm guessing outta habit."

"For evidence if she got busted?"

"Right. You know, they always ask the 'Are you a cop?' line just in case. Maybe one of her buddies advised her to do that."

"You sure she was a hooker?" Miller said. "Any chance of us talking to her?"

"Nope. I mean yes to your first question. At least that's what the doc said she told him. And no to the second thing you asked. Turned out she gave a fictitious name at the hospital, and she's already been released."

"So she's long gone."

"Yep. Probably figured that a hooker wasn't going to get a fair shake with a big-wheel diplomat. Besides, he's gone too. Left the country."

"So she brought you the tape thinking we could use something on it."

"That's how I see it. God, he was talkin' some shit. Not only sexual, but global-scheming kinda stuff. You know … The kinda stuff you boys deal with. I sent the original tape with the overnight I sent you."

"I've read the transcript. You did the right thing sending it here."

"You know, we see a lot of crazy shit in this business, but I have yet to see a hooker use an audiotape like this for revenge on some goofy diplomat."

Miller smiled into the phone. "We probably haven't seen the weirdest of the weird yet, Sheriff. It's a new day. Goofy's gone global."

He expected laughter, but the sheriff said, "Yeah, you got that right. Goofy in a bad way. But to tell you the truth, I never heard of this one before. Talkin' 'bout rulin' the world, runnin' all over the Chinese *and* the Middle East? Whew!"

After reminding the sheriff to keep this quiet, Miller ended the call and picked up the report again. The sheriff must have missed the recent news, where this particular goofball was mentioned. Also in a follow-up email from James Marshall. The name "Ivan Mitrofanov" was starting to show up in a lot of places, for the wrong reasons. And from everything he had read, Ivan Mitrofanov *could* turn out to be the biggest of the bad-guy dictators.

He sipped on his coffee, trying to quell the minuscule tinge of excitement that threatened to swell large enough to derail his thought process. He needed to get this to the CIA, he decided. That tape, as distasteful as it was, was a huge win for intelligence, a valuable knight in the newest of the violent chess games.

"I'm no chess whiz, but I bet that guy at the CIA is," he whispered.

"So this is where your father worked in his last days?"

Aria didn't reply right away. When James asked the question, she was leading the way down a steep trail. Her backpack jostled on her shapely rear end, and her thick, wavy ponytail bobbed as she walked. He wished neither movement were happening, at least in front of him. At least not right now. The rocks were treacherous here, and it was a long way to fall.

At last, they were over the rocky part of the trail, and he forced his mind from watching her backside to what she was saying.

"Yes, this was Father's last dig," she said. "He first came to this country in the late seventies, to study the Neolithic sites at Gobustan. He eventually shifted his work to the west, to this place. G'tichavank Mountain has some curious rock formations, and there were folklore tales about hidden caves. He was the first modern explorer to lay claim to them. Even now, few people even know this place exists."

"G'tichavank Mountain?" James said, confused. "The mountain stands out for miles. How could they not know?"

He heard her chuckle. "Not the mountain, silly. The *caves.* You're still crazy, I see."

Yeah, crazy. Crazy enough to be hiking into an unexplored cave for an oil sample.

While James silently exhorted himself to keep his focus on his mission, they worked their way down and around the side of the steep face of the mountain, encountering more rock-strewn stretches as they went. They first went to the monastery, built by monks in the fifteenth century but now abandoned, covered in graffiti. After wandering around its empty rooms, they came out front and stopped at an ancient well. A heavy door covered it. James noticed a small cutout panel on it. Out of curiosity, he pried it up and off.

"Looks pretty dark down there!" Aria said, and an echo came back to her. "I wonder if there's any water in it?"

James checked his watch. "Don't know. But let's go. We've got two, two and a half hours of daylight left, at most."

They came around a rock formation, and below them was a small, dark area on the face of the mountain. Aria paused for a moment. "Father named these, you know. Called them the Leaping Deer Caverns."

James noticed the tension in her body, but didn't comment on it. Instead, he said, "After what we went through to get here, I can see why the cave entrance went unnoticed for so long."

She nodded, but the sadness remained on her face.

They moved toward the entrance, but once there, she stopped and grimaced. "I … I haven't even thought of this place since Father …"

James could see her dread, could see she wasn't ready yet. But he also knew she wasn't going to sit idly by when she had a chance to find her father's killers. James was her best hope for that, and they both knew it. And once inside, the exploration would go much easier with her there. She'd been inside the cave, he hadn't.

"We need to go in there," he said, reached out a hand to pat her shoulder. "*You* need to do this."

His words seemed to steady her. She breathed deeply, in and out, then said, "Okay …. Let's do it."

It didn't appear anyone had been to the cave to break down the project yet. Aria picked up two lanterns sitting on one of several small fold-up tables just inside the entrance, handed him one of them. James lit them and checked the time. Then, he winced. *Any longer, and I'll be pushing a dusk landing back at the airstrip after I drop her off at the farm.*

Looking around, he noticed the cavern's true entrance, a few yards back from the opening where they stood. He noticed some objects laid out neatly on a nearby table, with sheets of paper beneath them. He walked toward it to investigate, but something else caught his eye.

He picked up the object and glanced at her. "A Neolithic spearpoint," she explained. "Very old."

He hefted it and ran his index fingertip over the dull point, thinking, *The tip of the spear. Wonder what my buddies at Special Ops Command in Tampa would say about this? That nothing's changed in the past thirty thousand years, probably.*

No, they wouldn't say that. Rather, they'd probably say, *Put that thing down, stop looking at that girl's tits, and keep trying to find the frickin' oil!*

He put the spearpoint down, then waved a hand at the dark entrance. "You're my tour guide, Mademoiselle. Show me the way."

She smiled. "I bet you say that to all the spelunkers."

"Only the gorgeous female ones."

Instead of pulling out the "crazy" talk again, her smile widened, and he allowed himself to hope while she led him into and through the cave's narrow entrance: so narrow, she had to turn sideways to slip through it.

"We won't get any sunlight in here until late afternoon, when the angle is right," she said. "Until then, the lanterns will have to do."

He nodded, turned sideways, and followed her into the cavern, whistling when he realized how huge it was. And how special.

"I can see why your dad named it Leaping Dear Cave," he whispered. All around the main room, the rock walls were covered with scenes of what appeared to be deer hunts. Hundreds and hundreds of deer were caught in flight as they raced for their lives from the crudely drawn hunters.

"The Caucasus Mountains are rife with both caves and Neolithic artifacts," she said. "The most famous being Gobustan, where Neolithic man left a pictorial diary of life. And death," she sighed, "in what was, in some ways, a decidedly more primitive time."

Nothing much has *changed between men,* he thought. *Hunters and gatherers, but also fighters.*

"You're looking at that spearpoint like you think it's important."

Startled, he looked up at her.

"Do you think it might have something to do—?"

"No, no. Not really," he said quickly. "No way to be sure, though. Just thought I'd take a close look at it while I'm here. You never know."

Nodding, she waved him on, deeper inside the cavern, where she stopped. He was pleased to see that her original tension was gone, replaced with eagerness to show him her father's work.

"Here's where it gets interesting," she said. She stooped over and walked through the shoulder-high opening of a tunnel, worn smooth over the eons. Like the main room, its walls were covered with more Neolithic artwork. "Isn't it beautiful?"

He nodded. "Yes. Just … amazing. There's no other word for it."

Under her proud gaze, he surveyed the variety of scenes depicted, ranging from animal hunts to spiritual rituals to dances. But he also couldn't help surveying Aria again. She glowed in the lantern's light, especially her eyes, which shimmered and danced at seeing his pleasure in what they were viewing. But a moment later, he saw the sorrow woven into her expression while her eyes moved from scene to scene.

After a moment, they continued. The tunnel opened into a taller, much broader chamber, and at one point there was a fork in the path through it.

"This way is the best," she said pointing left. "The right path is what I call the Bat Barn. Lots of bats." She shivered.

"Lots. And the ground is always so … slimy. Ugh! Father said it was because of the puddles of oily water in there. They mixed with the bat guano, I suppose. I just think it's gross."

Trying to not show a reaction, he peered into the smaller, more angled opening to the right, heard squeaking, and didn't argue.

After about fifty feet, the left path entered a circular room with a cavernously high ceiling. Startled, he said, "Is that—?"

"Yes, sunlight. From the very top of the mountain, I believe."

The light filtered down from a vertical, chimney-like channel that hovered above a circular stone hearth on the cavern floor. The hearth was scorched and littered with what looked like charred wood. All around, on the walls, were more deer images.

"Father thought this was where early hunters took their kill," she said while he looked around. When he stopped next to one large blackened section of the cave's floor, she continued, "Perhaps what you're seeking is somewhere around here, maybe in this room. There was apparently a great deal of ceremony around each hunt at one time."

He chuckled. "There still is. Just not the fiery-sacrifice kind. At least, I don't think—"

Aria's lantern hissed and gave out, cutting the light in half.

"Let's go back to the entrance and get another one," he suggested, and they worked their way back up front. When they were almost at the entrance, he said, "As soon as we have light again, we'll go into the Bat Barn. That's the only place we haven't checked, right?"

She winced. "Yes, but … ugh. You can go in there by yoursel—"

He stopped moving, reaching out a hand to prevent her from continuing. She looked at his tensed jaw and whispered, "What's wrong?"

"A shout," he whispered back. "I'm sure of it. Outside."

CHAPTER

17

It wasn't much, but there was some scrub at the cave entrance. Little foliage on the bushes; it was still early spring. But it provided cover while James carefully surveyed the area. Seeing nothing, he waved Aria beside him and, together, they moved to a boulder next to the brush.

This vantage point was better, and worse. Here, he saw the source of the noise: moving up the mountain, perhaps halfway from the ground to them, was a small group of men. Soldiers, possibly mercenaries, nine or ten of them.

They were a hell of a lot closer than he liked. Still, he took the time to squint at them for a moment, trying to get an exact count. They weren't mercenaries, he decided. But based on their ease of maneuvering up the mountain with so little noise, he doubted they were regulars either. Perhaps they were part of the militia he'd been briefed on, the one being assembled by Ivan Mitrofanov and his allies.

Whoever they were, they knew what they were doing here. And no matter what their intent, they were far too close. James didn't fully understand the alliances between the Armenian army and these brigands, but neither group would welcome him here … especially if they were after the same thing he was after. Considering the firepower those soldiers carried, he was all but unarmed. And, he had a vulnerable civilian to protect.

Neither he nor Aria had made a peep, he was certain of it. So it must have been the warrior's sixth sense that made the lead soldier glance up just as Aria suddenly raised her head. Or perhaps some sort of perverted fate kept him from pushing her head back down fast enough. Whatever the cause, he heard the soldiers shout excitedly at each other. A glance told him they'd begun a crawling, scrambling uphill run, directly toward him and Aria. One of them stopped, took aim, and fired a short burst at the boulder.

"Let's move!" He grabbed her by the hand and they started running toward the trail. He had found it, the source of that oil. But sample or not, he had to get her the hell off this mountain, like yesterday!

Using the too-thin foliage to hide behind, they made their way back up the steep trail. Not fast enough: a shot ricocheted off a boulder in front of them, and he dragged Aria with him behind a group of larger rocks, ones he prayed didn't offer a clear shot from below.

"What next?" she said in a panting whisper. He experienced a dual sense of relief, surprise, and admiration at the lack of panic in her voice. No doubt, growing up in a war zone had taught her survival instincts.

He glanced around, noticed they were near the top of the mountain: achingly close to the plane. But they still had to negotiate the rock-impeded section of the path, and there was little cover there to protect them on the final climb up the trail.

"Hate to say it," he said, keeping his voice low, "but I think we're pinned in this spot."

"No! Let's keep running."

He shook his head, but didn't explain there was no way he would put her in the line of fire.

Breathless, he reached into his helmet bag and pulled out his 9mm pistol and two grenades, which he placed carefully next to the bag.

"The pistol's no good at long range," he said. "The grenades, they're easy to throw downhill."

"But there are only two of those," she said, watching his face.

"Yes. That means I'll have to time the throws. Don't worry, I've had a little practice."

"That tells me two things," she said.

He looked up at her, curious.

"One, there's a lot I don't know about you."

"And two?"

"You really *are* insane."

He grinned at her. "Can't deny either right now. But if we make it out of here, I can't say I'll ever prove you wrong on the crazy part." He paused for a second. "But I hope we do make it out of here. I'd like it if we could get to know each other bet—"

Another shot rang out against the boulders. There was no longer any risk of revealing their location, so he took another glance. Not good news, but not the worst. Three of the men, clearly the fastest of the bunch, led the way. The others were well behind them, maybe as many as ten minutes behind. Yet they all moved feverishly toward the top.

James looked back down at his pathetic arsenal, did a mental calculation, decided he had a few minutes. Grinning, he said, "How's the phone reception around here? Any good?"

Her forehead wrinkled. "Huh? We're being chased by an army who's shooting at us, and you want to plan your next vacation here or something?"

He put down his pistol and shoved his hand into his inside jacket pocket. "Nope, just hoping my sat phone, which I just remembered, works up here."

"What, you're going to call the cavalry?" she sputtered.

He shrugged. "We've got about three minutes before those goons get here. I figured I'd kill a little time by telling my partner he'll have to find another ride home tonight."

She leaned her head against the boulder and closed her eyes.

* * *

At the moment the phone rang, Raffi had just looked at his watch and gone back to pacing his office. Something was wrong, he could feel it in his bones. He hadn't heard from James, but he wasn't about to call him like a worried mother. Raffi realized he had been wrong about this guy at first. But one part of his early assessment hadn't changed: James Marshall didn't really like jumping into a hornet's nest … unless it was one he created himself.

Raffi answered, and James spoke while he watched the advancing men, gauging the distance. "No time for chitchat, I'm in a world of shit. I'm not sure who's after me … probably the militia; shots have been fired, and more on the way. I'm pinned down with Aria about fifty feet from the top of the south side of G'tichavank Mountain. Hang on …."

He threw the first grenade, which exploded harmlessly about fifty feet from the three men. They ducked for cover, and then continued their ascent. He put the phone back to his ear with a muttered, "Shit."

"I just checked the map and called the Embassy," Raffi said, speaking quickly. "We have a contract helicopter on standby at the airport. We can get there, but not nearly soon enough. But I'm working on it. Keep your head down and—"

James wasn't listening. He threw the second grenade, and this toss was a lucky one. At that moment, the three men were bunched together. A friendly bounce put the grenade in their midst. The explosion sent them tumbling down the steep incline, lifeless.

He turned to Aria, saw her terror, but couldn't think of anything to assuage it. In fact, he was suddenly having trouble thinking at all. Behind her, a soldier he hadn't noticed stood on the trail, blocking their only path to the plane, training his assault rifle on them.

A second man appeared, and the first man gave James a rough smile that lacked a few teeth, then said, "*Lotfan…* (Please)," followed by the halting English words, "Put your hands above you heads. Now."

Not Armenian, or Turk, James thought, each thought stumbling over the next one. *Farsi … He's Iranian…., and I think I've seen that face before … outside a bar … with a drunk Russian— Oh, hell.*

Instinct drew his eyes to his pistol, which lay on the ground on top of the helmet bag. The Iranian's broken smile chided him, and the two soldiers exchanged a long look before returning their grinning stares to James.

The man's expression of smug conquest changed to surprise when a metal object struck the side of his head, and stayed there. His jaw dropped as his head jerked to one side, and he fell to his knees. After a brief wobble, he collapsed onto his face.

The same instant James realized what the object was—a six-pointed fighting star—the second man whipped around in the direction the object came from, as though to train his weapon on an unseen foe. So his back was to the knife-wielding man who leapt upon him from the rocks above and drove his blade down into his lung past his collarbone. The man gasped, and by the time he turned back to James and Aria, eyes and mouth agape, blood was bubbling from his lips.

James could hear a tussle just out of sight, behind the rocks from which their savior had appeared. During the scuffle, he'd grabbed his pistol. Now, he readied himself for the next enemy he saw.

"You won't need that. We are friends. Come up! Quickly!"

The words had been spoken in accented English from behind the rocks.

The man with the knife helped Aria to her feet and led the way around the rocks, where they were met by three more sturdy Asian men with crew cuts, all wearing the same sand-colored camouflage uniforms. No insignias, but James didn't much care. Unlike the Iranian militiamen, these guys weren't trying to kill them.

The leader, the same man who'd called them up, issued terse orders in a language James recognized as Japanese.

Then, he spoke to James in English. "I am Agaki. We must go. In your airplane. Quickly!"

"What the hell are you doing here?"

"No time. We must go now."

"Well, this is bizarre, but I'm in no position to argue," James said.

"Not *bizarre*," Aria sputtered at him. "This is just nuts!"

Agaki's comprehension of English must have been as good as his spoken command: He guffawed at that.

Agaki's men assembled their gear and they all headed for the Cessna. There were only fifty feet left to climb to the plateau, but it was far more difficult going up than when he and Aria descended the trail what seemed like a lifetime ago. Shock and depleted adrenaline saw to that. The group worked zealously, though; there were still at least half a dozen enemies behind them as motivation.

They topped the trail and were finally on level ground. Now, they ran toward the plane.

"We can't get everyone and the gear in the plane!" James said, panting. "We'll have to leave some of your equipment or we'll be too heavy."

Agaki nodded and issued more orders, and his men began tossing items from their bags. Mostly canvas covers, foodstuffs, and other nonessentials. They all trundled into the five-seater, with Aria in Agaki's lap in the front copilot's seat, while James fumbled with the keys and got the engine going.

The plane roared to life and James stood on the brakes and quickly set the flaps in their full position. He knew the plane would wallow on takeoff—six adults in a plane designed for five guaranteed that. But how much, he didn't know. At least he had some altitude to start with, a good two thousand feet of it.

"Hang on!" he shouted above the engine's roaring, then released the brakes and began a heavy, bumpy ride downhill. The Cessna felt sluggish as they neared the edge of the plateau, but it was far too late to worry about it. With a shouted, "Here goes!" he gripped the yoke and pulled back gently. The plane dropped precipitously as it left the improvised airstrip, and Aria and at least two of his other passengers screamed.

As the plane wallowed, it took gunfire. He could see tracers coming off the side of the mountain, near the top. The rest of the militia must have heard the plane's engine starting, and quickly figured out their next move. At their slow speed and relatively low altitude, the plane was a sitting duck.

He drew back on the yoke until the copilot's yoke, which moved with his, struck Aria in the stomach, then yelled "Suck it in!"

She attempted to make room. Fortunately, her effort was made easier by the plane's nose-up attitude. They were definitely in trouble from the extra weight. The prop strained loudly, and they lost all airspeed and began to slide back toward Mother Earth.

Screaming "Hold on everybody!" he stomped on the left rudder pedal and jerked the yoke over in the same direction, sending the aircraft into a hammerhead stall that took them straight down. Aria let out another long scream, this time accompanied by all her fellow passengers.

James didn't have time to explain his maneuver. If it didn't work, there would be no need to. He pulled the aircraft out of the dive, established stable, controlled flight, then made a steep turn out of the remaining militia's direct line of fire. He leveled out and sped away to the east, toward Baku, skimming the treetops of the forest.

Only then did he look over at his terrified copilots. "Learned that one from a buddy of mine," he said with a wink. "Crop duster … knew all the fancy moves." He couldn't see the men in the backseat, but he was pretty certain they shared Aria and Agaki's horrified disbelief.

The silence inside the cabin was the byproduct of intense fear, but James didn't try to allay it. Instead, he used the silence to evaluate their circumstances. The gunfire hadn't missed its target, as he'd hoped. Fuel was streaming out of the wet wing on the starboard side. The airspeed indicator showed one hundred and forty knots, but the fuel gauge was slipping toward E, if slowly enough to calm his nerves for now. Still, he needed to pick up some altitude after he was inside Azeri airspace, to allow time to find a suitable landing site if they ran out of gas. That would draw some unwanted attention to him, and at a time when he had a rogue's gallery of unscheduled passengers.

But first, he wanted to know why the hell they were even in the area.

"What was that all about back there?" He directed the question to Agaki.

"Yeah, why were those people trying to kill us?" Aria asked.

James gave a twist of his head and a weak smile as if to say, *Aria, I just asked him that.*

One of the men in the backseat moaned in pain. Agaki turned to him. "*Misete kudasai.* (Please show me.)"

The wounded man turned his shoulder to Agaki, revealing a bullet's shallow graze running across his shoulder and a few inches down his back.

"How is he?" James asked.

"It is … difficult to tell from here."

Aria peered at the injured man, then glared at Agaki. "It's only a scratch. Now tell me why those men were trying to kill us! And who are you guys?"

The aircraft hit some turbulence and jumbled everyone in their seats. Another loud moan came from the backseat.

"*Shitsurei shimasu.* (Excuse me.)" Agaki attempted to twist around to the backseat.

"Speak Azeri, or English, or Russian, or something I can understand," Aria said, angry now. "What planet are you from anyway?"

Agaki's features twisted in sudden anger. "*Shizukani!* (Quiet!)"

James looked at the fuel gauge, which had moved quite a bit in just the past few moments. He said, keeping his voice calm, "Back off, Aria. That can wait." Then, to Agaki, "But, how about some English please…?"

"I am an officer of the Japanese army, and these are my

men—"

Aria twisted violently in Agaki's lap and somehow managed to grind her elbow into his temple. "You? Oh, my god! It was you!"

Agaki cursed in pain as she continued to press, trying to face him. The airplane rocked with the motion, causing the wounded man in back to cry out again and forcing James to turn all his attention to controlling the plane.

Aria's eyes were now directly on Agaki's. "*You* were there when Father was killed! You told me they were after me too! You know who killed my father, don't you? Answer me!"

Agaki roared in frustration as she twisted again, and the shouting match continued. Finally, James pulled out his pistol and pounded it hard against the dashboard. "Quiet! Quiet, all you squawking wet hens.… Listen!"

Then the aircraft became silent. Completely silent, because the engine was no longer running.

They were out of gas.

He didn't explain what just happened, but didn't have to. Thankfully, the silence continued while he maneuvered the airplane into a southeasterly heading, searching for suitable landing sites.

Suitable, as in discreet, and quick.

He could land on a road and then coast off into the trees. The aircraft wouldn't be noticed, maybe for days, or at least until it could be recovered. Such a site would also allow for an easier discharging of his mysterious passengers. As though in answer to his mental plea, he spotted some fig orchards to the left that would do just fine.

He looked around the cockpit, which remained silent. It was now dusk, and everyone looked exhausted. But they all showed one unspoken concern on their faces.

"We're okay!" he said. "I can land us, even without an engine. I've done this before. I landed in the woods once, on a road, without an engine."

No one argued, nor was there an outpouring of confidence.

He'd have to prove it to them.

"Okay, hang on, we're going in!" he said. He directed the Cessna to glide silently toward the road he'd lined up on. As the plane continued its descent, the trees began to whiz by at eye level, and finally, they touched down on the bumpy dirt road.

They jostled along for about two hundred yards when James noticed a deep washout in the road ahead. He'd been pumping the brakes, but pushed the left brake extra hard now, causing the plane to swerve to the left and into the orchard. The right wingtip clipped a tree, and the craft turned to the right and came to a complete stop after ramming into a fig tree's trunk. The fight was out of all of them, and one by one, they tumbled out. James drew out his sat phone as he emerged. Miraculously, it was still with him, and still intact.

"No moah aipranes," sighed one of the Japanese as he surveyed the Cessna with James. It had been shot up pretty bad, and the damage inflicted by the landing left it a hulk. Hollywood's imagination would have made it a fiery crash scene. But in this case, there was no gas left to burn.

Agaki looked long and hard at James, then stumbled over to the crippled Cessna. No one spoke as he deliberately abandoned all sense of military professionalism, drew his pistol from his holster, and angrily pumped a round into the engine cowling.

CHAPTER

18

James finally cleared the vehicle inspection at the embassy compound's entrance, and he wearily drove ahead into the parking lot. Ordinarily, he appreciated the thoroughness of the Marines, with their mirrors under the vehicles and explosive-sniffing dogs. But after a long night of debriefing there, and being called back so soon now, he only found annoyance in the process this time.

He had been able to keep Aria out of this by getting Raffi's help. On the way back, Raffi had arranged to stash her in a safe house on the outskirts of Baku. She fought him on the idea, and she wouldn't be happy staying there for long. When he returned there in the morning, she would likely demand to leave. He hid a grin. What he was about to face might not be a total waste of time, after all. Perhaps it would help steel him for *that* upcoming confrontation.

Following through this morning with written reports was going to be tedious, but even more, he dreaded the meeting scheduled with the ambassador's chief staff officer, who had a reputation for coming down hard on any America citizens who rocked the diplomatic boat in Azerbaijan.

The four-story building, like many high-profile buildings in Baku, was an interesting mix of European and Asian architecture, nestled amongst trees that extended out to Azadlig Prospect, the main road. The eight-hour time zone difference with Washington seemed to keep the parking lot full around the clock.

He saw Roger on the way inside, unloading boxes from his well-worn but lovingly maintained Ford pickup, and gave him a friendly wave.

"Hey there, James," the big man drawled. "Top of the mornin' to ya, and all that good shit!"

"Morning." James looked, eyes narrowed, at the box Roger held. "What kind of contraband you got there?"

"This here's the primo shit. High-end rotgut brandy that'll give you hangover pain to rival a mother-in-law's bitchin'. But I'll tell *you*, this stuff can pull the thinnest hint of flavor out of a cheap cigar. You get yourself a good Cuban ... oh my God ...."

He chuckled at his joke and continued to unload cases of the brandy.

"Hangovers?" James said. "You know what, I'm sucking wind this morning. I've got headache pain that makes me appreciate that comment."

"I'll talk softly then," Roger said with a conspirator's grin, assuming he had a hangover. James chose not to tell him that he likely had hit his head while landing the engineless plane.

James studied the labels on the stack of boxes. "So who's all this for?"

"The big man himself," Roger replied, referring to the ambassador. "Sends this hooch by the case to his buddies back home. Cheap, but it's novel. So he gets some mileage out of that. 'Course, I make fourteen bucks a bottle, so I ain't complaining. Hey, you ain't married, are ya?"

"Nope. Not yet."

"You just wait. Young guy like you, you'll find you a honey. And there'll be this plump old hen two steps behind her when you take her home. Yes, sir, when I finished my tour in Desert Storm in '92, I just didn't go back. Left everything…"

James rubbed his neck and wondered if he could find a polite moment to head inside. He needed a cup of coffee. Badly. But Roger continued his story.

"See, Azerbaijan was about the farthest place from Texas I

could think of, and I wrangled a job with embassy security as a civvy working with the Marines. Retired from there. Things were tough here then for the local folks. Early nineties, you know. Turned out to be a good place for me, though. Can't complain."

He kept unloading the cases from his truck. "This stuff here keeps me busy, I guess. Augments that retirement check. Keeps me in the middle of things."

"Yeah, I hear you're the cumshaw king in this part of the world." James was referring to the old military term for the art of unofficially *procuring* things that were hard to get. This was usually done through trading of goods or favors, or both.

"You heard right, pardner. If you need it, ol' Rog'll git it for ya quick!"

James grinned. "For a price."

Roger paused, looked from side to side, then grinned back. "Hey, I hear you joined the flying club. Been out joyriding?"

James winced. "Cute. I suppose somebody else is going to be pissed off at me here."

"Sir, will all due respect, you do have a way of stirring the pot, so to speak. I just wish you'd consider taking me along as shotgun sometime."

Raffi had told James that Roger had been with the Green Berets' 10th Special Forces Group out of Fort Carson. Not a bad person to have riding shotgun. "Can you shoot straight while you're driving?" James said.

"So long as you hold my beer, I can hit anything you want."

"That was a serious question."

Roger grinned, but looked James dead in the eye. "You just say when, Commander."

"In that case, I'll keep you in mind, Master Sergeant."

Roger perked up, clearly pleased with James' recognition. "Thank you, sir. And … Roger works just fine for me. I'm getting to be an old coot, I guess, but I can still stand tall when it counts."

His headache forgotten, James smiled as he continued into the Embassy, even at the Marine who buzzed him into the building, snapped to attention, and greeted him with a crisp salute.

* * *

"You don't like me, do you, sir?"

James was just a few minutes into the closed-door meeting with the chief staff officer, and his headache throbbed harder than before. He had quickly discovered why Raffi was so reluctant to contact the ambassador's staff for anything, at any time.

"*Like* you?" the man replied. "I don't like your *kind*. The world is screwed up enough without people like you circumventing the rules at every opportunity. I got a phone call from the Azeri president's office this morning, wanting to know why they found our Cessna full of bullet holes in the middle of an orchard!"

The man began to pace the office. "You get here, don't check in with us, start a drunken riot, cross the border illegally, get into a shootout, wreck an airplane … The Islamic protests here have drawn reporters from all over the world. If they get wind of this …. Frankly, if you didn't have friends in Washington, you'd be on your way to Zambia. And I can't believe I'm allowing you leave time after you made this Embassy look so bad. If I had my choice, you'd be working in the file room in the basement. Understand?"

I don't work for you, you cocktail-guzzling State Department weenie. That was the silent voice in his head. A more rational voice came from his mouth: "I think I'm beginning to get the picture …, Sir."

"*Get the picture?*" Breathing hard now, the chief staff officer pointed a finger at James. "Here's your *picture*. If you find yourself in an Azeri jail one night, don't think we're going to be in a panic to get you out. I don't know why they sent you here, or what you're up to. But you're not as good as you think you are, *buddy*."

He sat down, snatched up a folder on his desk, and began reading it. "That is all."

* * *

James walked down the hallway, grateful that P.R. was apparently doing his part in Washington, fending off the State Department. He still had to see Aria. But that was tomorrow's trouble. Right now, he needed to come up with a way to find out Agaki's game. The man was holding back something, and James wanted to know what that was. The first step: getting close to him. But the dangerous edge he had also sensed could make it a difficult and delicate task.

He steered the car away from the compound, wishing Kranzer were still alive. Steve Kranzer could get anyone to talk. Never even had to threaten violence. *Well, not usually.*

He sighed bitterly and muttered, "On the downside, that might be why he's dead now."

"Come on, Chuck, work with me on this one." P.R. made the request of his old friend Charles Purvis, who shared his disdain for Ivan Mitrofanov. Right after his intended-to-soothe phone call with the enraged chief staff officer at the Embassy in Baku, he called Purvis to have lunch.

The U.S. Ambassador to the United Nations gave P.R. what he had, then asked, "The guy's a lunatic, but is he really stupid enough to trust the Chinese as much as he seems to? And do you really think the guy's going for the big brass ring?"

"Look, he's no aspiring banana dictator," P.R. said. "He's shrewd and cunning, and he's determined to be a power hitter on the world stage."

"A power hitter? Like *Mini-Me* in North Korea?"

P.R. suppressed a laugh and leveled a serious tone. "Chuck, the FBI report details twelve important commodities that will be part of STRONG…"

"One more time on STRONG? I've got the report here, but haven't had a chance to look at it."

"That's STrategic Resources Of Non-aligned Governments."

Purvis gave him a grimace. "Sounds like some damned Bond thriller."

"I *wish* it were fiction. Let me finish. Here's what STRONG boils down to in Ivan Mitrofanov's case. Let's say that this Caspian oilfield does fall into Ivan's hands. If he gets sixteen million barrels of oil per day under his control—combined with Venezuela and Nigerian output, that's the number we're projecting—that speaks all by itself. But then, thanks to STRONG, if you throw in eleven other hard-to-get strategic resources like chromium, platinum, and a few others? Then you've got a single, low-level dictator in complete control of a *super* OPEC … *an organization that prints money.*"

"And you picked this up off of a tape of him with a hooker in New York, huh?"

"God … it was ugly." P.R. drew in a deep breath. "Let's just say that he rhythmically announced each of the twelve resources during his session, followed by '*April Fools! They will all be fools in April when we meet.*' There was more, but you get the drift."

Purvis considered this. "April first. About ten days from now, he expects to know if the STRONG deal's coming through. And if it does, Ivan'll shake off China and Iran like a dog shaking off a flea dip."

"Yep."

"I'll nose around here and see if I can help figure out where the meeting is."

"Thanks."

"So where do China and Iran fit into all of this?"

"They don't," P.R. said. "Not as far as any of our operatives can find out."

"Ahhh. So if they knew what he was up to, that he's planning to cut them out if he can, then things might change for our friend Ivan?"

"That's the plan. Check out everybody's schedule, and we'll find that meeting place. You can bet your butt on it, and you'll still be able to sit down."

This brought a grin from Purvis. "P.R., you *do* have a nose for evil, don't you."

P.R. shrugged and gave Purvis a hard stare. "Thanks, Chuck, but this time we just got lucky. Pure and simple. And we've still got to find out where they're all meeting."

* * *

Even with the tension of anticipation, the prospect of dinner with Agaki seemed a welcome relief to James as he descended the elevator into his apartment building's elaborate lobby. The dusk enshrouding the lobby's huge windows offered a psychological salve after the grueling day at the Embassy. There was little activity here, save a few businessmen and other miscellaneous foreigners transiting the hallways.

Azan, the now-not-so-mysterious porter, met him in the lobby, giving James' lucky Cubs ball cap an admiring eye. "Sorry, James," he said. "The *Yankees* will win the World Series this year."

James laughed aloud. "Oh God, Azan … I travel to the other side of the earth, only to meet a Yankee fan. In the United States, we root for our favorite teams, not necessarily the one with the best record."

"You have made that obvious to me, Commander," Azan said with a grin.

"Ever see a game-saving homerun in the bottom of the ninth? From the stands?"

"No I haven't. Yet the might of the *Yankees* rules."

While James was rolling his eyes, Azan removed the package he'd been holding under his arm and held it out. When James' eyes came to rest on the box, he was overcome. They were cheap cigars by anyone's standards, but the gesture said volumes to him.

"Okay, I'm going to Americanize your thinking a bit tonight, Azan. The little guy with heart is what the Cubs are all about. The sooner you understand that, the sooner you're on your way to becoming a Cubs fan."

He pulled off his cap, gave it a longing glance, and then held it out in an offering. "Two stogies gets you a piece of genuine Americana."

Azan eyed the cap, an uncommon item in this part of the world. "Deal."

Two minutes later, Azan said, "Yes, my son will really

like this." Then, beaming, he walked off, fingering his new treasure.

"Wear it with pride," James called after him, waited until Azan was out of sight, tucked the cigars into his jacket pocket, and headed for the building's exit.

* * *

One hundred and fourteen meters away, across the square from the apartment building, a darkened third-story hotel window was slightly ajar. Inside the room, a ceiling fan rotated slowly over a man lying still on a bed covered with a plastic tarp. As he studied the comings and goings through the building's doors, the fingertips of his left hand manipulated a scope mounted on a high-powered rifle. A duffle bag was laid out flat on the floor beside the bed; several small items related to the rifle were neatly lined up on it.

"Patience, my friend. Patience is the virtue of the hunter." General Lu spoke softly to himself. He would lie in wait for hours, days if necessary, to have the perfect shot. They needed just a few more weeks, and this American was not going to spoil their plan. Not this American, or any other. And no underling could be trusted for this task.

Lu shifted his weight on the bed slightly. He'd been there for nearly three hours, and he could maintain this position, and his focus, for many more. Yet he couldn't resist thinking about the letter. His younger sister had mailed it three months ago from their childhood home in Bagou, a remote mountain village of southern China situated in a lush, forested valley. The letter spoke of family members and other local news, which was of little interest to him. That is, until she mentioned their train. As children, they rode a narrow-gauge steam train to school and to market. They'd sit together on bright-green-lacquered wood benches and take in the view of the thick vegetation on the steep slopes on either side of the train.

As it had always been, Lu thought it always would be. Always *should* be. But in the letter, his sister wrote that their train, his cherished childhood memory, would soon be reserved for taking coal to the city to be used in smelters and coal-fired power plants. Just for that. No more passengers, no more children dreaming of their future. Just coal. All of the China he'd known as a boy, and now as a man, was touched by a corrupting industrialization that seemingly had a life of its own.

And that was why he was here.

The plastic tarp crinkled audibly as he shifted his weight and refocused on his mission. The sniper is a human weapon used most commonly in combat, rarely in the assassination of diplomats, or even enemy agents. He'd spent most of his time in Karabakh posing as a diplomat interested in the country's business methods, while getting the new militia organized and in place to assume control of the country. But the current aspect of his mission, while unexpected, was something for which he had prepared for years. This was his moment, and he would not fail China. That the Chairman had personally selected him for this, and the Moroccan mission, told him his role was of urgent importance.

The rifle stock pressed against his shoulder so tightly that he could measure the rhythm of his heartbeat and its impact on his delicate aim. He would time his shot around the beating of his heart, at the exact moment of his choosing. He repositioned his trigger finger along the thin metal wisp that would soon set this powerful device into motion—and whispered, "Patience."

* * *

James opened the door to his building and smiled; the Lexus sent to pick him up was ten minutes early, and the driver stood quietly near the vehicle. James climbed inside, quietly agreeing with Agaki that a pickup at the building's rear entrance was a good way to draw less attention to their meeting. The car drove safely down the alleyway and then disappeared into the flow of evening traffic, while death waited at the front door.

Oblivious to the danger, he settled back and enjoyed the ride. Mercedes was the status symbol in this part of the world, but the Lexus was Japan's signature luxury automobile. And on the diplomatic social scene, Japan was always one big cocktail party. Each embassy would, seemingly in turn, host a function where guests enjoyed drinks and great conversation—and collected information to plow into a report the next day at work. So to some extent, they helped each other out with something to write about. Nothing that would compromise their national security interests, but interesting-enough tidbits nonetheless: a "word in the ear" that helped oil the moving parts of the international machinery.

But tonight was different. Tonight, James was Agaki's only guest.

His head still hurt from the plane ride, and he really needed a cold beer. He leaned harder into the plush leather interior and closed his eyes, remembering what P.R. had told him once: If you do the right thing in a tough situation, then you won't ever have to face your toughest critic: yourself.

Yet, during the Embassy's after-action debriefing, one of the staffers had actually questioned whether James was "good enough" to carry through on the secret mission the CIA Director had assigned him.

Long ago, Steve Kranzer and he had several conversations about what made a person qualified to engage in a particular mission. He recalled Kranzer's reasoning, the reasoning of a twenty-year-old who'd already been tested many times at the Academy:

'Not good enough.' Just whose place is it to say who's good enough? Einstein flunked math once because he wasn't good enough. Miles Davis flunked out of Juilliard because he wasn't good enough. Hell, Nixon couldn't get into the CIA because he wasn't good enough.

The car took a slow turn into the Japanese Embassy's compound. James barely noticed.

I might not be 'good enough,' he thought now, *but I'm a results guy. So go ahead and be pissed, but be sure to kiss my unworthy ass while you're at it. And, while you're blustering, I'm going for results. That's what I do. And if that sycophantic, blowhard ambassador's flunky doesn't appreciate that, it's his loss.*

James had had to repeat his story several times for the

ambassador's staff and a few others who wanted every detail to report back through their channels to Washington. He was sorry P.R. would have to field their crap, but there hadn't been time to contact him before the order came to visit the Embassy.

One thing that came out in the briefs was that Major Kishikawa Agaki, along with his special forces team, was hot on the same trail as James. James had already been grateful to him for saving his and Aria's lives; the fact that he shared James' mission made James eager to know him better. That— and finding out the unknown *something* that kept bugging him now.

Unbidden, thoughts of how Aria had affected him the first time he met her came into his mind. How devastated he'd felt at the mere possibility of her dying on that mountaintop. This reminded him that her stakes, and the risk she was taking in searching for her father's killers, were at least as high as his in wanting to find and kill the bastards who'd murdered Kranzer. He quietly wished he could have brought her with him, and perhaps he should have.

"But no," he muttered, recalling her fiery reaction to recognizing Agaki. "That would just complicate matters more."

The Lexus pulled in front of the Japanese Embassy, and he prepared to find out how deep Agaki's finger was in his pie, and why.

* * *

Agaki's blue blazer and dress slacks made him look much different than he had in his fatigues and combat gear. And this time, he greeted James with a firm handshake and a slight bow of the head. Then he said, "Welcome to Japan!" in a reference to his embassy's sovereign status

He motioned James inside. "Not quite home, but you will enjoy all of its comforts. And the ambassador sends his regrets. He was called to Tokyo on urgent matters."

They began with a tour, chatting while walking the embassy's floors and continuing after they took chairs in what James considered the study. Waitstaff entered on silent feet to serve cocktails and hors d'oeuvres. Somehow, they'd known his favorite beer was Amstel Light. "Gee, I wish we had the intel you have here," James said, raising his glass.

Agaki smiled, as did the young Japanese girl who served them and left as silently as she entered. But Agaki also raised his own glass, Sapporo beer.

"How is your wounded man?" James said when the polite talk wore thin.

"Not badly injured, but I've sent him back home to take leave with his family. Thank you for asking."

"When I saw you and your team on G'tichavank Mountain … it convinced me that postwar Japan has changed."

"Yes it has. I have deployed to Samawah, Iraq, and … elsewhere. Japan is an island, but like your country, can no longer think or act like one."

"Yes. The world changes too."

"And alliances with it."

James nodded. "I think you're referring to the … new cooperation between the Iranians and Chinese. And their new presence here in Azerbaijan."

"*Hai*. We are sensitive to China's involvement here. No, more than sensitive to—*vulnerable* to—China's actions anywhere on the world stage."

James understood what he meant. China had a distinct advantage in manpower and munitions, so Japan usually was first with the olive branch when relations became strained. But now, the olive branch dripped oil. Their relations were at a post-war low, and differences over natural gas resources in the seas between them didn't help things, especially in this environment of scarce energy resources. *Something has to give soon on that equation,* James thought to himself.

Agaki continued. "So where is the girl?"

"Oh, yes, I meant to mention that. She thanks you for the invitation. But Raffi, my partner, helped get her settled into a safe house here in Baku."

Agaki leaned back into his soft leather chair. "Is she all right?"

"Yeah, I guess. She was pretty shaken."

"I understand. I recall how difficult it was, seeing her react to her father's death."

James smiled. "She sure didn't forget you."

"No."

James cleared his throat. "Did you take a lot of heat for what happened yesterday?"

Agaki grimaced and quietly dipped his head.

"That answers my question. Same on my end. You guys got there ahead of us." He held up his Amstel Light. "You've got better sources than we do."

Agaki gave a wry smile. "You and I? We are just foot soldiers here in a bigger game. We did not know for sure what was going on there, just that China is *very* excited about a great discovery on that mountain."

James thought a moment. "So we find ourselves here for the same reason."

Agaki raised his beer in salutation. James smiled and nodded as he did the same.

"So, you guys were all set up on G'tichavank," James said. "Until the ugly American came bopping in and screwed everything up."

"I can't totally disagree with you. But you did bring a beautiful woman with you. One who thinks you are … out of your mind."

The two men shared a chuckle, then Agaki said, "Traveling with her has been a tough assignment for you, eh?"

James smiled and raised his eyebrows in agreement, but then changed the subject. Suddenly, he wanted to keep his thoughts about her to himself.

He became aware of appetizing fragrances wafting into the room. "Something smells delicious."

Agaki nodded and grunted, but seemed dissatisfied with James' attempt to change the subject. James decided it best to assuage his host's curiosity.

"Aria's been very helpful in figuring all this out. Between

you guys reading the Chairman's tea leaves in Beijing, everyone in Washington watching Fox News all day long, and the two of us drinking beer over here in Baku, we should have our arms around this problem in no time."

When Agaki only nodded, James noticed Agaki's *ka-mon*, the family-crest lapel pin on his coat. Typically, the *ka-mon* was worn by samurai warriors to identify friend from foe, or to distinguish social status or authority. "Is that your family *ka-mon*?" he said to break the silence.

Agaki reached up and gently touched the pin. "*Hai!* You are familiar with this?"

"I've read some Japanese history, mostly about the Edo era."

They were served another round of beers, and Agaki said, "This has been my family's *mon* for almost four hundred years. My family is from Kyoto. Each generation has served Japan, beginning with Yoshimitsu Ashikaga." Agaki bowed his head almost reflexively, as a gesture of humility. "The symbol is Plum. Most *ka-mons* are of the plant family. There are thousands of them."

Agaki spoke for several minutes about the battles in which his ancestors fought, then said, "Now, tell me about your family. A man such as yourself must have come from a great lineage."

"My father was from North Carolina, as was his father. Before that, it gets a bit sketchy. I come from a mix: German, Irish, French, and Welsh mostly. They all left Europe looking for something better." He grinned. "Guess that kind of makes me an all-American boy."

"John Wayne!" Agaki raised his beer glass.

James laughed, raised his glass, and acknowledged the toast with a hearty swig. Then he refilled their glasses from the fourth round of fresh bottles brought to them, and proposed a toast of his own. "*Toshiro Mirafune!*"

Agaki, visibly moved by this compliment, bowed again. James hoisted his glass as a challenge to accept, and Agaki did. He took a long series of gulps that drained his glass, and then slammed it on the table, bellowing in Japanese. James didn't understand what he said, but clearly the alcohol was starting to speak for both of them. He was grateful for the fellowship. He was also glad he had a ride home. If he expected to discover the *something* he sought, however, this was going to be a long, wet night.

* * *

"Someone has been playing your man in Washington the fool, *mon vieux*. He has been compromised, and now they are just playing with him."

"What do you mean?"

"Gobustan was a waste of my time. No one of interest was there. No James Marshall, or any sign of a pretty girl." His glass went to his lips, and after a few swallows of iced-down scotch, he continued. "I would pull him out if I were you … and tell him to watch his back on the way to the airport."

The man on the other end was silent for a moment. "You are sure of this?"

"I am sure. We have known each other a long time, and we both know how this works…."

"Then I will pull my man out." He hung up the phone, put his stockinged feet up on the table, and leaned back in his chair. As he did, the pistol hanging in its holster on the chair's arm swung back and forth, a slow pendulum. France had the best information, but was still in the dark. He would have to find another way to figure out what was going on with this mysterious oil discovery.

He leaned forward, groping for the half-empty bottle on the table, and muttered one word that summed up his feelings about the day before: "Merde!"

* * *

It had been a long day, but a good one. Azan had changed clothes and was headed for the hotel's front door, happy to be headed home, but stopped while he reached into his bag for one of the cigars he'd bought earlier.

His hand encountered something else first, and emerged

with his stogie, along with his newest prize: the Cubs ball cap. *Might be my last chance to wear it,* he thought. That was likely, after his son saw it. Grinning, he put it on and slipped the cigar into his mouth, then exited the building into the night air.

Just outside the front door, he paused again. Cupping the cigar with his hands, he had to lower his head while he pulled his lighter's flame through the tobacco leaves. The smoke curled around him in the dim light, until his head lurched back and his body collapsed onto the sidewalk in front of a door splashed bright red before the sound of the shot even reached the building.

CHAPTER

20

James surveyed the wooded area before he slipped out of the rental car. The secluded spot was perfect for a safe house. However, going to any safe house involved precautions that included being certain you weren't followed. And after what had happened last night, he wanted to be extra careful. Something, perhaps even that trip to the mountain, had drawn out the shooter. No matter what had brought it about, a killer was close, and dangerously so.

He was sick about Azan. That bullet was for him, and he knew in his gut that it came from the same man who killed Kranzer. He had to head south to follow up an urgent tip from Langley, one he thought might lead to the shooter's origin. But he couldn't delay meeting with Aria. Even telling her about Azan on the phone last night didn't quell her demands to leave the safe house. If he couldn't convince her to stay, she might be the next one to die.

He nodded to Frau Ketchel, the sixty-seven-year-old German woman who peeked between the curtains of the cottage's back door. According to Raffi, she had lived in this two-story house alone since her husband died seven years ago, and had been a friend to the CIA since her sister was killed in the Lockerbie terrorist attack. The agency had rare occasion to use this house; nonetheless, Ketchel maintained her proficiency with a pistol through monthly sessions at the Embassy range and was always eager to help out.

"*Good morgen*, Frau Ketchel," he said as he went inside.

"*Good morgen,* James. Your photograph doesn't do you justice."

"They say if you look like your passport photo, you need the vacation."

She laughed. "Would you like some tea or coffee? I have both."

"Black coffee would be great, thanks. How is she?"

Frau Ketchel frowned and shook her head as she poured a steaming cup. "She's been through a lot, that poor girl. And she doesn't deserve a bit of it."

"I couldn't agree with you more. Thanks for taking her in."

"You're most welcome. Your agency can always count on me."

"I've heard that about you. Again, I thank you." He sipped his coffee. "Where is she now?"

"Upstairs. First door on your left. She came down for tea earlier this morning, dressed, so she should be up for a visit."

"Did she make the call to her uncle?"

"Via satellite phone, as you instructed. They were relieved to hear from her. Her uncle wanted her home immediately. Yet he understood."

"I'm sure."

Frau Ketchel smiled. "She favors Earl Grey, like me. I like her."

James smiled back. "I'll be a few minutes."

"Take your time," she said, sipping her tea. "I was just about to start weeding in my back flowerbed."

He trotted upstairs. Rather than knock, at first he just said "Aria?" to the door. When there was no reply, he gave a few quiet taps. Still no response. A few more attempts, and he set down his coffee and pulled his pistol. With one hand on the doorknob, he held his Beretta up with the other, then turned the knob and threw open the door.

She was at the window, holding a fireplace poker she'd grabbed from the room's fireplace.

"Oh my God! I didn't know it was you. You scared me to death!" she said, returning the poker to its stand.

"It's okay! I'm so sorry. I didn't mean to scare you."

He put the Beretta back in his shoulder holster. Aria stood motionless, her eyes shifting, and he wondered if she was upset beyond being startled.

"I'll, ah … I'll wait downstairs," he said. "We can talk there."

"No. That's not it. You said it's okay. It's not okay. They're monsters," she stammered out. "They killed that guy at the hotel. They killed Father. They tried to kill me. And I still don't know what the heck is going on here. And that's … not … *okay!*"

He started to speak, but saw tears form and walked toward her. He stopped short of touching her, no matter how much he wanted to. She'd been through a lot of trauma over the past few days, beginning with her father's murder. No doubt, this latest murder brought it all back to her again.

"What could be that important?" she said between sobs.

"Nothing's more important than your love for your fa—"

"That's not what I mean." Her voice wavered. "My father loved old things, studied them. What could he have possibly known or had that was so damned important? What were you looking for in the cave?"

He fought for the right answer, realized at last only the truth would do. "Your father entered a game he didn't intend to."

She looked at him through tear-wet eyes. "What are you saying?"

He took a deep breath. "Your father stepped into a realm of ugliness most people either don't know about, or would rather avoid."

"Will you please get to it—?"

"Oil."

A long moment passed. "Oil? Those little puddles? Is that why Father is dead and I'm being chased all over creation? Over stupid *oil*? *Why*?"

"Aria, you studied business, you know how important oil is—"

"But why Father? And how the hell would he have had access to that much oil anyway? He dug for stones and bones, for god's sake, not oil! It was just an annoyance to him!"

He took a deep breath, blew it out slowly. "Your father found it. And some people … some very bad people … believe there's a lot more there."

She looked at him, not comprehending. "But there's so little there—"

"Aria, listen! Some people believe there's a lot more, under the mountain. And aside from you, only your father and one other person knew where it was. The other person was my friend."

He crossed his arms and shifted his weight as he continued. "And there are people who would take it away from its rightful owner: the people of Karabakh."

"Who?"

"Pick any country. The Chinese. The Iranians. Could be just about any government in the world."

Her face tightened. "Father is dead because he found some oil." She put one hand over her mouth and turned to the side, and then turned back to him.

He owed her more explanation. But what could he say to explain her unthinkable loss? "It's not just the oil," he said. "It's … a rapacious and cruel need for control … to control what they want."

It wasn't enough, he knew. He barely understood it himself. Why one country or another was willing to do anything, including declare war or commit murder, to grasp control of something they could learn to do without if they only tried.

Her hands dropped slowly to her sides, and he searched her face, her eyes, for what she might be thinking. As he did, he reached out and briefly touched her arm. Realizing his comforting gesture might not be welcomed, he pulled his hand away and backed up a step.

To his surprise, she walked toward him. Her lips parted, but she made him wait for words as she touched his arm in return.

The two of them didn't speak, but their eyes locked in a deep conversation. After a moment, she said, "It's so unfair. I …"

He hated himself for suddenly wanting her. Anywhere else, in any other situation, he wouldn't hesitate to pursue what his body was telling him to do. But in this place, under these circumstances—

She took a deep breath and spoke directly. "You wanted to see where Father found the oil … That's why you had me take you to the cave. Because that was his last dig. You thought it might be there … Admit it!"

Caught off guard, he could only say, "Yes, that's true. But I know how to find the cave now. If you tell me where to search inside the Bat Cave, I'll—"

"No deal. If you want to find it, you'll have to take me with you. You'll *never* find it without my help. That cave is *huge*. Full of crevices and nooks. It'll take you too long to find the puddles … That army. They're surely guarding the cave now. If you go back, those thugs, whoever they are, will kill you before you can find anything."

"Don't you worry about tha—"

She rolled her eyes. "*That's* exactly what I meant!"

"What?"

"You drag me off in an airplane, I nearly get shot by an *army* of killers, then you crash the plane, and then stash me away in this little … little … *bungalow* of yours. And now you want to take me completely out of the loop." She paused for breath, her face taut with anger.

"All right. I'll explain what I can. But I'll have to hurry it up. I've got a train to catch."

"Where are you going?"

"Down south to check something out."

Deep scorn flashed in her brown eyes. "My, you're just full of mystery, aren't you? So what am I supposed to do in the meantime? Sit here with the *fräulein*, drinking tea? Bet that would make you happy, wouldn't it?"

"Aria, you said it yourself … they tried to kill you, too. So they at least suspect you know about the oil. I'll be back in a day or so. Then I'll get you out of here. I promise."

She turned away, strode to the bed, picked up a shirt, folded it, and placed it on the dresser. "And when you do, I'm going with you back to that cave."

"No. You're not."

"Oh yes, I am." She whirled around and glared at him. "I don't care if you take an entire army to protect you. Once you get there, you'll have to hurry. If you don't know exactly where the big deposit of oil is, you'll waste time. No one else can get you straight to that oil. You *have* to take me. You will *not* shut me out of this!"

James paused, and then sighed deeply. "All right. If that's what you want."

She grasped his arm. "It's not just about what *I* want... I know where there's something *you* want. If you want to find that oil, be careful to keep that always in mind. I'll do your bidding and stay here for two days, and two days only. Fine. But keep your promise, James Marshall."

James recovered quickly and leveled his eyes with hers. "I always keep my promises."

With that, he turned and left.

CHAPTER

21

Get out of town, damn it, just for a couple of days! Go check out our latest lead to the south. I'll get a team in to investigate the hotel shooting while you're gone.

Those final words from P.R. echoed in James' mind while he trundled through the train station. He struggled to keep Aria out of his head, finally realized that was futile.

What is *it about her?* Certainly, she was beautiful. Intelligent too. But she wasn't the first brilliant, beautiful woman he'd ever wanted. No, it was some special chemistry going on with her. His loins tingled at the thought of her, but there was something else … something that stayed with him in a way that was deeply personal. Was it that she shared his passion to find the killers and bring them to justice? Or was it just her strength in general: that she had lost both her mother and father, but retained a burning passion to help her homeland?

Or … and this thought made him gasp quietly … could he actually be *envious* of her, because she had such a strong and close family even after losing both her parents? That, unlike him when he pledged his life to serve the military, *she* hadn't had to trade the chance to stay close to her family for her myriad other passions?

The train station was crowded, and he spoke just a little Azeri, but using the Russian he was more proficient in, he managed to get through the crush and onto a southbound train. He was even able to snag one of the stiff-backed seats inside one car.

The train tracks' broad gauge was Soviet, the widest in the world and supposedly the smoothest, but the train itself was crowded and noisy. He studied the people, who were mostly Azeri, but also Russians and some people speaking Farsi and French. No English. Most of the people wore western-style clothes, but some wore traditional garb, and a few wore the robes of the Muslim faith. James had made a point to wear simple, nonthreatening clothes that would help him blend in and make acquaintances along the way. *Or at least not stand out as an insufferable American wearing a baseball cap.*

He winced at the thought of Azan, and glanced at the people around him, whose enthusiasm for life seemed depleted. He thought of Azan's son, who'd just lost his father because he was wearing James' ball cap. Without a father to guide him, would he grow up feeling as disenfranchised as these people? The thought distressed him, and he tried to shake it off, hoping no one noticed his discomfort.

The train ambled along, sometimes jerking back and forth, but generally yielding a fairly stable ride. The people all seemed to smell of sweat and cigarettes, and their faces held an impassive yet unsettling weariness.

Then, it hit him. *It's her passion.* Yes, that was it. Aria's passion to find her father's killers, combined with her ardor to restore her family business and her country to what it had been before war ruined it. *That* was the chemistry, what made him feel so alive again the moment he met her. Once, he'd felt that kind of zeal about defending his country. Until Kranzer's death, his safe office job had worked to take it away from him. Now, knowing Aria, being in her sphere, he'd felt the stirrings return. And now, he regretted keeping her in the dark as long as he had about what he'd hoped to find on that mountain.

The train moved south. To the left, he could see the Caspian Sea from time to time, and on the right the Kur-Aras Lowland. The train made several stops, with waves of people embarking and disembarking at each one. None of them held any real interest for him, but he was getting hungry and decided to get off at the next stop. According to his map, it was close enough to his destination that he could walk the rest of the way if need be.

A few minutes later, the train slowed. The sign at the station said Saatli, a hamlet halfway between Baku and the border with Iran. It looked crowded, but where there were people, there had to be food. In spite of the rank odors on the train, his stomach was growling.

He stood, and a woman wearing a *chador* bumped into him. She'd been looking behind her, attempting to keep her children together.

"*Bebakhshid* (Sorry)," he said politely, using his best Farsi.

The woman gave him a blank look, and then tended to her children, calling to them in a language he didn't understand. He'd thought she would speak Farsi, being Muslim, but then he realized that the people of northern Iran didn't speak Farsi, but another Indo-Iranian language.

This reminded him of something else, something he'd learned in his briefing: While not as obviously as in some Middle Eastern and North African countries, the people of AZ were only *culturally* Muslim, and didn't rigidly adhere to the religious disciplines of Islam. The European–Russian influence was unmistakable here.

This place'll take some getting used to I guess, he thought as he left the train. *And this is a refugee town, for sure.* There were few buildings, mostly temporary structures, houses that clearly once were railcars and other makeshift housing.

Even with the feeling of impermanence and despair, he heard music somewhere close. He wandered through the throngs and headed toward the sound.

He passed alongside an area where rusting boxcars were parked on rail sidings, about eighty of them. Each appeared to house at least one refugee family. Various pack animals laden with plastic jugs of water ambled toward the dwellings. Children happily chased each other in between the cars. They wore well-worn but clean clothes, and seemed oblivious to their squalid surroundings.

surroundings. James recalled that these refugees had lived in this makeshift camp for nearly seventeen years. A generation growing up as refugees.

The music drew him closer, its tone upbeat and happy, yet sometimes wistful. He noticed, with surprise, that the farther he moved through the crowds, the lighter the mood around him became. Some of the clustered groups were even joking and laughing.

At the center of a group of perhaps eighty people, refugee children played the *saz*, a traditional instrument once used by wandering minstrels called *ashugs*. Others sang along with the modern-day *ashugs* as they skillfully worked the strings of their instruments.

James didn't see an obvious choice for food, so he approached a man who might be able to direct him. "*Salam. Ingilisce danis, iniz?* (Hello. Do you speak English?)"

"*Baeli!* (Yes!)," the man said, then his eyes narrowed. "You are with a nongovernment aid organization?"

James shook his head. "*Yox.*"

The man sighed. "Another journalist, then. You people keep coming and talking, and nothing ever happens."

By now, a few curious onlookers had gathered around them, and the man waved them away, disappointed.

James decided to lie. A Canadian journalist would be left alone. An American journalist would be pestered for money and support. "I'm Canadian," he said. "And I'm only looking for something to eat."

"I am Rasul. My uncle owns a restaurant right over there. Good food for you. Especially today. March 21st, our Spring Festival. Always good food on a holiday. Come, I will show you."

While they walked, Rasul gave James occasional sideways glances, sizing him up. After a while, he said, "The people here are losing their hope that they will go home. Saatli is the beginning of an area of much suffering. It is called 'Refugee-stan' by many, and it goes many miles to the south and west of here. Full of displaced people and empty promises. When you write about us, tell your people this."

James didn't want to announce just who he was, and besides, Rasul seemed like a nice enough fellow. "I want to hear what you have to say," he said. "Why not have lunch with me?"

The restaurant's walls were adorned with items of local color, not unlike ethnic restaurants that dotted the Washington Beltway. James gazed at them until Rasul called to a relative, who came and took their orders. Sort of. Rasul motioned in a circular gesture with his hand, and that was it. James had been with a Dutchman in Lisbon who used the same motion to order the *faire du jour* and bits of this and that to try. The memory brought a smile.

The area was so depressed he hadn't known what to expect, but the sampling of meats over rice and fresh vegetables was quite good. While they ate, Rasul continued a story he'd told many times before to anyone who would listen.

"These people, they come from the village of Marjanli, which is occupied since 1993. You have heard of what happened then, yes?"

"Baeli," James answered, nodding. That turned out to be the only word he would get in as Rasul continued his well-rehearsed but heartfelt diatribe on the area refugees' plight. James felt guilty enough to stop eating when he spoke of the malnutrition among the children, due to their diet of bread and weak tea.

"But it is just as bad in Barda, farther south," Rasul said, waving his hand to encourage him to keep eating. "Barda is where the ex-Turkish tent camp is."

James nodded in recognition. That camp was named so because of its abandonment by the Turkish Red Crescent in 1996. He'd also heard of the Lachin Wintergrounds, in the arid plains of the Agjabadi region. Rasul described that one as a one hundred–residence cluster of mostly underground dugout dwellings.

Eventually, when Rasul wound down, James asked the

obvious question: "What will become of these people? They've been here seventeen years, with no end in sight."

Beginning with a sigh James thought only partly melodramatic, Rasul blamed the lack of recovery and reconciliation on the United States. Between bites, he complained about the Freedom Support Act passed by the U.S. Congress in 1992, which denied all U.S. aid to the Azerbaijan government.

"We are bad guys to the United States? Why?" he said. "Do you see any guns here? Azerbaijan has been overwhelmed with refugees, most are Azeri, and many are Meskheti Turks from Uzbekistan. This whole place suffers."

Outside the restaurant's window, a lively tune started up and a troupe of girl dancers began a traditional Azeri dance. Rasul watched, his face now wistful. "They have tried to keep their culture, and their faith, but these things grow more difficult each year…"

Either there was no more to say, or what was left was too painful for him. Rasul stood and went to the nearby checkout counter, took a piece of paper and scrawled down his name and a phone number.

"You can call me here." He pointed to the phone hanging on the wall. "You are a man who might be able to help us one day. Perhaps you will." He came back to the table and sat down. "I hope that you will call me. I have hope, we all have hope, that someone like you will call us one day with good news."

With that, Rasul gave an expectant look. He was finished: He had earned his meal. After a few pleasantries, James picked up the bill and tipped Rasul's cousin handsomely before he left.

"By the way, which paper are you with?" Rasul called after him.

James turned around. "I'm, ah … freelance."

"Is that a newspaper in Michigan?"

"*Yox.*" James slipped into the crowd with a final wave and began searching for anything that resembled a taxi. Over his shoulder, he could see two men approaching Rasul. Definitely not tourists. Hopefully, they were just local security, and weren't connected to the sniper. They probably wouldn't figure out who he was. Just to be safe, he picked up his pace and went down a side street.

* * *

An hour later, James rolled out of an ancient taxicab and walked the last few hundred yards into a nondescript walled compound. A plainclothes guard watched from the rooftop, but only nodded at his arrival.

A massive wooden gate topped by razor wire was the only entrance to the roughly fifty-meter-square waterfront compound that housed several two-story buildings, one a warehouse on the Caspian Sea side of the facility. He passed unchallenged through the gate and walked into the small office building.

"Not a luxury suite, but it serves the purpose," Lieutenant Tom Teurell said in introduction. "At your service, Commander."

"James Marshall, nice to meet you, Tom." They shook hands, and Teurell led him into the warehouse's interior. James noted that the nametag on his coveralls had submariner's dolphins on it. Likely, he wouldn't wear the coveralls outside the building for security reasons, but wore them indoors out of pride in his profession.

They stopped at what appeared to be a makeshift data processing center. "This compound is where we stage some of our equipment for the sensor grid we're putting down," Teurell said. "We've been comparing notes with ONI, and thought it would be a good idea to track Iranian vessels threatening oil platforms. Really, any warship movements in the Caspian."

James smiled at him. "You make it sound so easy."

Teurell laughed in return. "Well, not quite as easy as just deciding to do it. But if you know your military history, the treaty of Turkmanchia helped us out."

James nodded. The early-nineteenth-century treaty allowed only the Russians to have warships in the Caspian Sea. But, the rule had recently been challenged by the Iranians. "And with the price of oil so volatile," he said to the Lieutenant, "this is more of an issue today than it was just a couple of years ago."

"Exactly. Come on, I'll introduce you to our bottom-crawler team."

They walked past the first row of computers, where several men crowded around a video display.

"I'm only guessing," James said, "but that might be the bottom of the Caspian Sea."

"Exactly. Guys, meet our new Defense Department attaché."

James shook hands and said hello to the group he readily identified as bubbleheads, a friendly but derisive term for submariners. "So what's this here?" he asked, and pointed at the screen.

"We've taken some images of the seabed," Teurell said, "but there's not much interesting on there. Not nearly as good as what you came to see."

James gave a wicked smile. "Now I'm curious."

Teurell pointed to a photograph of a ship. "It's disguised as a Kazakh fishing vessel, but it's really our, ah … research vessel. Serves as the mother ship for our operations over here. It lowers our submersibles into the water, and controls the ROVs from an umbilical line attached to its rear end. That's how we first discovered these guys … two days ago. Haven't really had a good look at it yet."

ROV stood for a remotely operated vehicle, which required another vessel near enough to control it. And of the ones James was familiar with, this one was a beaut.

As though hearing his thought, Teurell said, "The remote capabilities on this one are pretty incredible: The technology's come a long way in just the past couple of years. On this baby, the data feed and the control function can be sent to this workstation … or for that matter, to one in Oklahoma City. And the sub, which we call Peanut, is a great ride. But come see why you're here."

Teurell pointed to a bulletin board, where a series of long

printouts of seismic soundings hung. James studied them while
Teurell talked him through their meanings. When he finished,
James said, "Show me where you picked up that sonar."

The men circled around a large chart under glass on a
table. There were several grease-pencil marks on the glass.
James didn't recognize the symbols, but he did recognize the
geocoordinates scattered amongst them.

"It looks like *they*, whoever *they* are, are working a pattern
from here, to here … a survey," Teurell said. "From what I can
make of it, a pretty steady pattern. My guess? Tomorrow they'll
be working this sector, right here." He tapped his grease pencil
on the chart. "We were thinking of parking Peanut just below
and checking it out. Want to join us?"

James had a good idea now who *they* were, but decided to
keep it close for now. "You bet I would," he said, and touched
a fingertip to the spot Teurell had pointed out. "How deep is it
here?"

"Pretty shallow up on the northern end, at the Volga Delta:
The Volga has silted it up over the years. As shallow as twenty
fathoms. And just in case you've forgotten, being a spook and
all, a fathom is six feet."

Teurell gave a friendly grin and continued. "But down
here, it's fairly deep. In this sector? From three to five hundred
fathoms. We can go to the bottom, but this trip we'll drift
along at about two hundred feet, waiting for our friends to
show up. Sound better? And oh, I used feet for your benefit,
Commander."

James gave Teurell a playful shove. "So when do we cast
off?"

"I love it when you speak Navy, Commander!" he said,
which drew a few grins from his men. "To answer your question,
we cast off at oh-dark-thirty. So let's call it a day. I'll show you
to your quarters."

* * *

Bathed by the full moon, Kishikawa Agaki stood
motionless in the open courtyard. This place, in the center of the

Japanese Embassy, was normally used for ceremonies or social gatherings. During the day, the embassy staff would read or chat in small groups here if the weather was nice. But tonight, alone in the evening's silence, Agaki now focused on his breathing. This allowed him to clear his mind and train his thoughts.

His chest was bare. He wore only the *Hakama*, a split skirt worn by Kendo players that allowed great range of movement. He let his mind focus, abandoning all but the smooth, controlled movements now being executed in his mind. Each breath was measured, deliberate, acknowledgment that the greatest victory comes without a fight at all: vanquishing an opponent without drawing the sword.

But unfortunately, such a spiritual defeat isn't always possible.

In a single movement, he drew and advanced.

And then was once again motionless. He focused on his breath, and on being one with the blade in his hands.

He continued into a series of sword strokes, some swift, some slow, all equally graceful, showing that balance and position were as important as strength and speed. All these things combined with the blade and became a disciplined vehicle of death. He concentrated on the strength in the combination of strong, fluid movements and the rigidity of the steel blade. *The blade is rigid and does not yield, nor does it bow in the wind. But the hand, and the arm and the mind, they are as flexible as they are agile.*

He began another series of moves, and the moonlight flashed across the blade time and again. The sweat on his upper body now glistened in the moonlight.

Each day he made a decision to be one with this sword. Each day he practiced hundreds of strokes. He recalled James Marshall's mention of the Edo period, when the Samurai practiced thousands of strokes each day. He wished he could spend more time with this art form, as the ancients had done. *To become one, together, the warrior's character, like the blade, must be tempered … many times.*

He was truly alone. There were no lights on in the windows surrounding the courtyard. No one watched this demonstration. As it should be. The deep humility of this warrior-artist would not allow an immodest display, nor did his ego require the praise of an audience.

The American was a good man, and Agaki reflected on James' loss of a true friend. James would soon learn the identity of General Lu, and would want to kill him.

Agaki stopped and was once again motionless. *Unfortunately, he will not get the chance.*

He had lost someone closer than a friend to one of General Lu's bullets. When the time was right, he would kill the man himself.

CHAPTER

22

The hull creaked a bit, but not as much as James had experienced onboard the *USS Seawolf*, a nuclear-powered sub that had once taken him to a clandestine meeting. True to its nickname, Peanut was only about twenty feet long, but it had all sorts of scientific accoutrements hanging all over its otherwise sleek exterior. Commissioned during the Clinton years, it was said that Peanut was nicknamed in honor of President Carter, who was from the peanut-producing regions of Georgia in addition to being a submariner. The most persistent rumor was that, when then–President Clinton first saw a rendering of the vessel, he exclaimed, "Now if that don't beat all, that thing looks just like a peanut." And the name stuck.

At the exotic instrument displays, Lieutenant Teurell worked the fairwater planes and stern planes and his sonar technician, Chief Mansfield, worked the ballast tanks. James was pleased with the view sent into the monitors all around him, a sign of the crew's consideration of their guest. The seventeen-inch plasma monitors all over the sub were fed on command by any number of source inputs. A number of high-resolution cameras dotted the hull's exterior. Each one had extraordinary zoom capability, and they were all on.

As they descended through one hundred feet, the light on the screens faded, but this didn't alarm him; light doesn't make it very far in deeper water due to refraction, starting with red, and working through the spectrum until there was no light at all.

He heard a rushing sound as gas in the variable ballast tanks was remotely manipulated to fine-tune the sub's displacement and trim characteristics. Chief Mansfield let out a deep sigh at the sound, and began groaning as if experiencing pleasure.

"Don't mind him, Commander," Teurell offered. "He's a saturation diver. They're totally into gas."

Hearing that, the chief stopped his show as a sign of respect for their guest. James smiled at him, said "That's okay," and continued to study the sub's inner hull.

Teurell said, "These guys are different for sure. Ever heard of nitrogen narcosis?"

James nodded. "Yeah, I'm a diver too. But I didn't sound like Mickey Mouse when *I* went down."

All three men shared a laugh, knowing the effect helium had on a saturation diver's voice.

"So how did you avoid sounding like the balloon-blower at a children's birthday party?" James said.

"We rigged up a circuit board that translated the squeaky voice to a normal voice."

James gave an admiring nod. "Tell you what … you guys are on the fringe. That's something we definitely have in common. But where it stops is when you go underwater. I mean, the Navy, to me, means cruising the oceans, or even flying high above them. But sinking that far beneath the surface in a wetsuit, hoping everything works while you're down there? No thank you!"

Something large thudded against the hull.

"What the heck was that?" James asked, reaching out a hand to steady himself.

"Probably a sturgeon," Chief Mansfield answered. "Last century, there were several attempts to seed these waters with fish. Flounder around 1900, mullet in the thirties, and sturgeon in the late thirties. Now, these waters produce a huge portion of the world's caviar and sturgeon."

Teurell turned on the outside lights to reveal that the Peanut was in the midst of a school of the large fish.

James grinned at him. "You're just a walking encyclopedia, Chief."

"Hey, I do my homework before I sink beneath the surface!"

The men watched as the sturgeon gracefully moved around the vessel, until the chief reached up and placed a hand on his headset. "Skipper, I've got contact."

He put the sounds on audio, and there was a definite pattern. Nothing else happened. James asked, "Where did you send this off to get checked out, Lieutenant?"

"Office of Naval Intelligence. We should hear back any day now. My guess? This is their deep look at the bottom. It's very powerful, and it's a bit different than anything I've seen before. Some sort of deep-penetration seismograph, below the sedimentary layers. Like they're looking for something *below* what's already been probed."

James nodded, recalling what he'd learned in his briefing. "Can we get a look at these guys?"

"Happy to oblige." Teurell maneuvered Peanut into position. "Next pass, they'll be nearly directly overhead. We'll be as close as possible without showing up on their findings."

Another twenty minutes went by as the sonar pulses grew louder. Finally, the fishing trawler was nearly on top of them.

"Okay, let's see who's doing this." Teurell moved the sub closer. The overhead video cameras worked well at one hundred feet. The video display showed a panoramic view of a fishing boat's hull passing nearly overhead, attendant nets in tow, spread widely from each side. Only these nets weren't rigged to catch fish; they waved uselessly in the boat's wake.

James leaned closer to the screen. At fifty feet, directly below and behind the fishing boat's hull, was a bulbous torpedo-looking device with fins on it. And that was what they'd come to see.

Chief Mansfield monitored and recorded the sonar pulse, both as it left the machine and as it returned, and read a few technical readouts to Teurell.

"Want a peek at the transom?" Teurell said to James. "See the name of the boat?"

At James' nod, he took the sub to a shallow depth and raised its scaled-down periscope. Again, the video monitors' glow reflected the crew's excitement. James could see the typical profile of a fishing trawler, complete with seagulls and hands working the deck. And the transom was in clear view now.

Teurell zoomed on it, and James read: "*Yaxs, i Arvad* (Good Wife)."

"Guess we'll have to do some homework on this boat," he whispered. Beside him, Teurell nodded.

*   *   *

Oh God… oh God… oh God!

Bill Schoffner raced up and down the stairs of his McLean townhouse. *Where is it?* He tore open his desk drawers for the third time, and then rifled through the familiar items again. Again finding nothing, he went to his valise, quickly searched it, and then threw it aside.

Screw it! Just get out of here!

He grabbed his hastily packed suitcase and started a loping run for the garage, in such a hurry, the suitcase ricocheted off the closed garage door before he tossed it into the backseat of his car. He pulled out of his driveway and screeched wildly out of his complex's parking lot. On the far side of the lot, the man sitting in the mail truck adjusted his headset and kept his gaze on the series of monitors in front of him.

"Gotta hand it to you man, you called it. You nailed it, brother," the man said. "Now, let's see who's right about the next step."

He bit into a sandwich while listening, brushed a few crumbs off his postman's uniform, and mumbled, "Mmmm? Yeah, he grabbed his jump drives."

He chewed, listening again, then said, "He's loaded up with classified goodies. But he's missing this." He held up and waved a French passport, listened. "I'm betting on the Embassy. Why? The airport's too obvious, too hot, and he knows it by now. And without his passport? Where else could he go? … We'll see. Anyhow, you guys bag him … Nail that son of a bitch."

CHAPTER

23

When P.R. entered the room, Alexis Brown was already there, had clearly been there a while. He took in her young face, taut and furrowed as she studied the outline she'd put together, the one she had emailed to James' 'high side'—secret and encrypted—email account the day before. This thing in Karabakh was a project out of the blue that was taking on incredible momentum. Sharp-minded analysts like Alexis were critical to the team, and were a lifeline to guys in the field.

The screen finally came to life, and P.R. listened while she went through some opening pleasantries with James, signaling to alert him of P.R.'s presence just off-screen. P.R. gave a friendly wave and sat back. She jumped right into her delivery.

"We've got a pretty full set of answers for today, starting with the sonar," she began, speaking to James' image on the VTC screen. "We've identified the mysterious sonar pulse as a newly patented technology. Capable of looking deeper than any seismic system in existence. It can also image underground reservoirs. In other words, it's capable of figuring out, in detail, what's beneath the known layers of oil concentrations."

James nodded. "So has this whiz-bang technology found out what those guys are up to, then?"

"We've captured enough data from Peanut's sensors to get a good idea. Our techies are working on that part as we speak. But, their preliminary review suggests there's something big down there … really big."

She paused for a breathless sip of water. Chuckling, P.R. said, "You have more than two minutes if you need it, Alexis." P.R. could see that she quietly ached to discuss the cell phone incident with James, but couldn't … not yet. P.R. had ordered a lid on it until he heard more from the field.

"Since the Armenian government is practically bankrupt," she continued, China has essentially bought them off and is backing China's surrogate, Ivan Mitrofanov. There's no one else of substance to challenge him."

"No one still alive, that is," P.R. mumbled.

She gave him a nervous glance, then looked back at James, saw the mirth on both faces, realized it was a dark joke, and the tension left her face. Another sip of water, and she continued her brief.

"To that very point … you might recall that when the shooting started in 1992, Karabakh Parliament members began dropping like flies in mysterious accidents. Like Artur Mkrtchian." She glanced over at P.R., who gave a smiling nod to continue. "Well, the same thing's happening again. Three prominent members of Karabakh Parliament have died in the past three weeks, and our intel says most of the others are laying low in fear.

"More news: Sources tell us that Mitrofanov has a core group of Chinese and Iranian advisors, and those advisors support a paramilitary force with about five thousand members. Armenia is backing out, allowing Mitrofanov to fill the power vacuum unilaterally. His only legitimacy seems to be that he's a junior member of Karabakh's parliament."

James jumped in, saying, "Where are these militia men coming from?"

"Ex-Armenian military, stray Turks, some mercenaries, and some are just outright criminals. But the largest component is Iranians—Shia—and they're taking direction from Tehran. My assessment? This kind of coalition would make it easier to garner support from the international Islamic community."

"Any ties to Hezbollah?" James asked, referring to the Shia

organization.

"No, but the militia's starting to throw its weight around, harassing some of the small towns all over Karabakh. Not quite with demands for conversion from Christianity to Islam, but the Christians are definitely getting pushed around. But both sides of the Islamo–Christian struggle seem to keep beating up on each other."

James nodded. "Good intel, but any idea where the oil fits into all of this? And, is Iran trying to establish a buffer zone? What are the Chinese doing in there?"

P.R. leaned forward. "This is where I take over. Thanks, Alexis."

Deep worry crossed her usually implacable face, and she nodded to him, then to James.

He leaned forward and rested his elbows on the table. "James, I briefed the National Security Council on this yesterday. We've learned from a reliable source that China's chairman is focused on pinpointing a new oil discovery in Karabakh. *Intensely* focused."

James nodded, recalling the inadequacies of China's current energy sources.

P.R. continued. "Now, *convention* tells us there's no oil in Karabakh. But in the opinion of China's petroleum geochemists—and our people are taking notice of this possibility—it's the Caspian area's mother lode. Apparently, as we suspected, there *is* a deep field beneath the known fields in the Caspian Sea ... one that bubbles up *into* the others."

"Like a mother lode right under a mother lode?" James said.

P.R. nodded. "According to our sources, a geographic anomaly takes a vein of this oil directly into Karabakh."

"G'tichavank Mountain." James said this in the tone of a schoolboy recounting his caught-with-hand-in-cookie-jar story.

"Bingo," P.R. said. "You marched into something very big with that little escapade. Problem is, it's going to be a lot tougher to get back in there to get a sample. And ... listen carefully ... we need a sample of that oil. To make certain we have what we think we do: a common reservoir that feeds up to the known reserves. A sample can give us that evidence."

"Genetic evidence," James said. "Like Professor Denton told me about."

"Exactly." P.R. fondled his unlit cigar, his favorite vehicle into accelerated deep thought. "Thanks to your visit, the militia's doubled up the guard." He couldn't help grinning. "I'll bet you and Aria Palestinio were the last things they expected. They'd sealed the base of the mountain, made it off-limits to tourists. But they didn't expect anyone to land an airplane on top of the mountain."

"Ah ... sorry, sir."

He lowered his eyes to meet James' chagrined ones. "It's done. And on the upside, you got us a lot closer to this issue than we've ever been. So, I'm giving you a passing grade ... so far. You're just lucky as hell that those Japanese special forces were there. Otherwise, we'd have had to write you off."

P.R. saw James wince at his slang for leaving an operative for dead, or, worse, denying that he even existed if captured.

Now, he gave James a hard look. "The Japanese were barely one step ahead of us on finding that location. And we're not going to shut them out of this investigation."

James nodded. "After the, ah ... the front-row seat I had to give him during the escape, Agaki's earned a front-row seat in this deal. I definitely consider him an ally." He smiled. "That is, if he ever trusts *me* again."

P.R. chuckled. "Agreed. Now, our next steps: Get a sample of the oil from that cave, and check out its genetic makeup. I'll probably get Professor Denton in on that. If we prove that oil *is* part of a larger, deeper oilfield, this will get even more interesting. China would be in a position to suck that puppy dry over the next forty years. Iran will continue to influence a large share of the known oil reserves. And collectively, they'll have a virtual monopoly on the Caspian Sea's oil."

"So long as Mitrofanov's still around as their front man, since he's their link in the Karabakh parliament."

"Yes," P.R. said, his eyes thoughtful, then he added noncommittally, "If he's still around."

James leaned back in his chair. "Aside from knowing they can climb like mountain goats and they're packing some serious heat, how much do we know about the militia?"

P.R. sighed and ducked his ashes, took another draw. "The intel from where you are is … worrisome. They've stepped up patrols all around the border. Gonna be the devil's own game to get past 'em now."

"Thanks to me. Again, I'm—"

"No. *Sorry* is for past deeds." P.R. grinned. "Save *sorry* 'til you have a bigger batch of 'em to apologize for. And you will. But, I won't borrow trouble, so back to the situation. Alexis mentioned the minor clashes all along the frontier. The Azeri army's moving in response … they've fielded about five thousand men in company-sized groups. There've been some casualties. Unfortunately, mostly civilians caught in the crossfire."

"Having recently been trying to protect a civilian in a crossfire, I know a little about how unfortunate that is," James said with a pained smile.

P.R. loved a good joke as much as any other person, but he didn't laugh. He was too busy trying to come up with his next words.

Finally, he sighed and said, "For the record, and I personally commend his consistency, the President insists that *the people of Karabakh* decide who to sell the oil to. But all the while, he's got China in one ear and Iran in the other, squawking for his help to force Karabakh to sell to them. For the good of the entire world, they say. Ha!

"Main point: If Karabakh has oil, China will want it. Iran will want it. And to be honest, so will the United States. If the President tells them to lay off Karabakh, Iran won't like hearing that, and China sure the hell won't like it. We have to prepare to stomp on China's toes if need be. We don't care about Iran, but we have to be careful with China. Extremely so."

James said, "I can get that sample sir, but I'll need some help."

P.R. didn't quite meet James' eyes. "I haven't mentioned this before, but … the President's authorized military involvement. Marines and other assets. They're already at Vaziani Air Base in Georgia. *Who knows what the Ruskies think of all this*. If needed, the Marines will help you get in and out of G'tichavank—if anybody can. James … this is going to get hot."

"*Get* hot?"

"I mean in a big way."

James shook his head slowly. "What about Schof—?"

"He's off this project."

James smiled at that, and at how Alexis was squirming in her seat at the mention of the name … she didn't trust him either, and clearly, she knew why and how Schoffner was booted. But, there was no time to satisfy his curiosity. "Okay, so we have backup," he said. "Who's the Marine contact?"

"Colonel Rip Martin. He's picking you up … and Miss Palestinio. Tomorrow afternoon, 1400 your time. Mrs. Ketchel will bring Aria to meet you at the airfield." P.R. looked at James with playful concern. "I saw the photograph of Aria that Mrs. Ketchel so kindly provided. James … don't get distracted and miss the flight."

James averted his gaze and tried not to react. "I do have one question," he said quickly, "and this falls into the realm of speculation."

"Shoot."

"If this escalates, could we be at war with China soon?"

P.R. didn't answer right away. He leaned his head back and worked the cigar in his hand, then brought it almost to his mouth. "You just be *certain* you're on that chopper tomorrow afternoon."

"There you are...." The woman put down her binoculars, picked up her cell phone and walked away from the window, punching in a number she knew well.

"Maybe I am just a whore," she said, sighing. "All those years with CBS, and now I have to act like a low-class PI just to keep a job."

When the click came, she said into the phone, "Okay, here's the news flash you wanted. He just left the Embassy compound, headed toward downtown."

* * *

"So, you were saying that this is for a man in the mountains ... a Christian?"

In response to the man's question, James tossed some *manat* on the counter. "Does it matter to you what kind of man enjoys your tobacco?"

The tobacconist mumbled something under his breath and gave James his change. He and Raffi walked out of the shop and into the late-morning street of downtown Baku, and readied to light up their cigars.

"Touchy, wasn't he," James mumbled around the cigar.

"There's no love lost between Azeri's Muslims and the Armenian Christians, that's for sure," Raffi offered, along with a box of Russian-made wooden matches. The two strolled along tree-lined Karl Marx Avenue, a street flanked with ornate stone midrise buildings exhibiting late-nineteenth-century European architecture that contrasted with the drab apartment buildings from the Soviet era. Blended in and amongst the apartment buildings were shops, various places of business, and restaurants.

"So who *is* the pipe tobacco for?"

James smiled. "Kasim Beria."

"Aria's great-uncle in Karabakh?"

"Yep. He and I kinda clicked. Wanted to bring him a little something. Aria can get it to him, I guess."

Raffi smiled "Seems like you've *kinda clicked* with Aria too."

James returned the smile while Raffi waved his hand to the west. "I've got a ride waiting for us a block from here. Have you met Sergey yet?"

"No, I always seem to just miss your partner. You brought him down from up north, right? Chechnya?"

"Yeah, he's fairly new here, like me, but a good guy. And he knows this area much better than I do. You'll like him." Raffi sighed. "I'll tell you what, it amazes me how shorthanded we are in this part of the world—where we really shouldn't be."

James was window-shopping as they walked, noting nice leather shoes in one window and mentally trying to convert *manat* to dollars. By the price tags by each pair, shoes were shaping up to be a good find here. So it was by sheer luck that he saw, reflected in the angled store window, the black sedan bearing down on them, its rear tinted window sliding down and a gun barrel protruding through the opening.

Screaming "Get down!" he rushed at Raffi, pushing him against a parked car as bullets sprayed over their heads.

"This way!" Raffi shouted, and led him around a corner into an alley. Chunks of concrete flew from the building's corner when a new volley chased after them and ricocheted wildly.

They sprinted down the alleyway and cut behind the back of the building just as the attackers pulled up and into a clear line of fire. Their luck held when the car couldn't fit into the narrow alley to chase them. It accelerated rapidly and continued around the block, tires screeching.

Raffi and James continued their escape. "Sergey heard that," Raffi panted. "He'll have the motor running."

James kept the cigar clenched between his teeth and didn't slow his pace.

They raced out onto a main road, and Raffi yelled, "Over there, the black BMW!"

As Raffi predicted, the BMW was running, its front passenger and back door open and waiting.

"Move over, I'll drive!" Raffi shouted as they approached in a full sprint.

"But I am dressed for the occasion," Sergey yelled back, showing pouty disappointment as he held up his hands and wiggled his fingers, showing off his fingerless racing gloves.

Raffi piled into the front, James the back, and Raffi shouted, "Okay, you drive, *but drive fast!* There they are!"

James glanced where Raffi pointed, saw the black sedan turning the corner out of a side street.

Sergey yelled, "I can do that!" To demonstrate, he stomped on the accelerator and fishtailed out of the parking place. Burning rubber smoked from the rear tires as the car surged ahead. "Fasten your seat belt," he called out, laughing. "Safety first!"

The black sedan was already moving at a high rate of speed, and accelerated as it continued its pursuit.

"Guess those four Iranians still aren't happy about the introductions we gave them the other night!" Raffi said.

"Yeah, but that dead one's *really* unhappy!" James called back, referring to the one who died on the mountain while trying to kill Aria and him.

Raffi pulled out his cell phone and began to alert the Embassy while James pulled out his Beretta. James had only a moment to give Raffi's partner a look in the rearview mirror. Thirty-something and slight, Sergey's rugged Eastern European features weren't far from what he'd expected. Sergey's weathered face was wide-eyed in joy, not fear, and as he steered to avoid other cars on the busy street, he bounced in his seat as a small child would.

They sped down Karl Marx Avenue, and the sedan managed

to pull up alongside them. The front passenger-side window rolled down and the short-stocked assault rifle was now in Sergey's face. They all ducked, and a fury of 9mm rounds perforated the side and rear windows and whizzed over their heads. James' attempts to return fire were hampered by the bad angle, and by the sedan dropping back. "He's probably reloading," Raffi yelled.

James wasn't so worried about that now; their pursuer's actions pegged them as amateurs, something he'd suspected since that day on the mountain. If the men shooting at them were well trained, they would have shot into the metal sides of the car, not the windows. A rookie shoots at what he sees through the windows, so it is easier to duck and evade. That kind of bumbling was what had landed the fighting star in the first Iranian's temple.

Sergey whipped the wheel over as he hit the brakes. The car almost hopped at an angle and clipped several vehicles before he turned sharply down a side street.

"Now, the 318i series, that has better torsion bars," he called out, shaking his head. "A much better-handling package. I never would have hit that bus if we were in a 318i. That first car, maybe, but not the bus."

The next sharp turn lost their pursuers. The car surged forward briskly and the engine roared as Sergey worked the shifter.

"Did you notice how I downshifted back there? The manual is wrong. My way is much better. Driving like this is an art form." His face went from a stern look to a sage smile. With the sedan now out of sight, James kept his focus studiously on the clutch and shifting action while smoke still wafted from the barrel of his pistol.

"And I … I am an artiste," Sergey continued triumphantly. He didn't have an audience with Raffi, who had no appetite for his chatty dialogue. So he enjoyed a rare moment with an interested audience … until the sedan reappeared and stubbornly renewed its pursuit.

"I'm kinda surprised that dead guy's buddies want to keep playing with us after what happened to *him*," James said.

Raffi shrugged. "Idiots like that? They never want to let go of a grudge."

The BMW swerved across the double white line that served as
a demarcation point between opposing traffic, necessary to get past
the heavy, slower-moving trucks and local drivers. The car heaved
as it swerved in and out of traffic, terrified drivers honking at them.
Sergey looked over his shoulder at James. "So, how do you like it
here so far in Baku?"

"Not bad. But the drivers aren't very friendly," James shouted
over blaring horns. Chunks of glass dribbled off his shoulders
as he sat up straight, noting they were on the home stretch to the
Embassy.

"Where do you come from, James?"

"North Carolina. Yourself?"

"Chechnya. Born and raised, as you Americans say. But, I
needed a break. It was too dangerous there."

Sergey shifted again and again while he raced the BMW down
Azadliq Prospekti, dodging traffic. He looked over in inquiry at
Raffi, who nodded and yelled, "They are expecting us."

As he spoke, James could see the Azeri security force and
a group of foreign-service nationals, known as FSNs, taking
positions outside the compound's perimeter. Sergey hit the brakes
and whipped the wheel over as he again worked the heated
transmission. The car slid through the Embassy's open gates and
quickly came to a stop at a second gate just inside. The Marines
closed the outside gates and trained their weapons on the sedan,
which was already drawing fire from the FSNs while it sped past.

A lone figure stood in the embassy courtyard as the car
finished its flight in a cloud of dust just a few feet from him. As
the dust cleared, James could see that the figure was a man, and
the man was Roger.

Roger slowly surveyed the shattered windows, the bullet holes
that made the doors appear to be bizarre giant cheese graters, and
the many dents from glancing off other cars on their flight. Then
he came up close and looked at the occupants, one at a time, while
they brushed broken chunks of safety glass off their clothes.

He pushed his cowboy hat back on his head with one hand in
an act of mild disgust, then calmly leaned over where the driver's

window used to be. "Sergey … Beemer … fancy gloves an' all, you still can't drive worth a shit."

James leaned forward from the backseat. "Can you do any better?"

Roger looked up at him with questioning eyes. "Commander?"

"No, I'm serious. I need a ride, and fast."

Roger gave him a big Texas smile. "You reload. I'll get my truck."

Moments later James hopped into the passenger side of Roger's truck, which had barely stopped to allow him to climb in. Roger leaned out and yelled at the Marines, most of whom he knew personally, and they let them through the gate. Then Roger looked expectantly at James.

"Take a left. We're going to an uncontrolled airfield about twenty klicks north-northwest of Baku."

Roger nodded. "I think I know the one— Ha!"

"What?"

"If you could see what I just saw in my rearview mirror! The chief of staff cursing and swearing out in the parking lot … looking for you, I imagine. His secretary Mabel and I are buds … she told me about your last meetin' with him."

James gave a rueful smile as he grabbed his green helmet bag and checked his watch. "Thanks for the ride, Roger. And just in time. Got a beautiful woman I've got to meet."

* * *

The man fumbled with his wallet and nervously tucked the bills into it. The hotel clerk was polite while she refunded his five hundred dollar cash deposit, but she could tell something wasn't right. It wasn't just the name he'd given … even though no parent in their right mind would name their kid "John Johnson!" No, it was more than that. Like, it was rare for someone dressed like a U.S. Senator on vacation to work on a cash basis. Sure, some people didn't like credit cards … but he probably did. Least, he *looked* the kind who whipped out a Visa or Amex without thinking.

But credit cards can be tracked, she thought. This added to her certainty: This was a guy who didn't want anyone to know where he was, or who he was.

* * *

Schoffner didn't know the clerk's thoughts, and wouldn't have cared if he did. His main goal was to avoid using his credit card. Like an idiot, he hadn't thought he'd need one with a false name, so he'd never looked into getting one. No, until he could get out of the country—and that required finding his friggin' passport!—he'd have to live by a fake name, and use his dwindling supply of cash. His vital currency, his main leverage at his destination, was locked up tight in his suitcase.

He climbed into his car, cranked it up. And then, it hit him. He'd been so careful to keep track of his passport, just in case he ever had to move out of the country quickly. Just like what was happening now. It was unimaginable to him that it was missing when he needed it most.

The realization was a physical force, one so strong that it threw him back against the car's leather seat. *Could someone have taken it?*

Didn't matter. What mattered was how to get out of the country. His head had been swimming with ideas, but kept going back to only one. The call from his handler, coupled with that icy look from P.R. That look was unmistakable. How the hell his boss found out was beyond his best guess. But that steely bastard *knew* … and it was time to get the hell out of Washington. He put the car in reverse and slowly released the brake.

Moments later, the voice came from a van a block away. "He's on the move. Let's see where our boy takes us next."

* * *

Roger's truck slowed to a stop on the desolate runway apron.

"You sure there's a chopper coming?" He looked over at James with an apprehensive eye.

"Certain," James said, his focus trained on something off to his right.

"Hey … I've got a little somethin' locked up in my toolbox." He motioned to the back of his truck. "Not much … a few guns and grenades, shit like that. I figured you might need a little extra edge."

James turned his head to see Roger's smile. "You never know. Thanks for all your help, Master Sergeant."

"I'm here for you, Commander." Another grin. "And I'm still lookin' forward to ridin' shotgun."

Their attention was drawn by the approach of another vehicle, this one a dark green sedan that slowed to a stop twenty meters from them. Mrs. Ketchel emerged from the driver's side of the vehicle and cast a nod of recognition their way.

Watching her, Roger muttered, "Hey, I know her. She's at the Embassy a lot. Somethin' tells me that ain't the woman you meant."

James chuckled and was about to answer when Roger sat up straight at the faint throbbing of helicopter rotor blades, which rapidly grew louder. As the throbbing became a roar he stepped out onto the tarmac, just as Aria did from the other vehicle. He watched her looking at the Black Hawk, whose skids were searching for the firm ground beneath them.

"Now *that's* a little closer to what I had in mind," Roger shouted into James' ear, keeping his eyes on Aria. "She's a pretty one … where's she from?"

"Vank. And she's as brave as she is beautiful."

Normally the loud rotor-wash and engine noise would steal the moment, but both men choose to admire Aria's seemingly unflappable presence in the face of the roaring wind.

"So where you all going?" Roger shouted near James' ear.

Where are we going? To hell's gate, that's where. But he said only, "Can't say. But it's not going to be fun when we get there."

A crewmember wearing a flight suit, helmet, and gloves hopped out of the chopper and pointed to Aria and then to James, then waved them to the aircraft. They ran in a trot to the chopper and climbed in. Roger watched as the helicopter turned as it rose, then surged northward, and the wind and noise faded away.

Vank, eh? Got a friend near there I need to go and visit, right quick.

He grinned. *I hate to miss a good fight.*

* * *

"Tell me why you wanted to meet here of all places?" As he asked the question, Laurent Makumba's eyes warily scanned the tables of the crowded restaurant. Except for his two bodyguards seated at a nearby table with Ivan Mitrofanov's men, he was the only black man in the room.

The restaurant was one of Ashgabat's hidden secrets, offering visitors to the Turkmenistan capital gourmet dining and an atmosphere that was both elegant and discreet. The two men shared an excellent bottle of pinot noir, as well as a relentless drive for power.

"Why here, my friend? Because no one ever looks for anyone here." Ivan gave a sly smile as he hoisted his goblet in a toast. "To my good friend Nizayov … the ironfisted man *here* … he died so suddenly."

Ivan's eyes met his guest's, then again drifted over Laurent's shoulder to continue some meaningful eye contact with a woman seated alone at the bar. He gave his glass one last raise in her direction before he drank, and she responded with a smile.

"So, let's talk some business, shall we?" Ivan leaned back in his chair while the waiter cleared their plates. Laurent also leaned back, in contentment, and raised his eyebrows, an invitation for Ivan to speak.

"Two cognacs please," Ivan said to the waiter. The waiter nodded to him, and left them alone.

"I understand the Congo's Katanga province has $300 billion in mineral wealth that will be realized over the next twenty-five years."

Laurent shrugged. "Give or take a few billion. But there is much competition out in the bush for those dollars."

"Your backers in London tell me that you have the potential to take a larger role in the Congo." He paused in anticipation of his guest's response, which was calm and quick.

"They also tell *me* that *your* ambitions exceed well beyond your borders. STRONG, eh? Good name. I like it."

"It seemed an appropriate name for our alliance," Ivan said, accepting the compliment with a nod. "Think about it … without key raw materials, the industrialized powers are helpless."

"I have thought about it, a lot of us have. It's been a long time coming."

"Agreed. So, you are their man on the ground in Katanga … and you will also have a country of your own soon."

"Yes, that is the way I see it," Laurent said, watching the waiter place their cognacs in front of them. "The transitional government has lost its support, and things will be happening there soon."

Ivan shifted his eyes away, then back to the man he hoped to do business with. "There is a lot happening soon around the world. Tell me about coltan," he added … I've never heard of it, until recently."

"Most people haven't, but without it, cell phones just couldn't happen."

"And Katanga is one of the few places where it can be found?"

Laurent nodded. "Most of the attention is focused on Katanga's diamond and gold production. Important also, but there are other minerals that don't get as much publicity. Coltan is one of them. Without them, the circuitry in such things as cell phones and video games wouldn't be as possible."

"Which is why you have been invited to my little summit in Istanbul, Laurent."

"Something I look forward to, Ivan. How about dessert?"

"I was just getting to that…." He drained the cognac and patted his ample waist, then fixed his gaze over Laurent's shoulder. "But after that sumptuous meal, I should skip it."

Laurent looked over his shoulder, and was smiling when he turned back around to Ivan, who continued.

"I appreciate this chance to get to know one another before next week's summit. We will talk some more over breakfast."

Ivan stood and extended his hand as his eyes moved again to the blonde in furs at the bar. He wondered if she was from Belarus, like the last woman he was with here. "Let's make it a late one, say eleven?"

"Okay." Laurent chuckled as he shook Ivan's hand. "You have yourself a good evening … partner. Enjoy your sweet stuff … a man's dessert."

Ivan smiled at him. "I intend to."

* * *

Bill Schoffner looked at his right hand, which had just shifted his car into park. It was clammy, and shaking. *Pull yourself together, man! Almost there. Cool and calm, and you'll make it*

He stepped out of the car and looked around. The U.S. French Embassy looked like a concrete fortress, and truly, his safe haven was only one hundred yards away. And thankfully, the surrounding Georgetown sidewalks had only the usual Washington foot traffic. He pulled his suitcase out of the trunk and headed down the street toward its entrance.

As he did, the voice inside the van spoke again. "Jim, you called it. Damn, I owe you that beer after all. Okay, team, it doesn't look like we're going to get anyone else. Go ahead and take him."

* * *

Schoffner switched the suitcase from one hand to the other, and then put his free hand into his pocket. His fingers searched for, and found, the five portable USB drives that would insure his value to his handlers for some time to come. He knew it didn't matter any more, but still he wondered how P.R. knew. *Too many coincidences? Or maybe that damned nose of his …*

He looked up. Only fifty more yards to go. He picked up his pace a bit, but his heart raced when he noticed the bearded man seated at an easel on the sidewalk, painting.

Easy, Bill, easy, he's just one of a thousand outta-work guys trying to make a living drawing pretty pic—

He stopped thinking, could no longer think. The angle of the sun showed him something else, something he would've missed if sunlight hadn't glinted off it at just the right instant: A hair-thin wire dangled from the man's ear and disappeared beneath his windbreaker.

The man stood and stretched, and began to amble in Schoffner's general direction. Schoffner made brief eye contact, but that was enough.

Shouting "No!" Schoffner broke into a sprint. The artist did too. Schoffner threw the suitcase at his feet, but gained only a short lead on the man, who adroitly hurdled over the tumbling luggage.

"Freeze! FBI!"

The single shout seemed to come from all directions. He kept running for his life. He could see figures looking out from the embassy's gate; male or female, he couldn't tell. Not that he cared. He was so close. *So close!*

He felt his legs stop moving, and realized it was because of the vise grip of the agent who'd tackled him. His face hit the pavement and his arms were yanked behind his back. He struggled to turn his head toward the gate, where a large group was gathering just inside it. Schoffner recognized his handler amongst them, and pleaded to him for help.

"*M'aider! M'aider!* Oh God please help me!"

It wouldn't be obvious to a casual observer, since all of the action was around Bill Schoffner, but the subtle motioning by the man behind the embassy's doors spoke volumes. The man who'd served as Schoffner's handler wore an expression of disappointment at losing such an important source. But there was something else on the man's face, something that only a perceptive trained eye would pick up on: the subtle contemptuous smile that expressed profound disdain for a man who had gotten his just desserts for betraying his own people.

CHAPTER

25

"Would you bet your ass we can rappel into that chute?"

"Yes … and I'll double the bet, 'cause I'm gonna do it with you."

Rip scowled at James. "James, *our* asses might not be worth much, but we up the ante with our lady friend here … and my men."

"So… what am I … sushi?"

They turned to Agaki, and all three burst into laughter. As soon as it died down, Rip looked at the lone civilian in the room and locked eyes with her. "Ms. Palestinio … this might not be pretty. You sure you want to do this?"

She brushed her hair back and said, her voice solemn, "First, I am Aria. Next, lots of things in life aren't pretty, Colonel. I absolutely want to do this. And as I've mentioned, I grew up in this area. I've been scaling these mountains since I was a toddler."

"It's not the rappelling I'm worried about, and I think you probably know that."

She didn't reply, but there was no need. The makeshift conference table in the Vaziani Air Base headquarters building was littered with classified materials, including a Joint Operational Graphic offering a relief map of G'tichavank Mountain and recent overhead images from an unspecified source. The images were annotated, highlighting landmarks, the monastery, guard posts, and a host of other detail. Clearly, the mountain's defenses had been reinforced since James and Aria's infamous joyride. Two representative pilots from the helicopter detachments also looked over the table, took in the plan, and deferred to the third pilot on their right. The hour's worth of briefing they'd all just heard guaranteed that everyone in the room knew what they faced.

Sparky Lyle, representing the Hogs, leaned forward and smiled. "You know … you don't have to go in hoping nothing goes wrong. I can hit these sites first."

"With regrets, but nothin' doin'," Rip said. "We've been ordered to let them take the first hostile act. Otherwise, I'd be with you on that call. We're not at war here, just making a pickup."

Sparky's eyes rolled. "We'll be there when you need us, Colonel."

"On the other hand, if they *want* a fight with us," Rip stood and began a slow pace of the room, "then we'll give them a fight. Nagorno-Karabakh is officially a breakaway province of Azerbaijan … not recognized as a sovereign state. Azerbaijan has given us over-flight rights. So, according to international law, it's okay for us to be there. Not that international law will keep them from shooting at us."

He stopped and pointed his finger at his audience for emphasis. "If they shoot at us, we'll deal with it. But they shoot first. That's the deal."

"So, you want us in a high-spin pattern overhead waiting for your call?" Sparky leaned back as he asked the question.

"Not even that. This is a low-profile entry and exit. We don't want to alert the whole world. Like I said, you guys loiter near the border … here." He pointed to the spot on the map.

Sparky nodded. "Got it."

Rip felt confident in his instructions to hit the front of the cave as a diversionary measure, while the real target, the oil sample, was obtained by going in the back door, down the chimney like Santa Claus. Still, one more round of explaining wouldn't hurt.

"Okay, kids," he said. "We arrive at 0330, a couple of hours before dawn. The Cobras go in first, drawing attention and fire, if it comes, from my Blackhawk, which will hover over the chimney while we insert." He glared at Aria. "You said five minutes to get the sample once we hit the ground?"

"Get inside the inner chamber and get the sample. Five minutes. No more."

He nodded, then continued. "We extract in five minutes, then get the hell out of Dodge. If you need to, you Cobra jockeys can use the mountain as cover, but I doubt there'll be a need. This should be a short in and out. The Black Hawk will have its lights out, and with all the noise, maybe it won't be as noticeable."

He looked around the table. "Last call for questions."

"Why don't they just put a quiet SOF team in there?"

"No Special Ops team available. We're it. And I'm told that we've just got a few days to get that sample and get it back stateside for analysis." Rip's jaw clenched as he looked from side to side. "Any more questions?"

No one spoke.

"Then we'll do this together, as a team." He stopped pacing and surveyed his silent audience. His eyes stopped on Aria, James, and Agaki, and he smiled. "Okay then, how about if I introduce you guys to my Marines?"

As the group exited the building, Rip contemplated being ferried in and out by Army Rangers flying Black Hawk helicopters. Not usual fare for the Marines, but Rip didn't have any Marine H-53 Echoes available to him right now.

He rolled his eyes at another thought … *just like SOCOM didn't have a team available*. Knowing that even the U.S. Special Ops Command was stretched too thin wasn't exactly reassuring. At least he'd have the detachment of four Marine Cobra gunships as additional support. He'd swung that by calling in a favor from a friend at the Pentagon. Those gunships would provide relentless close-air support as needed, if needed.

Coming out of Vaziani in Georgia, they would pass into the

Nagorno-Karabakh region from the north, with minimal time in Azeri airspace, and follow it in a southerly route down to G'tichavank Mountain. Rip worked through the scenario for the fiftieth time. The helos would keep a lower radar signature, hugging the Lesser Caucasus Mountains when possible.

He sighed deeply, and for the first time noticed how his neck ached. He could smell a fight. And his least-favorite way to fight was with an innocent civilian like Aria Palestinio in the fray.

CHAPTER

26

"Spidey, you gotta see this to believe it." As he spoke, Gomer looked through the open barrel of the gun he was cleaning.

"So … whada'ya see, Gomer?" Even after several years in the Marines and months at Vaziani Air Base in Georgia, Spidey's born-and-bred Queens accent just wouldn't go away. His head was shaved clean, beyond the requirements of the Marine Corps, and a tattoo of a spider graced his muscular right forearm. Once he was Stateside again, he was considering adding a Spiderman tattoo to the left arm, just to even it up a little.

"I dunno what I see," Gomer replied, "but it's big, really big." As he answered, he continued to peer through the M-16's sleek barrel, twirling it slowly with his slim fingers and muscle-roped arms.

"Are there bad people in there, Gomer?" Spidey continued to clean his own weapon.

"No. Just this one *really* big thing," came the reply. "Never saw *anything* like this in East L.A. You know, there are just two things that can be seen from outer space. Did you know that?"

"Okay. Great Wall of China, and what else?"

"It's really big. Like, I've gotta move this thing around a lot to see all of it."

"So? What? What is it? I give up."

"Remember that girl you were datin' when we were back at Twenty-Nine Stumps in California?"

Spidey nodded, then remembered Gomer wasn't looking at

him. "Yeah, I remember her. So what'ya see?"

"I'm looking at her ass. It's huge!"

"An' I'm gonna kick yours, you asshole. Only a Mexican would come up with some bullshit like that!"

Gomer pulled back from the barrel and gave him a grin with gleaming-white teeth. "Don't you forget, I'm an American now. And that's only because I signed up to share a barracks with your sorry snorin' ass. Talk about *sacrifice*, padre."

The two of them leaned forward, pressing their foreheads together in half-hearted braggadocio, just as Guns walked by.

"Stand down, you two." Under his threatening look, they went back to cleaning their M-16s. It was a nice, sunny summer afternoon at Vaziani Air Base, but it was a busy one too.

Guns kept his eyes on the two men under him, but his gaze softened. Gomer, also known as PFC Hernando Gomez, one of thousands of noncitizens who'd joined the military to stand up for this country. Gomer once told him, "This isn't only the land of economic opportunity, sir. It's also an ideal. I know I'm new here, but I see too much complacence in this country."

Gomer was right, Guns knew. He suppressed a smile, remembering Gomer's story about his mother. She had promised to say twelve rosaries when he came home to her safely. He carried a scapular she gave him the day he left, a Catholic symbolic keepsake bearing a picture of the Blessed Virgin Mary. Gomer kept it in his pocket when he went on patrols. "For my mom," he'd explained with a shrug. "Just in case, ya know."

A boom box pumped out Radio Free Europe in the background, and the disc jockey in nearby Tbilisi was spinning a lively mix of American music in between his broken-English renditions of each song's title. Hip-hop, rock, oldies, whatever … what he played gave a welcomed taste of home.

"Spirit in the Sky," the classic from a year that preceded their births, belted out a rough bass guitar that resonated with Guns' mood. They all knew they'd probably take some heat in a hot zone, yet were just as certain it would be for something very important. There was some kind of monkey business with the

Iranians and the Chinese. They didn't totally understand it, but if the President said go, they went. That was what they were there for. They had faith in their Commander in Chief, and, perhaps more deeply, in each other. They would do their jobs.

Guns walked on, wondering when the call would come.

* * *

Agaki, James, and Aria followed Rip past the shaded area beside Vaziani's hangars where the large group of Marines prepared their weapons. Rip sensed their tension, knew it came out in different forms: frivolity, keeping busy, focusing on routine acts. These men were all brave, but none of them was fearless. Including him.

"Crank it up man! I love that song," he heard one of them yell.

The volume went up.

A group of men carried heavy belts of 20-millimeter ammunition to the four Cobra gunships. As the deep bass of the music split the air, they loaded the ordnance into pods slung beneath the Cobras' short wings. Fuel trucks maneuvered along the runway apron, and the Predator aircraft were getting a workout, as well as the A-10s, just in case they needed that little something extra. A world-renowned war machine, the best of the best, was setting up for action, combining to put the fist in the glove that carried the blunt-force trauma of a sledgehammer, and in a way that had made their tactics in Iraq the study of foreign agents the world over.

He waved at his small group to continue, and led them to a wooden structure with ropes and harnesses hanging along its side. The two Marines there were doing their level best to maintain stone faces at the beautiful woman they were about to teach rappelling tactics.

"Aria, these men are going to spend the next couple of hours showing you the ropes. Pun intended." Rip smiled. "Particularly what you'll need to know to rappel out of the helicopter. I'm sure you'll do fine," another smile, "especially since you said you were raised as mountain goat."

Grinning back, she said, "Thanks, Colonel." She introduced herself to the two polite, but stunned, men and turned back to Rip. "You don't have to worry about me, I'll be okay."

She smiled at the two Marines. "Okay, guys, show me how this works."

* * *

Late that night, seated next to Aria in the Black Hawk that held Rip's team, James watched the other helicopters as the rotor wash blew all around them. The song he'd heard on the tarmac earlier resonated in his head, the deep loud bass in complement to the rhythmic *whump-whump* of the helicopter rotors. He felt her grip his arm as all six choppers, laden with extra fuel tanks, lurched into motion at the same time, pulled away from Vaziani Air Base, and turned south, toward Nagorno-Karabakh. When a steady breeze rushed through the cockpit, James could feel her grip easing. His mind raced with distant memories of Afghanistan and Iraq, and the recent events that had brought him here. Especially the death of his friend. At the Academy, he and Kranzer had had many excited conversations about going on missions just like this one.

He shook his head to clear the memories and returned to planning. He and Aria each carried three sixteen-ounce containers in their backpacks, which they would use with a small manual pump and its attached plastic hose to quickly gather the oil samples. The lights were off, but there was just enough moonlight to see. He looked around the bay, and then at Aria, who offered a reassuring smile. He felt pain in his right arm that faded quickly as he loosened his grip from the side of his seat.

* * *

"We're taking machine gun fire."

Shit, James thought. *This soon?* He'd heard the Cobra pilot's announcement via the headset he wore. He looked over at Rip, whose face was smeared in green and black, saw him listening intently on his own headset. He glanced over to see Aria gripping her seat, eyes forward.

The wild array of tracer fire had erupted as the Cobras came roaring in overhead, and they responded in kind, launching a series of 70mm air-to-surface missiles that systematically took out the heavy machine gun emplacements around the mountain.

The militia's troops were scattered around the area, so they were difficult targets as they traded fire with the Cobras, which jinked defensively back and forth in the night sky. James glanced at Aria at one point and saw her wide-eyed stare at the battle. She noticed him looking at her and gave him a thumbs-up and a smile. Only then did he return his attention to the Cobras' attempts to clear the area of troops.

One of the Black Hawks stayed at a distance as backup while James and Aria's ride hovered neatly over the chimney. Rip hung out over the side of the door and helped another Marine lower the rappel lines down the shaft. He took off his headset and hooked up. As he went over the side into the dark hole, eight other men quickly followed him down, their weapons at the ready. Their job was to enter the caves and make sure they were, in fact, clear of any threats.

A faint green glow emerged from the chimney's mouth, illuminating both James' camouflaged face and the way down. The glow came from three trail-marker light sticks, Rip's signal that the tunnel was clear and ready.

Aria took off her headset, and winced when the rotor blades' roar became deafening in her ears. James joined her at her side. She gave him a look, as if searching for reassurance, and then, to her great credit, hooked up as she'd been taught and hopped over the side as the rotor wash whipped at her. As she neared the bottom, she glanced up, saw him on the next line, keeping a protective eye on her with his pistol in a chest holster, ready to draw if needed. A quick nod, and she continued her descent.

After ensuring that his men were in position, Rip trotted back into their section of the cave. He unhooked Aria, and led them swiftly toward the Bat Barn. They made an almost–U-turn into the other chamber, and were twenty feet inside it when sounds of gunfire erupted in the cave behind them. A firefight had started in the main cavern up front, disturbing the bats, which swarmed by the thousands. Everyone ducked to the cave floor and hid their faces, and for the next thirty seconds, the night creatures roared past, then thinned out into more sporadic fits of flight.

Aria's discomfort with the bats didn't lessen, though. When James saw that her eyes were wild as she looked from side to side at James and Rip, he grabbed her arm to reassure her.

"Let's go!" Rip shouted as he and James helped her up. They ran into the main chamber and pressed on with Aria's direction to "the pit," the place where the oil had pooled on the surface. "We've got a little unexpected resistance," he yelled. "Gotta move quickly!"

While he held a flashlight over the oil pool, James and Aria ripped off their backpacks and went to work. Even though they'd rehearsed several times back at Vaziani, Aria fumbled a bit as she hurried to fill the containers. James didn't blame her. He didn't know of any scientist collecting specimens who could stay cool with gunfire echoing all around.

"Four minutes!" Rip yelled, looking at his watch. "Hurry up!"

"One more minute and we're gone," James called back.

There was shouting down the tunnel. One of Rip's men ran up into the cave and up to them. "Nasty surprise, Colonel. The militia's moving in some heavy machine guns and more men."

Rip scowled at him. "Status?"

"We're good for another three minutes, tops."

Rip turned his eyes to James, his face grim.

"Got it, Colonel, got it!" James said as he stuffed Aria's backpack with the last sample container.

"Let's go," Rip said, making a hand gesture to make it perfectly clear in the noisy cavern.

The only way out was straight through the mouth of the cave, which right now was probably the least safe place to be; booming gunfire grew louder with each of their steps in the direction of the main cave. James looked at Aria, saw her growing panic, grabbed her arm and said, "Ladies first."

"Kiss my ass, you crazy—"

"No time for screwing around," Rip said. "Just keep moving!"

They started down the tunnel together, then turned back in the direction of the hovering Black Hawk. Here, the air was thick with gunpowder smoke and shouting.

Without warning, Rip grabbed James and Aria and pulled them to the side of the cave. "Incoming!" A Russian-made RPG-7 round flew past them and slammed into the wall of the cave near the split. Ahead of them, the ceiling began to collapse.

Rip signaled his men, and the Marines fell back into the Bat Barn as dirt dumped into the tunnel in a steady flow.

"Move!" he bellowed. As each of his men raced past him, he counted them.

Bright-red tracer rounds began to whiz through the thick waterfall of dirt and dust as the defenders' heavy machine guns came into action. Rip gasped as he looked over his shoulder, and then backed up with his people. James understood why. Their escape route up the chimney was closed. Fortunately, their foe was now blocked as well, but the Marines, James and Aria were now trapped inside the cave's rear chamber.

Rip barely avoided being covered by the ceiling's continued collapse in heavy loads of dirt. Shouting "Goddammit!" he led the way into the deep part of the cave. Here, it was as dark as it gets, and the only noise in the vast, dust-shrouded space was coughing and the sounds of faint gunfire.

Rip turned on his flashlight, and several other flashlight beams began to dance around through the dust. "Let's get a head count."

One of the Marines murmured, "Anybody got fifty pounds of C-4?" A rhetorical question. Fifty pounds would blow the top of G'tichavank sky high.

Rip's flashlight lit up the group. Heavy dust still swirled still around them, along with the familiar scent of fresh earth.

Other flashlights went on. Rip spoke into his headset, "Getaway, this is Bandit, over."

It was no good.The signal was lost. Not that it mattered, James knew. The helicopter had drawn considerable fire, and surely had had to pull back until it could return for the extraction.

Guns spoke up. "All present and accounted for, sir. We have two casualties, but they're mobile. But we're low on ammo, sir."

Rip nodded, but said, "We don't have anybody to shoot at in here." Then he looked around. "Where does that direction lead to?"

He asked the question of Aria as he pointed to a long dark open area.

"I ... really don't know," she replied, following his pointing finger. "I only came in here once, and didn't like it. I don't like it much now either, if you want to know the truth."

"Let's take a look anyway. Might be another way out there. Even though those guys will dig into this chamber in an hour, maybe less."

He opened a lifted balled-up fist, then extended the fingers outward, the sign to fan out.

The men moved around the large cavern Rip had directed them into. It was roughly the size of three basketball courts, and was littered with boulders, stalagmites, and wavy, uneven dirt layers that reminded James of sand dunes.

James looked over the stalagmites. "These things usually mean water—although the water could have dried up a million years ago."

He held Aria's hand as they moved between two large rocks, testing the ground with their flashlights.

"This was a fairly new discovery for my father," Aria said as they walked. "He had opened this chamber up a few months before ... he died. I guess the tunnel walls were too soft for it to stay open."

James nodded, but didn't answer, keeping his focus on

their deliberate advance over the uneven dark ground. A moment later, he turned off his flashlight.

"What are you doing?" she hissed, startled. "Don't you realize how dark it is in here—?"

"Shhh. Look straight ahead, and up!"

He pointed, but she said, "I can't see— No, there's something … what is it?"

"I'm hoping it's the moon. You'd look great in moonlight." He leaned over and grabbed her shoulder. "Let's take a look."

When they drew closer, it became clear that he was right. A thin shaft of moonlight peeked down into the cave. They moved closer still, and looked up.

"The well!" Aria whispered in wonder.

"Yep," he whispered back. It was the well at the mountaintop monastery. The cover panel he'd removed the week before allowed in the moonlight … and the sporadic reports of gunfire.

He swiveled his head and softly called out, "Rip, over here!"

After the echoes of his called faded, he heard sound from what had been the tunnel. Digging sounds … and those told him they'd be sharing the cavern with unwelcome company in a few minutes.

Rip arrived at the well, followed by his men, and looked around, immediately understood. "Is there a bucket?"

All flashlights scanned the well shaft. A heavy, rusted chain went down one side.

Rip looked at the smallest of his men. "Test it out, Parker."

Parker climbed onto Guns' shoulders, gave the chain a slow and steady pull, and turned and nodded to Rip. Rip gave the signal for him to go on up.

Parker swung a bit on the climb; and his feet didn't have anywhere for footing until he was about twelve feet up, where the bottom of the well shaft formed. The base of the well pit itself was a dry hole that disappeared down into the floor of the cave.

Rip looked at Spidey, who had forty feet of rope looped across his shoulder. "Get him the rope when he reaches the top."

"Yes, sir." Spidey shucked off the rope and began tying a foothold on the end.

Parker had reached the top. His head barely fit through the open panel with his helmet off. He looked around carefully, and then gave Rip a thumbs-up. The wooden cover would have to be fully removed to yield an exit, but the area around the opening was clear.

From the far side of the cavern, about eighty meters away, more sounds came. There was a shout in Farsi, followed quickly by three explosions. Probably grenades, James thought. While harmless at that distance, the noise reverberated throughout the cavern. He leaned over and whispered to Aria, "They've broken through the cave-in, and they're attempting to disable any resistance to their entry."

"What does that mean?" she whispered back.

"They'll be coming soon."

She nodded, and her eyes showed worry for the first time since the Bat Cave.

"Guns," Rip ordered, "you and Walker take positions, forty meters, and hold them back with M-203s. Get me five minutes."

"Aye, aye, sir." The two men disappeared into the dark cavern. The M-203, also known as "the Bouncing Betty," was a high-explosive round launched from a special barrel positioned just beneath the regular barrel of the M-16 rifle. Both men carried this type of weapon, and while Walker had six rounds in his web belt, Guns, who liked the M-203, carried a bandolier full of them.

Parker now had the well's lid off, and was keeping a lookout while the rest of the group began their climb, one at a time. Spidey's rope, now firmly affixed to the end of the chain, made the climb easier, and one of the men held the bottom to keep it steady.

Rip examined the two wounded men. One had a hole in his leg that looked made by an AK-47's round. The other, who Aria was tending to, had shrapnel wounds across the side of his head.

"They'll need some help to get up the rope," Rip said to her. "How are *you* doing?"

"How am I doing? We got the oil sample! Let's get out of this place—"

Bang! BOOM! A Bouncing Betty round had gone off,

followed by its detonation at the far side of the cavern.

James ran up to them as Rip drew a deep breath and looked up. "Get the hell out of here? That's the plan, ma'am—"

Bang! BOOM! Bang! BOOM!

"Come on, Aria, you first," James said.

She looked hard at him. "These men—"

"We'll get them out," he said, and pointed. "Put your foot in that loop."

With a quick, reluctant glance back at the wounded, Aria obeyed, and Gomer and Spidey pulled her up while Rip and James began staging the wounded men. The oil samples inside her backpack clanked on the side of the well as she nervously clung to the rope. Gomer called out gentle encouragement as he strained with Spidey to get her up. Aria closed her eyes and took a deep breath as she slowly twirled on the rope.

"Don't worry, senorita," Gomer cooed as she approached the top, his Mexican accent a lullaby, "Ole Gome and Spidey got ya ... don't ya worry."

"Thanks, but I'm not worried about me ... the samples ..."

His eyes widened, and with a nod, he made each tug even gentler.

As soon as she was up, the rope came back down for the wounded men, and their recovery was smooth. Watching them ascend, Rip gingerly rubbed his own leg, which had acquired a hot graze from one of the heavy machinegun rounds while he was dodging the cave-in.

James noticed andasked, "You okay?"

"Yeah, just a scratch. You go on up, I'll be right behind."

James grabbed the line and hoisted himself up.

* * *

Up top, the men had already called for the helicopter to pick them up. The pilots had been thoroughly briefed on the area, and the flat space around the well was a perfect HLZ— helicopter landing zone pickup site. The Black Hawks had fallen back to a predesignated holding pattern, but were waiting for orders to swoop in.

At the call, the first Black Hawk roared into position with the pickup lines already down. The two wounded and Aria went up first. The entire time they were being pulled up and inside, glowing scarlet tracer rounds whizzed past the fuselage. The pilot leaned over and looked down at James, who waved him off. As quickly as it had arrived, the Black Hawk disappeared into the night.

* * *

Only Rip, Guns and Walker remained below. Rip had been listening intently to what was going on above, and while his headset couldn't speak directly to the pilots because of his location underground, he could hear the dialogue between them and his men. When he heard the Black Hawk leave, he whistled loudly, and Guns and Walker trotted back to him. Rip sent them up.

Just as he began his hand-over-hand ascent up the rope, gunfire erupted in the cavern. Rounds ricocheted off the stone walls beneath him. He paused his climb and reached for two grenades rigged onto his chest straps, one after the other, pulled the pins with his teeth, then threw them over the boulders where the fire was coming from, yelling, "Have some of Rip's bling, baby!"

While the explosions echoed in the cavern, he continued his ascent to the top of the well.

CHAPTER

27

He was in the midst of his scheduled quarterly meetings, but not being able to keep his mind settled, P.R. Nicholson had skipped them. Micromanagement was the kiss of death, he knew that; but ignoring something like this was impossible. He'd been monitoring the mission's progress to the extent reasonable. Finding that delicate balance between the two approaches was the tricky part. P.R.'s mind now struggled with that, and with the broader picture as well.

He paced his office and marched his mind again and again through the timeline— not the mission timeline, but the one in play on the future of Karabakh. The Chinese had really upped the ante with the timing of the U.N. vote on support for Karabakh's independence, and the National Security Council, most notably the Secretary of State, was demanding answers, and quickly. He only had a few days left.

He had to make things happen faster. He'd worked this thing from twenty different angles, even had people in Houston, catcher's mitts open, waiting for this stuff … had convinced a company to push aside all of its testing to put the genetic work on that oil sample on the fast track. Thank God there were patriots in the business sector; otherwise, these kinds of things just couldn't happen.

Unable to bear not knowing any longer, he picked up the secure phone and pushed the speed-dial button for the Chairman of the Joint Chiefs of Staff. The two men went through the standard protocol of going secure, turning keys on the side of their phones, and confirmed that they both had the secure line operating.

"General, I need a favor...."

P.R. heard a familiar cracking as the man at the other end tightened his jaw. When the CIA wanted something—it wasn't all that common to get these requests—it usually involved the redeployment of Department of Defense assets. Sometimes it was no big deal, sometimes it was. But, in the spirit of 'getting it done,' the general cooperated whenever possible, especially with the all-encompassing, laser-like focus on the Karabakh situation. They'd talked only once about additional support for this mission, and he'd already brought it in to support P.R.'s big gamble in Karabakh.

"Whatever you need, if we can get it," the general said in reply.

"I need the fastest thing you've got to pick up my small package at Vaziani Air Base," P.R. said. "Time is now too critical for the conventional transport that we set up."

"I'll take care of it. I'll call you back in ten."

P.R. knew his last warning wasn't needed. The general knew exactly what that package was, and where it was going, and why ... and, while he didn't know all the fluid details pushing the timing of things, P.R. knew that the General was ready to call in the alert F-15s that he'd promised if needed.

* * *

"Follow me! Let's move!" Rip had to shout above the gunfire as he hopped out of the well and pointed at the trail behind the moonlit monastery, the one he recognized from James' account of his first escape from this place. The trail led to their alternate pickup point on the cliff.

Rip's men broke into a full sprint. Rip followed, but a bit slower, using his headset to call the other Black Hawk helicopter to arrange their extraction.

Two militiamen standing at the other side of the monastery with rifles were caught off guard when Parker sprinted by, unloading two bursts of three rounds into each of them. They dropped as he passed them, already dying, and everyone else jumped over them on their frenzied dash to where the chopper would land.

Gunfire came from behind them as they ran, bullets hitting the trees around them with dull thuds. Flecks of bark flew as the men zigzagged toward the cliff, using the moonlight to guide them as they occasionally hopped over rocks and bushes on the open trail.

The running group could hear but not see the chopper when they reached the cliff. Then, as if it were a great serpent emerging from the ocean's depths, the Black Hawk rose before them. It had been nestled against the cliff's steep face, out of the line of fire, and was now right in front of them. The door gunner opened fire with his pintle-mounted M-60, sending rounds over their heads and toward their pursuers, providing cover as best he could. Agaki and his men, along with several Marines, were positioned in the open bays, trading rifle fire and standing by to help them board the chopper.

Not needing the rappelling lines this time, the men began jumping right into the chopper. Rip waited until he was certain everyone was onboard. He made the jump, but a sudden pain in his injured leg prevented him from completing it, and he landed half-in, half-out of the chopper's open door, rifle in one hand, hanging onto the skid with the other, just out of reach of the Marines at the door.

RPG-7s were whizzing past them, way too close for Rip's comfort. The pilot, who now had a red emergency light flashing on his dashboard, heard Rip shouting, "Go! Go! Go!" and pulled away quickly, leaving Rip with his good leg over the skid, his wounded leg dangling over the same steep precipice where James had performed his hammerhead stall just a week before.

As the Black Hawk moved away, rotors screaming, Rip emptied what was left in his clip into the militiamen now charging out of the dark woods. The helicopter lurched and he hung on as best he could, the merciful darkness not allowing him to see the two thousand-foot drop to the rocks below.

James and Agaki were leaning forward, desperately grappling to help pull Rip in, but the chopper's deliriously jerky movements to avoid incoming gunfire made it impossible to maneuver in the cabin. Rip could hear the pilots shouting to each other, and what they were yelling wasn't good.

"We're gonna have to put down! We've got maybe five, ten more minutes tops of airtime in this baby!"

James heard the same calls, and it wasn't hard for him to see why … flames continued shooting out near the tail rotor section, a fire that had crept up the tail and to the rear of the cabin. Guns and the crew sergeant were busy with fire extinguishers. The helicopter was leaking various fluids like water out of a colander and seemed to be steadily losing altitude. But at least they were making good headway. He did a mental calculation and thought, *Even if our altitude keeps dropping, we can gain some distance before we have to ditch—*

Gomer did a sudden, belly-to-ground crawl across the Black Hawk's slanted deck—so sudden, all James could do was watch in horror as the soldier headed out the door to a two-thousand-foot fall and certain death. When he saw the door gunner's long safety belt around his waist go taut, his relieved sigh was more like a hoarse grunt.

Gomer's head had jerked when it hit the 140-mile-per-hour wind just outside the cabin, but he managed to keep his hands extended toward Rip. No good; Rip had already slid back to the rear of the skid, out of reach. James watched Agaki slide down the pitching deck as it angled downward again, grab hold of Gomer and roll onto his back in a single motion, the action forcing him out into the furious stream of air in a macabre rendition of an extension ladder.

But Agaki wore no safety belt.

Gomer's fingers looped over Agaki's web belt as Agaki extended himself and beckoned to Rip. They locked hands, but the floor's downward slope was making it impossible for either Gomer or Agaki to pull backward, into the safety of the chopper.

There wasn't even time to pray. James grabbed a headset and shouted into it, "Hey, on my command, we need some pitch to starboard to bring our man off the skid."

James had little hope anyone up-front would get the message; he was certain the pilot's entire focus was on every red and orange caution light flashing on his instrument panel.

It was. But he still heard James' plea. "Roger that. Gotta get him in. We're losing controlled flight. Call it … and we'll do our best."

"Do your best quick, we're losing oil pressure." The copilot's words were bland, but his voice was just as tense as the pilot's.

Wind continuing to blast at him, Rip had managed to get his injured leg over the skid. Hot oil sprayed down on him from the main rotor housing, burning his arms and shoulder. He roared in pain, but held tight to Agaki's hand.

James nodded to Spidey, who advanced to kneel beside him. Then James yelled into his headset, "Execute!"

The chopper took a hard roll to the right, and James and Spidey jerked all three of them into the chopper in one tremendous heave that ended with all of them in a tumbled landing on the Black Hawk's deck.

Moments later, Rip leaned back in his seat, lungs heaving, shouting, "Oh, Gawd!" while Agaki and Gomer slapped him on the shoulders, hooting in triumph. James gave him a quiet thumbs-up and Rip winked back, just now able to muster a faint smile, then he pushed himself out of the seat to get up and check on his men. He'd barely attained a standing position when Guns gently pushed him back, then strapped him in, yelling, "You just enjoy the ride home, sir!"

The pilot and copilot continued their conversations on open mic, for all to hear, dealing with the panic of the fire.

Listening, James and Rip looked at each other. They'd gotten out, but weren't home just yet. But, more importantly to both of them…

"Mission accomplished."

They'd spoken in unison, and meant every syllable. Even if

they didn't make it back, Aria had three samples in her backpack, and her chopper was already across the frontier to meet whatever transport was waiting.

The fire was spreading, and Rip and James struggled to hear what was transpiring at the front of the chopper. The pilot had been fighting the problem while the copilot spoke to the other helicopter and navigated. Both grinned when they learned another Black Hawk was hovering just across the border as backup, and would pick them up if they had to land somewhere.

"Always hope we don't need Plan B," Rip said, "but it's good to have." And they both turned their attention back to their headsets.

Because of their inability to gain altitude, they had to follow the terrain north through Karabakh, which eventually led them along a valley. They were some distance from the mountain now, perhaps forty or fifty kilometers—not as much as any of them would've liked, but they needed to land.

Smoke began to fill the main cabin. The men in the rear leaned forward to get away from the heat of the fire as the crew sergeant and Guns continued to work the fire extinguishers. The pilots decided to settle on the heavily wooded valley floor, trying to find a break in the trees so they could put the Black Hawk down where she might be at least partly obscured by the forest.

Once the skids touched ground, smoke billowed out of the main cabin, and the flames illuminated the valley floor, creating a noxious funnel that made breathing unwise. Everyone bailed out, salvaging what they safely could as they left. Black smoke swirled harder now, but at least the flames offered some light on the dark valley floor while they consumed the whole of the Black Hawk's tired fuselage. Luckily, the landing site was clear enough to spare the forest from the searing flames.

SSgt Vickers looked over at Rip after checking in on his radio. "Sir, this is actually a pretty hot spot. There's a Mitrofanov garrison about six kilometers to the west, and they've got patrols all over the area. We've been advised to stay put for an hour until we can get extracted. Help's on the way, sir."

"An hour? Bullshit," Rip said. "Get me General Mathers."

Ten seconds passed before Vickers passed his handset to Rip. "Here he is sir."

"General, what's the holdup getting us extracted?"

"Hot as hell where you just landed. God, Rip, you couldn't have put down in a worse spot. Every hostile in the country must've seen you go down."

Rip trusted his word. "Then we'll march outta here to a good HLZ."

"Not before we deal with a group headed your way."

Rip paused, glanced at James, then Guns. "How many?"

"Looks like two companies actually, coming in from the West. You'll see them in about twenty minutes. Also, they're expecting an extraction attempt, and they're chatting on open coms about setting up on the ridgelines to take down the next bird we send in."

Rip winced. "What kind of help can we get here, sir?"

"Hawgs are rolling in hot. They'll give you plenty of cover, and they'll also beat up another group of trucks moving in your direction from the south."

Rip nodded, satisfaction crossing his weary face. "I like the sound of that. Keep talking, sir."

"Cobras are about to land here, and the civilian's been dropped off at her home. That Blackhawk's also inbound here with the sample. Good work, Rip."

"All good. So let's talk about an exit strategy."

"We'll punch a hole and move you through it in a couple of hours. They'll have trouble moving in reinforcements in these mountains, especially with the Hogs."

"Get me some directions outta this valley, and we can march out if we have to."

"Working on it. B-52s inbound as backup. We'll work the ridges and fire teams with them."

"Roger that, General. We'll dig in. Let's keep talking."

"I'll check in with you soon."

Rip passed the handset back to SSgt Vickers. "Okay. Set up

perimeter, we have unfriendly company on the way from the west. Contact estimated in fifteen minutes."

He saw James's worried face and grinned. "Don't know about you, Commander, but I just love a good, old-fashioned ground fight."

28

The Chairman of the Joint Chiefs was direct and to the point. "Sir, I've got two F-15s climbing out of Incerlik Air Base as we speak. They'll be on deck in Vaziani in about twenty-five minutes."

P.R. stood up and began to pace his office. "That's great, General. I'll arrange the pickup in Houston." He had his shoes off; his toes nervously curled into the thick carpet.

The Chairman continued. "We'll have to tank these birds a couple of times, and that will add to the trip … three-and-a-half hours after takeoff from Vaziani. That will put them on deck Houston around fourteen hundred local. Call sign is Air Force–247."

"Cute. 24–7… I get it. Thanks, General. Now I owe you one."

"Humm. Let's see. You're CIA. I've got an ex who works over at State—"

"Sorry, General, we don't do exes. Ha!"

"Until the next big one, then."

"Roger that, thanks."

After hanging up, P.R. picked up another phone on his desk. "Confirm that we have the lab ready for this afternoon, and notify me the second our cargo arrives."

* * *

Roger knew that Napoleon Bonaparte was right about two things. First of all, kill all the damn lawyers…. For damn sure, he was right about that. Second, screw all that about marching to the drummer. Nope, good ol' Napoleon said to march to the sound of the *cannon*. That was something Roger had done a time or twenty in his life.

He gripped Betsy's wheel, felt her shudder as she ambled along the moonlit, washed-out dirt road. Vank was a good starting point after all. It was just a few miles farther 'til he got to where it was all happening.

It pays to have friends who know what's going on, he thought, pressing through a particularly rough and bumpy washout. He was just glad he trusted his instincts. He wanted badly to be there when it went down. Whatever it was.

"An' good thing I got me an American truck," he muttered to the windshield. "Nobody makes trucks like in the good ole U.S. of A. Come on Betsy, get me there baby."

The road twisted along the night-darkened mountainside, but Roger had been over it a thousand times, so he let his attention drift, wondering what James had been talking about. The implication was, it wasn't any of his business, but instinct told him James might be dead wrong about that.

Nope, the good Commander Marshall hasn't been around long enough to know all of what ol' Rog can do.

Considering his line of work, Roger usually had his ear pretty close to the ground. But with the doings of fellow Americans, he had to be like an Indian tracker: go in fast and stealthy, all senses working at once, then put the pieces of the jigsaw puzzle together as he went. This frustrated him sometimes. Sure, he knew the *big picture* of what was going on in his adopted country, and he didn't like this thing with Ivan Mitrofanov. The guy was just an asshole looking out for himself. Ol' Ivan, no matter his big talk, didn't care one bit about the people of Karabakh. Hell, anybody could see that. And now Mitrofanov was tangling with Roger's own: Americans.

"And that just don't cut it with ol' *Rog*," he muttered, downshifting on a particularly steep grade. Here he was, at 62, and even though he no longer wore a uniform and he peddled bootlegged liquor for a living, he still was a patriot. He'd chosen his ground, and at this point, he just plain didn't give a shit what anyone else thought. But he was determined not to let the likes of Ivan Mitrofanov ruin any more lives than he could help.

Problem was, how? That's why he'd decided to make the trip. He couldn't be certain; his informal circles weren't talking. But he had a deep-down feeling that James had something to do with keeping ol' Ivan down.

The truck slid a bit on the steep, angled short cut, not enough to scare him, but enough to make him wish these people could build *roads,* for cryin' out loud! Finally, he came up on the main road, if you could call it that.

Knowing he was close to Vank, sensing he was nearing the action, he stopped Betsy on the deserted road and tipped back his straw Stetson hat. Not for any reason in particular, just a last look-see at things. In daylight or dark, this area was a breathtaking sight. But that's not why he stopped. This was a moment. *A moment … one that defines a man's life.* He wanted to savor it a while, like a fine Cuban.

A moment later, he drew a deep breath, glanced in the rearview mirror at his precious cargo, then exhaled deeply and put the truck back into drive. Based on what he'd overheard on an officer's radio right before heading off, he was pretty darn sure something big was about to go down in Vank, and whatever it was, it had to do with James' mission. Perhaps in Vank, he'd get a better clue as to what that *something* was, and how he could help James in his task. Whatever it was, not knowing more, he felt as ready as he could be.

He continued down the road with a quiet but excited resolve until he saw three men ahead at a checkpoint: a spot usually deserted this time of night. He slowed down. "Yep, James just might need somebody like me on shotgun," he muttered, slowing to a near crawl. From this vantage he could see a lingering wisp of black smoke on his right, down in the valley. From the size of the fading gray plume, a chopper had gone down. A big one. "There she sits," he muttered. "What's left of her, anyway."

These three fellows with Kalishnikovs in front of him didn't want company. And that might just be a problem too. *They're sealing the perimeter, hoping to keep someone in and everyone else out. It just don't get more obvious that that.*

Didn't matter. Roger had friends in need, and he was here to help them.

He came to a stop at the checkpoint, rolled down his window and gave his best good-ol'-boy smile. "Howdy."

"You are American?" said the one nearest.

"No, sir."

"You speak English, you drive American truck, you wear cowboy hat … let me see your passport." The man couldn't help the smile, but looked him over and brandished his weapon. "Yes, you are an American. Your passport."

"No siree, I am pure, blood, Texican. And here are my bonafides." With that, Roger pulled the trigger on the Colt he'd eased out the minute he saw the checkpoint manned. It was a replica 45-caliber Confederate Navy piece, and he was proud of it: so proud, he kept it in perfect working order at all times … as in loaded.

The man reeled backwards and Roger stepped on the gas, taking a second but ineffective shot at the next man as he passed the checkpoint.

"Git it girlie, come on baby," he said lovingly to Betsy as she struggled to get further up the incline.

The road curved to the right, and, unfortunately, both the men in front of him, ones he hadn't noticed before, and those behind him now, had him in a neat crossfire.

The Kalashnikovs roared to life, and poor Betsy took more than her fair share of hits. Flecks of her metal skin popped up and her glass shattered. Bullets ripped into the engine compartment, and while an AK-47 wouldn't penetrate the engine block, it sure put holes in things that made it run good. Soon after she'd been bled of fluids, a rod shot through her hood like an obscene, slanted flagpole.

Equally unfortunate was the fact that Roger was still inside the vehicle, and couldn't all together avoid the onslaught of hot lead.

He looked down into the valley, and now he could see those who were about to be shot at.

His people, just as he'd feared.

He steered the truck to the right, hoping to get as far as he could, bumping along down the mountainside, toward his friends, his people. He felt burning in his chest and legs where he'd been hit. He knew he'd be better off if he could get to them. But infinitely more important was what was in the back of Betsy: his personal arsenal, lovingly gathered over time and kept for a day just like this. Those Marines, and the good Commander, would be short on ammo by now, and ol' Rog had to deliver the goods.

He bounced along, constantly swerving to avoid trees, hoping to avoid rocks, freefalling a little more than he'd planned on, and, after a tumultuous ride, a ride to end all rides of his lifetime, he slammed into a big tree and was done. But, good Lordy ... Lordy Gawd, he had made it to the bottom of the valley!

He was able to take three huge gulps of air before slumping over the wheel.

CHAPTER

30

In the heart of Nagorno-Karabakh, the cliffs of Kelbajar Pass obscure the sunlight for most of the day. But at night, it didn't matter much. A canvas of springtime moonlight managed to stealthily creep past the cliffs and glide down the craggy rock in a silent caress that silhouetted the lonely hulk next to the main road through the pass.

Manufactured in the Ukraine over sixty years earlier, near the close of World War II, the tank had been on patrol in conflicts all over the region until disabled during fighting in 1992 and abandoned on the spot. Rust had worked its way all over and through the lifeless and ruined vehicle. Now, it only kept vigil by the roadside. Its last owners, the fourth generation of ownership, had hoped, like the three previous, that it would give them a competitive edge in conflict. It had no visible markings or insignia, and the measure of its success in battle wasn't obvious. Its only remaining value was to serve as a reminder of the destructive power of war. The sad-looking relic didn't receive even a glance when the newest generation of war-fighting vehicles rumbled past with their headlights on. Eight trucks, most of them transports filled with soldiers, eagerly worked their way through the narrow mountain pass. They were in a hurry to get to the valley, thirty or so kilometers away, where eighteen intruders had just hopped out of a burning Black Hawk, where they'd show these American Marines what happened to those who stick their nose where it doesn't belong.

The lead vehicle was a convertible staff car holding four uniformed men. The two in back spoke in excited voices to the man in the front passenger seat, unaware of the discussion happening above them …

"Baker two, five niner is rolling in hot."

"You are cleared to fire. You are cleared to fire."

"Fox one."

None of the men in the convoy heard this conversation, but in an instant, their car was shattered by a thunderous blast and burst into flames that mushroomed sixty feet into the air. Simultaneously, the last vehicle, the convoy's gasoline carrier, was consumed in an even more spectacular explosion. The other drivers, confined by the narrow pass and confused by the smoke, frantically attempted to maneuver around and get out of the pass. But the men leaping from the back end of the transports, getting in their way, wiped out any hope of escape. In the melee to flee the conflagration, none of them noticed the two Wart Hogs once again bearing down on them from the sky above.

In a classic attack maneuver that disabled front and rear vehicles in a column, the Hogs stopped the parade, then picked apart the poor devils trapped in the middle. This tactic had been successfully honed in Operation Desert Storm in 1991 in Iraq, and used there again in 2003 when Saddam Hussein was removed from power.

There were other explosions, lots of them.

The seven barrels of the Wart Hogs' GAU-8 cannon were adjusted for the wind by an onboard computer as they, one after the other, roared into action, spitting out hundred-round bursts of 30mm depleted uranium bullets in less than two seconds, every sixth one being a high-explosive incendiary round. The lethal projectiles thudded and reverberated in the tight quarters between the cliffs, until the aircraft had finished their mission and turned back toward their base, knowing that their squadron mates were streaking into position above Rip and his men thirty kilometers to the north.

But here, the work was done. There would be no further advancement for this column. There would be no more fighting for these men. And now, the downed Marines would have considerably less to deal with.

And many years later, people might pass by these rusting vehicles on the side of the road and wonder about what had happened to these eight hulks that used to be trucks. With a leisurely inspection, they might also notice the tank. Just as its purpose had faded into long-lost memory, And like the tank, any purpose the other vehicles had served would be long forgotten.

* * *

"Get out of my way! Please!"

"Aria, dear, be reasonable—"

Ignoring his pleas, Aria fought to get loose from Uncle Lev's bear hug, but her frenzied passion to help James and the rest of the group was no match for her uncle's burly arms. Her hair flew wildly and her arms kicked as she shouted, "Didn't you hear the crash? We can't just sit here and do nothing!"

Themieux stood alongside them with one caring hand on his sister's jerking shoulder, a distressed expression on his handsome face. "Aria, calm yourself. I'll go to them."

He glanced at Lev, made sure he had her subdued. "Take her to the hunting cabin, Uncle Lev. *Keep* her there. I'll keep you informed."

"Nooooooo!" With a final yank, she freed herself and began pummeling her brother's chest with open-handed slaps. "You don't understand, you don't—!"

Themieux sighed and grabbed both of her hands, stopping the blows and forcing her to look up at him. "Aria, my sister, I believe I do understand."

She looked up at him, and he smiled at her. Her thrashing stopped.

"Yes, I do understand, dear sister. From the moment you walked in and told us how you foolishly risked your life to help the Americans, the only time you cried was when you spoke of the one named James."

He forced his arms around her in a tight hug, and finally, she relaxed into his arms, sobbing.

"Oh, yes, Aria, I understand. And I swear to you, I will do anything I can to help them. Father would have done the same. But you and Uncle Lev have to leave here while I go to them. Those horrible men are still after you, Aria. And we still don't know where they are. We must keep you out of sight until we do."

Fighting back sobs, she pulled away and nodded. "All right. All right!"

CHAPTER

30

Captain Randy Carter sat in his Air Force F-15D Eagle on the Vaziani Air Base runway apron. His wingman sat next to him, at the ready. They'd just landed and were getting their three external tanks topped off. The maintenance chief and his crew were still checking out his aircraft when a Black Hawk helicopter came into the runway pattern. Carter's pilot ears pricked up when he heard the chopper's crew speaking to the tower. As they maneuvered to land near his jet, the chopper pilot's voice was intermittent, as if he were stuttering. But this didn't concern Carter; electromagnetic interference of the rotor wash often hampered their transmissions. Even so, he noted the edge in the pilot's voice.

A truck pulled up to the chopper just as it set down, and a Navy chief and airman raced to it, were handed something from the back of the chopper, and then got back into the truck. Carter watched as the truck headed toward him and performed a tire-smoking stop. The excited chief hopped out and headed his way. Now, Carter could see that the object was a backpack slung over the chief's right shoulder, its sides making a flopping bulge each time his foot hit the airfield's hard-packed runway.

As he ran, the chief gave Carter the signal to raise the canopy: one hand pressed flat on top of his head, and then a lifting of all of his fingers together in a single motion, holding them up. Nodding, Carter raised his canopy as instructed.

Holding the backpack, the chief trotted up the maintenance ramp alongside the aircraft until he was level with the cockpit, and then leaned over to speak.

"Here's your cargo, Captain," he shouted over the engine noise. "I'll secure it in your av-bay."

Carter gave him a thumbs-up and nodded. The chief opened the door on the side of the fuselage and wrapped a blanket around the backpack, fitting it in nice and tight. He paused at the pilot's cockpit after closing the door, gave another thumbs-up followed by the close-canopy signal with his hands, and waved to the tower as he trotted down the ramp and away from the jet.

The tower began giving taxi instructions to Carter, who was now going through the pre-takeoff checklist attached to his kneeboard—essentially a notebook attached to his thigh, containing headings and contact radio frequencies, which saved the pilot the trouble of scrambling for them while in flight. As he taxied off the runway threshold, the chief and the rest of the maintenance crew snapped smartly to attention and rendered a crisp salute. Carter continued on, working the cockpit.

While his wingman performed identical operations in his own jet, Carter completed his checklist, including the engine run-up, and received final clearance for takeoff. He and his wingman pressed their throttles forward, pumping jet fuel into their two eager Pratt & Whitney F100-PW-100 turbofan engines, which now roared to life in full afterburner. One after the other, each released their brakes, and their jets lurched forward and accelerated rapidly as they roared down the runway.

* * *

Chief Bates slowly dropped his salute and watched the F-15s climbing off the end of the runway.

"Those Air Force guys," he grumbled. "Don't know how to return a salute."

"You forget one, Chief?" The airman next to him held up the container of oil the chief handed him while they were in the truck.

Bates took the container from the airman, hefted it gently in his hand. "This is in case he don't make it. Now, if he were a naval aviator, I'd'a given him all three." He snorted a laugh, but he'd actually been instructed to keep one of the samples … and while he wasn't told why, he was sure his guess was correct. It *was* just in case Captain Carter didn't make it.

* * *

They were both near the 68,000-pound weight limit for takeoff, so it was a relatively sluggish climb out to altitude. Because of the drop tanks hanging under the wings and fuselage, neither jet could quite achieve its full speed-potential of 1,875 miles per hour. But they'd be able to climb to their 65,000-foot ceiling as they turned northwest toward the Black Sea. From there they would pass over friendly Ukrainian airspace, then over Poland, in a great circular route that would eventually bring them to Iceland. There, they'd get refueled in flight and continue on, over Newfoundland, then through the Midwestern United States, and ultimately down into Texas.

"And all of this to deliver a backpack," Carter muttered to his wingman.

He heard the wingman's static-filled chuckle, then, "Yeah, but we're a heck of a lot faster than FedEx."

He nodded, chuckling back. And they *would* deliver the backpack, and well under their time parameter. But first, he had some unfinished business to tend to—something that just wouldn't wait.

* * *

While Chief Bates was grousing, the F-15s had begun a slow turn back toward the airfield, gaining speed and now coming at them head on. As the aircraft accelerated, the chief glanced up to see shockwaves forming along the wings as the jets approached the speed of sound. The jets were low, very low to the deck now.

"Stand by to hit the deck," Bates told the airman, tensing. "I don't know what those fools are up to."

They found out less than a second after Bates finished his sentence. Flying over the far end of the airfield, both jets dipped a wing toward them, giving a clear view of the pilots as they roared past, shaking every window in the nearby town, and awakening every sleeping dog this side of the Volga River. And as the jets passed, Bates could see the pilots rendering crisp salutes with their right hands as they gripped the flight controls with their left.

The airman looked at Bates, grinning. "So, Chief, will you take back what you said about Air Force pilots?"

"Naw, hell no. But I will say this…." He pointed to the aircraft, which were now fading into the distance. "Those two there? They'd 'a made a fine pair of naval aviators, yessiree."

* * *

Now that the social niceties were out of the way, he could concentrate on the next stop in his mission.

Yep, there's a big steak dinner waiting for me in Houston, Carter thought while he watched the altimeter climbing through fifty thousand feet.

CHAPTER

31

Just over a hundred yards away, James could hear the crushed radiator hissing at the tree it was wrapped around. The tree won that fight, but the rest was still up for grabs.

Rip heard it too. "Who the heck is that?"

"Roger … from the Embassy." His eyes narrowed. "My guess? He was trying to bring us a gift."

Rip looked over at James. "A *gift*?"

"Weapons … I'd be willing to bet he's got an arsenal in his truck bed."

"Let's check it out, and we need to be quick about it," Rip said, and turned to SSgt Vickers. "Get us an update from Snoopy on the visitors the general was telling us about. That Reaper's gotta be good for somethin' And I hope Sparky and his boys aren't too busy right now. We might need 'em."

A few moments later, Vickers said, "Sir, the Snoopy team reports some movement. Two company-strength elements, one from the west, one from the south, both about two klicks out."

Rip smiled. "Plenty of time. Let's check it out." He waved his men forward.

James pried open the passenger door and there was Roger, bloodied and slumped over the wheel. James gave a sad shake of his head, recalling the intense curiosity in the older man's face when he'd left him at the Embassy. The truck was in terrible shape and Roger not much better, but he'd made it into the heart of the firefight, just where he wanted to be.

Roger didn't move or make any sound. His heart nearly paralyzed from fear, James wondered if he'd made a terrible mistake in playing mum, in not telling Roger he was leaving the Embassy for a mission that could turn sour, and therefore, not to try to follow. But he hadn't, and if Roger didn't make it, James would make sure he had a hero's funeral.

Miraculously, the dashboard and overhead lights still worked. While Chief Kautz and the others stormed the back of the truck, James felt for a pulse, gave a relieved sigh—weak, but definitely there. Then he ran his fingertips along Roger's neck to see if it was broken. Feeling nothing obvious, he risked gently leaning him back into the seat. His reward was a moan and a wince from the grayish-pale face. At least he could see where the blood was coming from now. Three grazes sliced through the iron-gray hair on one side of the man's head. Thankfully, they'd already stopped bleeding.

Roger opened his eyes and blinked several times.

"Welcome to our little party, Master Sergeant," James said softly.

Once he made sure Roger could wiggle his fingers and toes, he helped him out of the truck. Even as banged-up as he was, Roger's only response was a long and painful gasp as he stood.

"I, uh, I forgot to mention," he panted. "Took a little fire on the way in. A couple to the leg … one in my chest. Nothin' big."

"A chest wound? Oh, hell …" While Agaki dropped to his knees to check Roger's leg wounds, James half-unbuttoned, half-ripped Roger's shirt open. That's when he saw a miracle; the man's chest was covered by a bulletproof vest. The gunshots had ruined it, but they hadn't fully penetrated it.

Roger gave another feeble smile. "Didn't get to be this old by bein' dumb. No way would I haul that kinda ordnance without protection." He took a breath, and groaned. "Might'a broke a couple'a ribs, though."

James and Agaki shared a glance and an admiring

headshake, then James said, "Yeah, I'll definitely call *you* to ride shotgun sometime."

"Not until his legs are healed," Agaki said. "The bleeding is bad. We should hurry."

As quickly as they could without hurting him, they hustled him to the group's medic, then headed back to the truck, where Guns and Gomer were rummaging around.

"*Geezuzzzzzz*, we hit the jackpot, Commander," Gomer blurted. "This guy's got enough weapons in here to take East LA...." He grinned. "Well, maybe not *thaaat* much firepower. Check this out, sir...."

He hefted an AK-47 and handed it to Rip.

Rip trained his tiny flashlight over the weapon, then scanned it over the items in the bed. "This guy came loaded for bear, all right."

In the flashlight's glare, James saw two boxes, each filled with six AK-47s, another box with assorted handguns, two boxes mounded with claymore mines, several filled with clips and cartridges, grenades, and six RPG-7 launchers with two dozen rounds. The coup de grace was a heavy machine gun, an M249 squad automatic weapon complete with several boxes of belted ammunition.

Rip handed the AK-47 back to Gomer, then pointed to the truck bed. "Pass this stuff out. Take your pick. Miller! Get us some psy-op tunes going here."

As he worked the dials on the pickup's sound system, Sgt. Miller said, "Oh, yes, his stereo's just as potent as his weaponry. He is *wired*, man!"

The men worked feverishly to arm themselves, several of them joining together to trundle the M249 out of the disabled truck and onto the ground. A perimeter was set up based upon the feedback from the Predator surveillance crew. Once all was in place, it was a waiting game.

High up on Granpa's knee, beggin' for a tale of adventure.
He leaned back and told me of a tale of
Belt buckles and boots, cowboys and rustlers...

The twangy country tune echoed on the walls of the valley. Rip looked at Sgt. Miller and called out. "That your first choice?"

"The only choice, sir."

Rip leaned over to James and whispered, "That mean he likes that music, or that's all he could find in the truck?"

"Probably better not to ask," James replied as Agaki approached and stood next to them. They watched as Agaki ceremoniously folded a scarf, tied it around his head, then lowered his arms with measured, swanlike grace, all while keeping serious eyes on Rip. James wanted to ask what was on his mind, but Agaki's solemn face stopped him.

Agaki finally spoke after the two had exchanged a long look. "Guys, first round's on me when we get back."

Rip beamed at him. "And I've got the second. Let's go check on our injured man."

* * *

From where he lay on the ground next to the medic, Roger looked around him, then saw the three approaching. "Put me down right here boys," he said weakly between coughs. "I us'ta wanna be brought home, but, hell, after kicking around so much … just lay me down where I die. That's the way I want it."

He looked at Rip, and Rip nodded. "You did good, Roger. Gave us a chance to get out of here in one piece. If there's a way, we'll return the favor."

Roger offered a thin smile back.

All growed up, tall and free, all hankered up for some adventure

I stood tall in a different kinda uniform, with

Belt buckles and boots, it was, cowboys and a different kinda rustler.

SSgt Vickers' radio came to life. "Sir?"

Rip listened for a few moments, and looked to the west and replied as he scanned the western side of the valley. "We're clear, get it done."

A few more static-filled words, and he looked around

frantically and shouted. "Incoming!"

The men ducked and waited.

Giving hope and a little taste of freedom.

Their side of the narrow valley erupted in thunder as the A-10s hit their marks. Their brilliant flashes overcame the pale moonlight while the shockwave boomed over them, followed by the intense heat of the blast. The flash had made them all turn away and hunker down reflexively, and chunks of metal shrapnel could be heard thudding into the trees around them as the smell of incendiaries hung in the air. James winced when shards of hot metal streaked into his scalp and right arm.

The radio again came to life. As soon as its squawking ebbed, Rip called back to Guns, "Focus your fire teams on the southern flank, and quick. The west looks pretty clear at this point."

He continued his dialogue with Vaziani Air Base, his strident voice competing with the music that continued to echo around the canyon.

Makin' friends, rackin' stackin' memories

"Okay, men, be ready. They'll be coming in now, expecting to do cleanup work on unarmed troops."

Sharing a lonely togetherness, far away from home.

He hefted the AK-47 and grinned. "So when they get here, be sure to pull the trigger a few times."

The men looked at each other, all of them knowing it was show time. A few faces showed anticipation mixed with uncertainty. None showed fear. Before the glow faded from the first strikes on the western flank, Guns motioned the realignment of the fire teams into a shallow gully behind a fallen tree. Rip had two men dash around to set up additional claymores on the southern flank, just in case their air support didn't hit home.

"We're having trouble hitting the group approaching from the south," came over the radio. "They're using the cliffs as cover. Can you see them yet? Closing in at just a few hundred yards."

"Don't see anything," Rip called back, scanning the thick

trees with his night scope. "But they'll have to break out in the open to charge us. Hit 'em when you can."

"Wilco. For now, we'll light them up for you from their rear. Stand by."

"Roger that." Rip brought the handset away from his face and turned to his men. "We're getting some flares dropped. *Fire at will* when you have a target."

The two men who had been setting the claymores came hopping back over the fallen tree, leaving a trail of detonator wire.

The quiet was too short: Another series of smaller explosions from the A-10s popped off, lighting up the valley sky from the south, allowing them to see a group of roughly a hundred armed men running toward them. The claymores were both tripped; simultaneously, the line of Marines opened up with all they had. The militiamen took heavy losses, but their charge was undeterred, and they returned fire as they advanced.

James hefted his AK-47 and began sending single rounds into the group. Agaki's men were mixed with the Marines against the fallen tree. Agaki looked at Rip and said, "I will take those who cross our firing line."

Rip looked perplexed as Agaki slowly took four paces backwards and drew his sword, then assumed a fighting position.

"No rifle?"

"No rifle."

Belt buckles and boots, cowboys and rustlers

Spidey, who was out on the left flank, reeled and dropped his weapon as a bullet grazed the side of his skull. He slowly stood up, shaking, and a second bullet hit him at an angle, passing through his body armor and ripping into his chest. He slumped to the ground.

Guns stepped over him, checked him out, saw his friend was in serious trouble. "I got your back," he said, his voice firm.

The fighting continued all around them. Most combatants

were now locked in hand-to-hand combat as the two lines began to meet. Rifles popped everywhere, broken by screams and grunts and the tinny sound of the country music that still twanged in an eerie backdrop to a surreal setting of furious life-and-death struggle. Fresh flares once again illuminated the valley floor.

Five men burst into the clearing in front of Guns and charged him. He pulled out his nine-millimeter and took aim. The first two fell in rapid succession while hot tracer rounds sped over their heads. A third dropped and took a shot to the knee. The remaining two continued their charge as Guns ejected his empty clip and pulled out his knife.

CHAPTER

32

Moving silently along in the dark sky ten thousand feet above the battlefield, a robot served its masters, masters who were comfortably seated miles away, inside a trailer that served as a command center. The sleek drone cruised gracefully along through the moonlit sky over the Marines below it, and, thanks to advanced optics and a multimillion-dollar electronics package, it provided information that served as the only hope to turn the tide of battle below.

A second robot slipped up behind the first, unnoticed. This one bore a similar profile. Indeed, much of what made it successful in flight had come from the same engineers. Only this one's technology had moved through an ally's friendly hands into less-friendly ones.

* * *

"Major Bishop, I have something unusual here sir."

The Major turned at the tech's statement. "Wha'cha got?"

"I'm ... not exactly sure," SSgt Farrington said. "Take a look."

They both peered at the display showing the UAV Reaper.

Bishop studied the screen for a moment and waved it off. "Probably an echo. Or maybe electronic scatter from something. I'm not too worried about it, but keep an eye on it."

"So, we just continue the mission?"

"That is correct," Bishop replied, knowing that the pilot, who was comfortably seated nearby, overheard this conversation.

The Major's answer would have been far different if he had seen the second robot slowly close in on the first, if he had seen the tiny aperture move on its underbelly.

Seconds later, Farrington blurted, "Holy shit, we're being painted! We're lit up by fire-control radar! It's locked, it's got tone!"

He looked at Bishop for guidance, but saw only astonishment.

A single shot was fired from the second drone, and a specially designed hollow-charge warhead made its way toward the Reaper. Upon impact, it punched through the drone's lightweight skin, and a stream of molten yellow metal moved almost effortlessly through the Reaper's sophisticated electronics suite. The link between slave and master foundered, then died.

Bishop looked at the screen, incredulous, as the second drone peeled off and began making its way to the edge of the display.

They looked at each other, and finally Bishop broke the silence. "I'm going to see the general. I'll be back in fifteen minutes, probably with him and a gang of people. Look sharp. Bring the relief drone off-site and into a low spin pattern. No, better yet, follow that guy at a distance. Let's find out where he lives."

"Aye-aye, sir." Farrington's tone now held disbelief, and a growing horror shared by Major Bishop. Without the drone's help, Sparky and his gang of Warthogs would have to target the militia on their own. Even worse, as of this moment, not only could they no longer give tactical support to the men on the ground who were fighting for their lives, but also it appeared that the United States was no longer supreme in the airways over its theaters of combat. Somewhere out there, someone had found a way to best their best technology to date.

CHAPTER

33

At first, Spidey could only see Guns' boots. They shifted from side to side next to him, kicking up dust as he fought the two men. Occasionally, the men's feet kicked at him and pressed up against him. He tried to get up to help Guns, or at least move away from the thrusting boots, but couldn't even turn his head to look up. All he could do was lie there and watch while his buddy fought for both their lives. One of their attackers fell to the ground, and Spidey could see him holding his stomach. The remaining two men continued to fight over him.

One man, then the other fell to the ground next to him, making the ground shake. A man's leg landed on top of him, but he couldn't feel its weight, and this terrified him. This time, though, he was able to turn his head to identify the fallen man. Now he could see into Guns' dead eyes as the second man stood up, triumphantly glaring at him in hate.

"I like killing infidel Marines!" the man blurted. "I killed men like you in Fallujah, and I will keep killing you!"

The man brandished his bloody knife and came after him.

"Not on my watch!"

As the words were spoken, four bloody holes ripped into the knife-wielding militiaman, who fell limp to the ground. This time, he didn't get up.

Rip stood there grimacing, holding a smoking nine-millimeter, and yelled, "And by the way, you're a liar. I don't remember seeing your sorry ass in Fallujah!"

Rip knelt next to Spidey. "Shit! Medic!"

Spidey looked up at him with a weak smile, the best he could offer, and Rip tapped on his boot, checking for a response. The foot didn't move, but the light faded from Spidey's eyes as he lost his final battle to stick it out with *his* Marines.

As gunfire continued around them, the medic knelt on the other side of Spidey, checked his vitals and wounds and gave Rip a solemn look, his head turning from side to side. Rip stood, the grimace back on his face, and rejoined the fray.

* * *

Agaki saw the first man just as the man planted one booted foot on the fallen tree. The man didn't see the sword in Agaki's hand, and Agaki did nothing to prevent him from springing into the air toward him. Agaki did, however, make a side-to-side swiping motion that nearly cut the man in half before he fell lifeless to the ground.

Agaki pulled the sword back so quickly, the second man never saw why his comrade fell. He soon found out, though, when he crossed the tree and launched himself unknowingly into a direct, tip-to-hilt thrust of hardened metal.

A third attacker, landing with both feet confidently planted, saw his comrade impaled on the sword, leaving Agaki weaponless. He gave a taunting smile, as if to say, *A sword to a gunfight! Fool!* Then he turned his weapon toward Agaki.

Agaki's free hand whipped across his body, releasing a shirakin five-pointed star toward the man with the force and speed of a major-leaguer's pitch. Before the attacker could train his rifle on what he'd assumed was a hapless foe, the star hit the attacker's chest with enough impact to press its pointed edge into his aorta.

Agaki pushed the second man off his sword with his boot, keeping his eyes trained on the third man during his collapse. The recently impaled man watched in stupefied horror until he, too, slumped to the ground.

When he realized that the cries and grunts behind him had faded, Agaki whirled around and checked the body-strewn area, looking for hostile survivors. Dawn was breaking, and soft if indirect sunlight now replaced the moonlight, allowing him to vaguely see the battleground. What he saw and heard was an occasional volley exchange with the fleeing remnants of Mitrofanov's men—that, and Rip standing silently over Spidey, holding his canteen, his face grim.

* * *

Rip shifted his eyes from Spidey to Guns, realizing the Corps had just lost two good men. He lowered his head, exhausted, but struggled to fight his fatigue. *Come on, Marine, you asked for a fight, and a fight you got. And there's miles to go before any damn body sleeps.*

He looked over at his remaining men, who were settling down, and heard one of them whine, "Man, I could use some *Rip It* and a stogie right about now." Memory lightened Rip's exhaustion a notch. The soldier was referring to a soft drink in Iraq, a favorite energy boost.

He saw movement and tensed; one of the five who had rushed Guns and Spidey still lived. Rip headed over to the man and found him holding a chest wound, so weak from blood loss that he could only lay on his back, motionless, while the wound made gurgling sounds with each labored breath.

The dying man eyed Rip's canteen. Rip glared back at him. "Best friend, worst enemy. That's the United States Marine Corps."

The man gave no response, but Rip felt an unexpected wave of compassion overtake him. He knelt next to the man. Through this closer look, just a boy. He poured some water on his lips. The kid coughed a bit, and then drank some more. Life came back to his eyes, briefly, and he said in surprisingly clear English, "You shall be vanquished, and driven together to hell.…"

"…and evil is the resting-place," Rip finished. He recognized the passage from *Surah III* in the Quran. Rip was not a particularly religious man, but had studied the book so he would know his enemy.

The boy's eyes grew wide in surprise at Rip's words, and

he struggled again to breathe.

Then Rip said something he was surprised to hear himself say. "Allah is with the believers." It was said only to comfort the boy. His next thought was not: *But he's not with me ... and that's my choice to make, not yours.*

The boy's focus slipped from Rip to the sky above them. A moment later, he stopped breathing. Rip surveyed his body, ravaged and drained of blood by two bullets, and then took inventory of his things. The Pakistani passport showed the name Abdul al-Salif, with a recent entry stamp into Tehran, and nothing else. Rip wondered why a boy with his whole life ahead of him would choose such an end, what his life had been like before today, why he felt the imperative need to wage war on anyone who didn't strictly obey *his* interpretation of God's law.

Then he wondered just how long this most-recent wave of militant Islamic fundamentalism would continue.

He continued to survey the battleground, and noticed a rifle with a large scope. Closer, he recognized it as an Austrian-made sniper rifle. A short distance away, next to another dead man, was a pair of British-made night vision goggles.

"Sold to Iran to combat drugs with a seal of approval by the UN," he muttered, his voice bitter now. He didn't have to wonder why a dealer would sell these items to a country that sponsored terrorism. For many, profit superseded principle.

And that money was now soiled with the blood of his men.

It had gotten very quiet. His attention was diverted by James and Agaki. James was signaling for him. As he neared, James said in a low voice, "We saw something moving ... over there."

Rip looked through his ocular night scope and muttered, "Well, glory be."

"What is it?"

"A horse. Looks like a stray." Rip looked at James with a bitter smile. "Finally. Here comes the cavalry."

"Or maybe not," Agaki said.

"Yep. Could be a decoy." Rip returned his eyes to the binoculars, watched the beast wander for a while in the trees, and eventually toward them. Both men tensed when the horse drew near enough for them to realize the horse wasn't stray, or riderless.

"Oh, man, oh Lord, I recognize that horse," James whispered and started running. Rip and Agaki followed, Rip drawing his weapon and yelling, "What is it?"

Their questions were answered when they neared the horse. A man was hanging from the horse in a stealthy riding position. As they ran up to him, he slipped off the horse, glanced at Rip and Agaki with a cheerful smile, then turned the smile toward James and said, "I think my sister has grown entirely too fond of you, Commander Marshall."

Rip glanced at James, then back at the man. "Where the hell did *you* come from?"

"Unless I miss my guess," James explained quickly, "This is Aria's brother Themieux."

Themieux nodded and smiled again, and Rip pointed his weapon down.

"Yes, that's who I am. And, like Aria, I grew up in these woods. I brought some beef jerky and water," he pointed to his packs, "and can show you the way out of here to safety."

Rip looked at the sky, figured that whatever had happened, their evac would be delayed. Then he lowered his eyes to their mounted rescuer. "Best offer I've gotten this morning. Let's get outta here."

CHAPTER

34

Dawn came on schedule, even if nothing else made sense to Rip.

He stood next to Themieux, brushing the dirt off his hands after helping James and Agaki move Roger onto a makeshift stretcher. As he did, he scanned the cliffs and trees. No signs of trouble. There was no movement, no motion, no more things in the night to check out. All the mystery and mystique of the darkness was gone as the light of day crept farther into the valley.

"These Marines come out with us," Rip said as he nodded to the bodies of Guns and Spidey. "We'll put them over the back of your mount."

He looked over to his men and called out, "We're marching out of here, ten minutes." Dried blood streaked his neck and parts of his uniform. He continued to survey the area as his men slowly but decidedly shifted into gear. He could tell they hurt, just like he did, but they still moved in unison, a team. There was no coffee, no room service, just a cold dawn littered with dead bodies. He knew they could handle it. This was something they'd prepared for since their first day as Marines.

The group marched out together. Parker led the way on point, followed by Themieux, who had given his laden horse to one of the pilots and now offered guidance to Parker. The men studied the high ground from left to right as they followed the Khachen River's bank down toward the nearest village. As they marched, they encountered no hostile resistance.

Agaki looked over to Rip and James and said, "They respect your air supremacy!"

Rip noted that Agaki didn't say they "feared" it. That didn't matter. The two men now beginning their last journey home had fought bravely and stubbornly last night. They hadn't been afraid to die, and they had died honorably for their country. What was going on with this militia was somewhat of a mystery to Rip, however. He knew all too much about the Islamic militant movement, but still couldn't get it. Not understanding was something that haunted him, but deep down, he felt this enemy was misguided.

The riverbank wound along for a few kilometers, and the farther they went, the more comfortable they all became. The valley was a tough spot, but they were out of it.

"Hey, Gomer, you got termites, man?"

Rip glanced over to see one man tousling the back of Gomer's collar. It had been burned during the helicopter ride the night before.

"Hey man, I guess this scapular thing don't make you fireproof, just bulletproof eh?" the Marine teased.

They both laughed, and Rip relaxed even more when Gomer said, "I tell you what, when I get home, I'm gonna have the biggest plate of tortillas and enchiladas ... and at least one *cerveza*." With that announcement, he bit into his piece of beef jerky.

Suddenly, the man on point held up a fist, the sign to stop. The laughter and talk ceased. Two more hand signals, and the men melted into the shrubs and rocks along the riverbed.

In the tense silence that followed, Rip saw what he hadn't before. Ahead, a stone bridge crossed over the river. In less than a minute, a car drove onto it and stopped. Two soldiers got out and began to survey the area with binoculars. None of the Marines moved; there was no need, since they were out of the vehicle's line of sight. The only sounds were of the car's idling engine, and closer, the dribbling of water over stones in the shallow river. One of the soldiers pulled out a walkie-talkie and spoke into it, then both got back into the car and continued over the bridge and down the road.

A counted minute later, Rip gave the signal to move on.

Themieux led the men up a gradual rise, and they now overlooked another valley. When Rip came alongside Themieux, he saw his horrified expression and asked, "What's wrong?"

"It's … my village." Themieux pointed to rising smoke. "That's where I was taking you. For … safety."

Themieux made as if to start running down the hill. Rip stopped him with one hand. "No. Wait."

Through his binoculars, he surveyed the scene below. The village was on fire. There were three military vehicles parked just out of range of the flames, vehicles that looked part of Mitrofanov's army.

There to stake a claim. Shit.

As Rip watched, one heavily armed militiaman shoved the back of a frail old man, who landed facedown next to three others. He thought it best not to mention that to Themieux yet. Not until he had to. But he told them about the military vehicles.

"They're looking for Aria, I'm sure of it," he heard James say. "We never should've dropped her off here. The helicopter's what drew those men. Mitrofanov must know about her father finding—"

"But … Aria is gone."

At Themieux's words, the other three men whirled around to him and spoke at once. "Where?"

"My uncle … Uncle Lev took her by horseback to his hunting cabin, higher up … to be safe. They won't find her."

James glanced at Rip knowingly. "Well, those villagers are going to need some help."

Themieux sputtered, "I must help … my people, I—"

"Themieux," Rip said, "take my two men, and Roger, over to the glen. Helicopters will come for them in one hour." Rip's tone and hard stare sent a clear message.

Themieux nodded in reluctant agreement and led the horse away while Rip looked around his exhausted, rag-tag group. "What do you guys say? We can move into the HLZ, or, we can do something about this."

None of them spoke, nor did they exchange glances. They didn't have to, Rip was certain. None of them would be able to live with themselves if they left that tiny village to be slaughtered. Rip gave a slow nod, feeling a wave of pride that he couldn't allow them to see. Not yet. Not 'til it was over. "Let's go, then."

He led the way. However, one by one, the men all looked back as they left, seeing Themieux busily laying the two dead Marines under the shade of a tree near Roger's stretcher, his movements gentle and careful. Blood and dirt soiled his shirt, but it was the sorrow on his face, not the blood, that made him appear deeply wounded. Each man knew that in a matter of minutes he might be the next person laid over the back of a horse.

* * *

"You must remember who is in charge here, Mr. Mayor!"

Considering the circumstances, Sattar's reply was calm. "Who is in charge? You have my head under your boot, but you are nothing."

The burly sergeant, whose name was Karl, laughed, and his men joined in. "Well then, old man, if I am *nothing*, and you are prostrate before me and I have my boot on your head, then what does that make you?"

"Sattar, let him alone," Kasim said. "He doesn't know what he is doing."

This brought another laugh.

Sattar joined in mockingly. "Okay, I will let him go … when his foot gets tired."

Again the men laughed coarsely, then Karl's voice lost its lightness. "The girl, Mr. Mayor. I'll only ask this one last time."

Similarly restrained next to him, Kasim could only hold his breath and pray that they would leave his brother alive.

* * *

From a distance, Rip, James, and Agaki watched and carefully counted Karl's men. Knowing their voices would carry, they kept their abbreviated discussion brief and quiet.

"I count eleven," James said. "Five by Kasim, four behind their trucks, two inside the house."

Rip and Agaki's nods were cut short by a cry of pain from one of the old men. One of the soldiers was grinding his boot against the man's pinned-down head.

Rip said, grimacing, "Let's do this quick, this is getting bad fast." He looked around at the others and signaled them closer. "Okay. Listen up, here's the plan …"

While giving instructions, he drew in the dirt in front of him, and then split the men into two groups. On his signal, they began a loping race down toward the village.

* * *

"Sattar, I think your days of *backtalk* are behind you. This bullet does not like your *backtalk*."

With that, Karl drew his pistol, pressed it against the back of the old man's head and pulled the trigger, and then gave a deep exhale and a gratified smile at the report. He looked around and called out, "Who else in this village would challenge Mitrofanov? Let that be a lesson to the rest of you."

When he neither heard nor saw a response from the terrified villagers, he lifted his foot from Kasim's head and holstered his pistol with an exultant grunt. His triumph faded as he pointed toward the porch of one of the unburned houses, next to where they'd parked their vehicles. "These people don't know where the girl is. Let's get out of the sun and decide where to search next."

* * *

Now released from the heavy boot that had kept his head pushed into the stone-filled dirt of the village square, Kasim wept quietly while he crawled to his brother's lifeless body, pulled himself to a kneeling position, and covered his face with his hands, his furious tears clashing with the angry growl that didn't match his tiny, age-gnarled figure. He leaned over and caressed Sattar's back with trembling fingertips, unable to comprehend the loss of the big brother who had been his mentor and protector and friend for so many, many years. He could only keen, "Sattar, my good brother Sattar …"

His grieving, yet rage-filled mind didn't flinch at, didn't even register, the noises behind him.

* * *

Striding toward the porch, Karl heard Kasim's cries of grief, shook his head and half-turned to rebuke the old man. He never had the chance. A grenade went off behind their vehicles, followed by a barrage of gunfire. The dazed militiamen stopped in their tracks; some fell where they stood. The rest were thrown into a battle they didn't expect and weren't prepared for.

His pistol drawn, James approached from the woods behind the house, his destination some sheds and the corral. Gomer stayed beside and just behind him, to assist him in cutting off any retreat by the militiamen.

James was just moving behind one of the sheds when one of Mitrofanov's militiamen raced past, obviously headed toward the noise. He didn't see James, who stepped forward and took aim. James shouted, "Hey!" but the man kept running.

Perhaps it was the sleepless night, or tension, or the stress of his first close combat in years. Whatever the reason, James could *feel* his old pistol instructor, CWO4 McDaniels, standing behind him, quietly instructing, "*Sight alignment and trigger control…*"

He led his shot a bit ahead of the man, squeezed the trigger deliberately, and felt the pistol's jolting recoil as the bullet flew out of the muzzle in eerie slow motion, striking the man in the side. The man fell forward to the ground, roaring in pain and grappling for his weapon. In one split-second motion, it appeared in his hand and he turned toward James, ready to shoot. A second shot from Gomer finished him.

Exhaustion had driven James to a level of numb clarity: He stood there, still in firing position, and felt a hollow click inside him. Not in his head, or in his heart, or his gut, but in all three. He'd come close during the war in Afghanistan and been nauseated by twinges of distaste the night before. But at this particular moment, he'd had enough of it all. He'd just shot a man, killed another human being who wasn't, at that instant, trying to kill him.

Gomer looked at James expectantly, concern on his face. "Sir? He'd'a done you the same … or worse …. Commander?"

When his heart and mind stilled and his gut released its torment, he managed, "Yeah, I suppose …. Let's go."

The pair continued toward the sounds of the firefight, which were rapidly tapering off.

* * *

Karl and most of his men had, by now, succumbed to a blistering line of gunfire, and Agaki's three men scanned the area from positions on the roof of the main house. While they kept their vigil atop the house, Agaki edged around the corner of the house and onto its front porch, his sword drawn and held over his head in tight, sinewy arms.

One of the two remaining men charged out of the house, screaming to Allah. Agaki's blade crossed the man's chest, and as the stunned militiaman dropped to his knees, a grenade tumbled out of his hand and rolled off the front porch, landing only a few feet away.

Agaki whirled away from the grenade, avoiding the blast, strode to the edge of the porch, and turned back toward the front door, his eyes wide open in anger and his bloody sword once again held up in an offensive posture, awaiting the second man. Flames and smoke roiled from the vehicle behind him.

At his call, his men slid down the front porch's roof and stood beside him, their weapons at the ready. James, along with Rip and his men, converged out in front of the porch, sensing that the battle wasn't yet over. The shooting had ended, and in the odd silence that followed, all eyes were now on Agaki, who didn't move, his breathing steady as he held his sword in the ready position.

Whooping as his comrade had, the last man came out the front door, brandishing his weapon at Agaki, then the group.

Agaki advanced toward him. The man dropped his weapon and stepped back against the porch wall.

Agaki charged, shouting fiercely in Japanese. His men advanced alongside him toward the surviving militiaman, who had backed up against the wall, terrified, as Agaki's men held the angry samurai back, just inches away. Agaki began to shout in English, startling the entire group.

"Where are your Chinese advisors? The Chinese? Tell me now!"

"Lachin! Lachin!" the man screamed. "Just south of Lachin. Next to the Goris-Stepanakert Highway! A compound …" A wet spot appeared on the man's pants, a puddle quickly formed around his feet.

Agaki turned and strode off the porch, and two of Rip's crew cuffed the terrified man. James followed Agaki, watched him share bows and quiet laughter with his men. And then, James figured it out: Agaki's cries in Japanese had been frightening, but were merely instructions to his men, who had happily obliged his ploy to terrify the cornered combatant.

Admirable, James couldn't help thinking. *Melodramatic, but very effective. Wonder if he gives lessons?*

* * *

As he wiped blood from his sword with a rag, Agaki saw James but quickly returned his gaze to his task and said, "So, when will you hit the Lachin compound?"

James reflected for a moment. He was still thinking when Rip came off the porch and joined them. James turned to him and said, "Lachin?"

Rip grunted and rubbed his hand over his scalp. After a few moments, he replied, "Lachin's the old name. It's officially known as Berdzor now. But locals have a hard time with the new name. Habit, I guess."

He gave James a curious look, then looked at Agaki, realizing that Agaki was going in on his own, with an agenda that Rip didn't understand.

With the oil samples safely on their way, Rip's part of the

mission was over. Still, he wanted to know.

"When'll we hit Lachin? Twenty-one-hundred hours, maybe. We knew about the compound, and several others. But until now, we didn't know for certain who was in there. Mind if I ask what you're up to? Why you don't wanna wait and go with us?"

Agaki looked at Rip and James. "A personal matter." And then he clammed up.

They looked at a map together, and Rip pointed out the location where the Chinese advisors were based.

James looked at Agaki, who wasn't looking at the map, but at a nearby truck, one not immolated by the fire. The vehicle was intact but had a series of bullet holes through the windshield. Also, the paint on the front had been melted off by the vehicle in front of it, which had burned during the firefight and was still burning, now in a relative smolder.

"Nice truck!" Agaki said, his voice light. He walked up to it, opened the door, climbed in, and started it up. "Twenty-one hundred?" he called out to Rip and James. "That allows me eleven hours and twenty-one minutes. Take care of my men."

"Bullshit!" James spat out the word as he strode toward the truck. "You're not taking him, I am!"

Agaki gripped the wheel and stared straight ahead. And then James realized something he couldn't believe he hadn't picked up on before now.

He grabbed the door handle. "You knew who the sniper was all along, didn't you?"

Agaki continued to look straight ahead. "Yes."

James fought to keep from reaching through the open window and grabbing Agaki's throat. The thought that Agaki had withheld such information from him—information Agaki knew from the beginning that he wanted—enraged him. But to avenge Steve Kranzer's death, he had to keep his anger directed at the one who deserved it.

He forced a deep breath and said, "That asshole killed my friend. He's mine. Get out of the fucking truck."

Agaki slowly shook his head. "This is my war, not yours."

"Get out, or I'll take you out."

Agaki glared at James. "You lost a friend to General Lu. He killed my younger brother. My *family*." He paused and took a solemn breath. "Therefore, I must do this alone. If I fail, then it falls to you."

James looked at him for what could have been an eternity, then punched the side of the truck as hard as he could and walked away, back to stand next to Rip.

"You okay?" Rip said, not quite understanding the exchange but easily recognizing the passion in both men's words.

"Yeah. I'm just tired as hell I guess," James replied without meeting his eyes. Then, he turned to Agaki and pointed at him with lingering rage, "But don't you fail …!"

Agaki's nod was solemn.

Rip studied Agaki's face, and then gave him a grim reminder: "Eleven hours and twenty minutes now. Better get a move on."

Agaki popped the clutch and the truck lurched down the dirt road. Rip checked his watch, moved a dial to mark the time. James noticed, and he explained. "I'll advise the general to respect that timetable. If our forces bomb the compound sooner, Agaki might be inside."

He turned to his radioman. "Let's check in on the pickup." He referred to the Black Hawks he'd summoned. They would first pick up the fallen men with Themieux, and then him and the rest of the troops.

He jerked his chin toward where some of the troops were resting under a tree. "It's been a long two days, pardner, and we're all tired. Let's have a sit-down."

They joined the group and reclined in silence for awhile, just resting, until Rip finally turned to James and nodded toward the sky. The two Blackhawk helicopters were now in view. "So, you ready for a hot shower and a good night's sleep?"

James smiled, just now realizing that two days with no sleep had left him ready to collapse. "Yeah, that sounds good. But I think I'll stay here for the night. Aria's family's here. I really need to …

to see Themieux while I'm here, to thank him for the bailout." He nodded toward Kasim, who now stood next to his fallen brother. "And Kasim might need help. Besides, I'm done. Stick a fork in me as of now. I'm a long-distance fighter, not so much a ground warrior like you."

Rip smiled and nodded. "You did good, secret agent man. You enjoy your stay here at Casa Karabakh. I'll take care of the rest."

Rip signaled his group to rise and follow him to the open field, but there was no need. They'd all heard the distinct sound of the rotors of the approaching helicopters. When they were a bit closer to the spot where the choppers would land, one of Rip's men tossed a smoke flare into the field, to help the pilots determine the wind's direction.

A tiny clutch of villagers who hadn't yet fled inside the houses watched the Marines leave. A larger group encircled the open flatbed of an old truck, which now held Sattar's body, covered by a wool blanket. James was desperate to see Aria, to beg her forgiveness for leaving her in a place that turned out to be so tragically unsafe, and to make similar pleas to her uncle. But first, he had to sleep, to rest, to try to get past the horrible images of the past forty-eight hours. He went over to Kasim. "I am so sorry for your great loss," he began, then asked, "would you like some company tonight, or would you rather be alone, my friend?"

Kasim lifted a face made heavy with grief to him. "Come, James, have a drink with me. I have plenty of time ahead to be alone."

The two men walked away slowly, arm in arm, toward Kasim's house, each carrying burdens that would lighten with time, but never fully lift from their shoulders.

"Air Force 247, contact ground control on 213-point-7."

"213-point-7. Have a good day, approach control." The speaker grinned. "At least *my* day's over."

The air traffic controller keyed the microphone twice quickly, an efficient *back at you* that was readily understood.

The F-15's wheels touched the runway of Ellington Field, and as the plane shuddered on contact with the concrete under them, relief and excitement surged through Captain Randy Carter's body. He knew his wingman would share the same feeling once he completed the pattern and landed behind him.

Ellington Field lay about fifteen miles south of downtown Houston, and Carter knew the rather nondescript airfield held a rich history that dated back to its use as an airbase during World War I. Today, Ellington supported a mix of commercial activities in addition to the military, most notably NASA, was home to the largest flying club in Texas, and hosted the annual Wings over Houston Air Show.

Yeah, he definitely liked the idea of being home.

He shut down the Eagle's hot engines and opened up the canopy. Three men, two of them in desert-camouflage uniforms, approached the aircraft, and the ones in uniform raced up to the avionics bay to retrieve the backpack. He was surprised to see that the uniformed men were Air Force generals. The one not in uniform, an older man with a distinctly British accent, was referred to by one of the generals as Professor Denton. They each offered him hearty thanks when he descended from his cockpit to the tarmac.

Man, what I'm delivering must be something special to get not one, but two *generals out here to say hello. What's up with that?*

Carter's wingman had just come to a stop nearby, and his engines still turned out heated exhaust that filled the area with the warm smell of jet fuel. Over the jet noise, one of the generals shouted, "Captain Carter, job well done." As he did, the second general looked over the oil containers with Professor Denton.

"Please do not make any mention to anyone of what you see here," the first general said to him. "Is that clear?"

"Yes, sir."

The other jet's engines began to wind down, and the noise along with it. The general turned his head to the other two and called out, "How we doin' over there, Professor?"

"We are, as you say, *in business*, General." Denton beamed, and his eyebrows were dancing. Carter couldn't tell if he was more excited about the oil sample or his geeky wit. But the oil sample clearly was the winner.... Denton cradled it like a baby.

"Let's get going, then." The general gave a last look at Carter. "Welcome home. Ft. Walton Beach, right?"

"Born and raised sir." Carter couldn't help but stare at the three stars on the center of the man's chest, a departure from the collar display that made it harder for snipers to pick off leadership in the field.

"You be sure to have a good time over there tomorrow," the general said. "You've earned it. In the meantime, get some rest."

"Thank you, sir. I will, sir."

"No, thank *you*!" The general's eyes made it clear to Carter that he genuinely meant it.

After sharing sharp salutes with him, the three quickly left in the van that had brought them to his aircraft.

Carter's wingman finished in his cockpit, and then the two of them headed to the transient aircraft line shack, where they would close out their flight plan and get some rest. Tomorrow, Carter had a much shorter hop, to Ft. Walton Beach, Florida and two weeks of R&R.

He stood at the counter in the transient line shack, and shook his head as his wingman walked over to him. "You know, I wanted a steak really bad ... but now all I can think about is a big fat cheeseburger. We need to find a good burger joint."

The wingman grinned. "As long as they serve beer and take plastic ... all I've got is Turkish lire in my wallet."

Carter laughed, slapping the pocket in his flight suit that housed his wallet. "Me too. Okay. Let's hit it." The two men gathered their belongings and exited the terminal.

CHAPTER

36

Half a world away, a cultured voice said, "Well, well … look who has come for tea."

Agaki didn't immediately respond to the taunt. His sword made his intentions clear enough. Instead, he assessed the man next to the desk while slowly changing attack positions. At last, he said, "You kill from far away, like a coward. I kill up close, General."

Lu began maneuvering toward his desk, surprised when the man allowed it. "You misunderstand me—"

"There is no misunderstanding here, General. You killed my little brother six months ago."

With an aching slowness borne of caution, Lu slowly sat and lit a cigarette. "Really? Mmmm … where did that happen?"

"East China Sea. On an oilrig. His name was Saburo."

"Saburo? Interesting name." Lu pretended to think. "Oh, yes …. I remember that boy. A college student on an engineering internship. Admirable. He shouldn't have been on that oilrig, however. That oil belongs to China."

He gave Agaki a thin smile. "And I made that point through your brother. I'll admit I relished the encounter."

"Just like I will relish this short time with you." Agaki's hands worked the handle of his sword, as if in anticipation. "Besides, that rig drills Japanese oil."

"You can't prove that."

"I am not here to *prove* anything. Only to kill you … up close. But not just for my brother's death. You also killed my friend's friend in Morocco."

Lu found himself enjoying this banter, which felt so much like the foreplay he enjoyed in torturing his victims. He did not know who this Japanese man was, but the fellow had a warrior's stance he admired. Also a certain … *panache*. Lu had no idea how he'd gotten past security into the compound, or into his heavily guarded headquarters. No matter. That was simply more proof that this opponent was first-rate. And that made the game deadly, deliciously so.

"Friend of a friend of yours?" he said. "Oh, yes. I recall Commander Marshall. You are most well connected, my friend."

Agaki stared hard at him. "Your *assessment* means nothing to me. I simply wanted you to hear this before you die."

Lu laughed confidently, sensing that the man would give him the first move as a sporting gesture. He also figured the man would expect him to go for a pistol in the desk: Allowing him to move behind the desk was almost an open challenge to see if he could get to it in time. He would not disappoint.

"I like to kill up close too," he said in a lighthearted way, and kept his eyes on Agaki while he flung open the drawer and snatched the pistol. His trigger finger was quick, sending a copper-sheathed round on a deadly track toward the center of Agaki's torso. And in spite of Agaki's beginning a turn in anticipation of this, the bullet penetrated his uniform easily and found soft skin beneath.

What Lu didn't anticipate was that Agaki's reflexes matched his own. The bullet's force accelerated his turn away from Lu. The instant he completed the circle, he charged.

* * *

"Striker One is rolling in hot."

"Roger that, Striker One," came the reply from the ground. "You are cleared for a live shoot on target Lima."

"That's affirmative. I have a lock on target Lima. I have visual."

"Striker One, do you see any collaterals near the target?"

"Negative. The area is clear."

"Proceed. You are cleared to release ordnance."

"Fox One!" With that, the Hog released the five-hundred-pound JDAM precision munition, keeping his eyes on the target outlined on the cockpit's video screen.

The pilot chimed in again. "I see a lone figure leaving the building … hauling ass! Look at him go!"

A five-second pause, then he added, "Wait, there's a large group headed out of the building. I think they're chasing that guy. Yeah, definitely after him. What do you want me to do?"

"Striker One, go ahead and hit the group. Striker Two, take the primary target."

"Striker Two Wilco. Tally on primary, no collaterals."

"Striker Two, you are cleared to release ordinance."

"Fox One."

The first JDAM hit in the midst of the fourteen men. Striker One's pilot watched the shockwave overtake them all. The lone man, well in the lead, was knocked down into a ravine by the blast.

The second JDAM impacted just as General Lu's aide was entering his boss's office. The last moment of this man's life was spent staring at Lu's head, which was neatly centered on his desk. The body remained seated upright, behind the desk in his leather chair. The look on Lu's face was one of shock and surprise, and above all, intense fear.

* * *

Agaki stood slowly, gritting his teeth at the shrapnel in his back and pulled his backpack from his shoulders. Luckily, the backpack had caught much of it. He straightened up, favoring the fresh bullet wound in his side, and walked toward the battered truck, a mile farther down the road and hidden in a stand of trees.

He didn't look over his shoulder when the next three JDAMS hit the barracks and parking lot filled with armored vehicles, but allowed himself a smile at the roaring that told him the compound was engulfed in flames.

He walked on.

CHAPTER

37

"Oh no, heavens no!"

"You Brits don't do pizza?" The lead technician rubbed his neck and scowled, but used a deferential tone with the project's only expert on Caspian oil.

"Weak tomato sauce on flimsy bread and covered with rubbery cheese?" came the passionate reply. "How can you eat that ghastly stuff? That's almost as bad as thinking about a place like this, so technologically advanced that doesn't have a single chalkboard anywhere in it!"

The tech sighed. "Professor Denton, sorry about the chalkboard, but … pizza's an American tradition. When you pull a late night working a rush job, you order pizza."

"I would have preferred shepherd's pie." Denton peered over his glasses with an impish smile. "Perhaps I could try your Texas barbeque? I've heard a great deal about it."

The tech considered this. "We've got twenty-three people to feed. I'll order both."

"When in Rome, as they say. And oh, could you get me some tea?"

Grinning, the tech replied. "Yes, sir, *that* we can handle. You drink it hot, right?"

"Correct, young man."

Not quite successfully hiding his amusement, the tech exited the office.

Denton was finally alone again and settled back into intense thought, studiously poring over the initial readouts from the tests. Several jumbled thoughts fought to coalesce in his mind, but the answer, the core answer he was seeking, wouldn't jell for him.

"Mmmm… I don't quite think so," he mumbled after a while. "A most intriguing possibility to consider … but I don't think so."

He began to pace the large office they'd been given: the CEO's, who was on leave, they'd told him. His finger waved in front of him as he paced, as if writing on an invisible chalkboard—and he was. The rest of the team was in the facility's huge labs, busily running additional tests to confirm their initial findings. Yes, the oil sample confirmed a common genetic base … and that had sent a wave of excitement throughout the team. However, Denton had a gut reaction upon hearing that, which had forced him into sequestered thought.

With a resigned sigh, he pulled out a pad of paper and began working a pencil over it. His eyebrows went up and down, and he rubbed his temples with his free hand. He hardly noticed the tea that was brought in, and later ignored the white Styrofoam container that held a steaming sample of some of Texas' finest pork and ribs.

Two hours later, he put the pencil down and stared blankly ahead. The once-spotless desk was now cluttered with paper, some of it crumpled up, some folded over at specific equations and placed near the computer printouts.

He stood and stretched just as the Air Force general in charge of the testing and the senior American petroleum engineer walked into the room.

"How are you doing, Professor?" the general asked, noting the unopened tray.

He finished his stretch and faced them with an unaccustomed smile. "How am I? I've come to a conclusion I think will astonish both of you."

* * *

Aria paced the wooden floors of the cabin with a fury that unnerved Lev. "I can see for a hundred miles in any direction, and I still don't know what's going on," she complained. "This is driving me crazy!"

"Patience, my dear, patience."

She stopped and gave him a stern look, and then turned away to continue her pacing. Lev watched her, thinking of how she had reacted when her brother forbade her from accompanying him to rescue James Marshall. Recalled the way she'd spoken of James in the time they had been together here. He was certain Aria didn't yet realize it herself, but, somehow, his pragmatic, levelheaded niece had fallen in love.

And with an American, no less!

When he was certain she couldn't see him, he allowed himself a smile. *But an American that her dear father and mother would definitely have approved of. Brave. No, more than brave. Loyal. Steadfast. A warrior's spirit.*

For the first time since his sister's death, Lev's heart, at least as it concerned his niece's happiness, was at rest.

* * *

Even now, a full day after the attack, a thick quiet drifted around the buildings and mingled with the misty, early morning fog and smoke from the smoldering ruins of the house and truck destroyed the day before. From the chair in front of his house, mercifully spared, Kasim Beria leaned back and took in the beginnings of a first-of-the-season's fine summer day. It was early, even for him, but his slender hands poked and tapped his pipe, and his medals clinked together when he pulled the tobacco pouch from his vest pocket. He struck a match, and with well-rehearsed ceremony, pulled the flame through the fresh tobacco. A smile came across his face as he surveyed the landscape, also luckily spared from the attack.

This was still his home. One day, perhaps soon, he would die here, and be buried beside his courageous brother.

He noticed someone approaching, recognized James a moment later. "I am surprised to see you up this early after a hard day's fighting," Kasim said, his tone the knowing one of one warrior to another. "You know how to liven things up, do you not?"

James gave a small smile in acknowledgement of Kasim's gentle humor, then said, "I have to leave today. Back to Baku, and then on to Washington. My work here is complete."

Kasim did nothing to hide his curiosity. "Someone in Washington sent you here, then?"

"Yes. His name is P.R. Nicholson."

Kasim nodded and puffed. After a moment, he said, "This P.R. Nicholson … is he a man that makes difficult decisions that people criticize?"

He drew softly on his pipe with an expectant look, and James nodded.

"He does not change his mind when they try to push him around, no?"

"No, he doesn't. Not one bit."

"Your boss, this P.R. Nicholson, is a man like us, I think. You know, my brother was given a medal for bravery. He fought in the Korsun-Shevchenko battles. You probably have never heard of them."

He looked at James, who only shook his head.

"In the Ukraine. But the battle for which he earned the medal was in a town called Mergus, in Romania, where he fought Nazis when he was surrounded. The men with him thought they would die, like many before them that day—an awful time. But Sattar would not give up. He rallied them. Sattar always said you are never truly beaten until you agree with your enemy that you are. He was a warrior just like us."

The smile he gave James was only to help hold back a tear as he continued. "I was fighting somewhere else, in some muddy ditch. We shot at the Germans, they shot back at us. We ran out of bullets, and when they joined us in our ditch, we fought them with our bayonets. They made Sattar's commander, General Mamedov, the Hero of the Soviet Union. Mamedov was from here: Shusha." He waved his pipe in the direction of Shusha. "And they gave my brother this …."

He pulled out the medal he had removed from Sattar's body, stared at it for a moment, and then held it out to James. "Give that to your P.R. Nicholson, and tell him to think of Sattar the next time he is surrounded."

James reached out and took it from Kasim's hand, holding it

with reverence. "I will, Kasim. I know he'll be grateful."

Kasim smiled and again looked at James expectantly. The smoke still swirled, the sunlight still danced, and his wizened face now sported a sly smile. "And I want you to have something else."

From a breast pocket inside his coat, Kasim carefully pulled out a worn felt sack, then pulled open the drawstrings that secured it. From the bag, he pulled out a ring. The center was two pear-shaped diamonds side by side, flanked by three smaller diamonds. The settings, and the ring itself, were platinum.

"This belonged to my wife, Kara." He studied the ring as he spoke. "It is all I have left of her, and of our three children. I lost them all."

He reached out, holding the ring with one unsteady and, and attempted to take James' hand to place the ring into it. James pulled away, saying, "I can't take this from you. It's too much. Lev is your lifelong friend. Perhaps his children would—"

For a moment, Kasim considered if he should tell James what he had seen: Aria's shining brown eyes, so like his own daughter's, as she spoke of James that day.

No, he decided. *If God is willing, he will know in the fullness of time.*

Instead, he said, "Make an old man happy, James. I am eighty-four years now. The ring is a small thing, compared to what it stands for. I would be pleased if, after I am gone, it continued to stand for two people's love for one another. Please…"

James took the ring, held it a moment, as if deciding, and slipped it into his shirt's breast pocket at last. The two men shared a smile, and he said, "Thank you, Kasim. I'll cherish it always."

Kasim nodded, then shifted his gaze to the expansive mountainous countryside of Karabakh. "Karabakh has produced many warriors. One … his name was Farhad bey. He was a warrior, like us." Kasim leaned back proudly and drew again on his pipe.

"I'm not a warrior, Kasim."

"Oh, but you are!"

James looked away. "Nah. I'm just a little guy out trying to do big things."

"We are all just men at the end of the day, James. Some act like they are better than others. But you are a warrior, and that is because you are willing to stand up for what you believe. You would be surprised at how many people in this world wouldn't do that. They simply do what they are told."

The frail man drew again on his pipe, and continued with his story. "Now, the Ottoman-era warrior named Farhad bey … he was a very brave man, and people still speak of his cavalry charges. I will never forget a poem about him that my mother read to me as a young man. Written by Pushkin, something about war making you lose forever the modesty of your behavior and charm of your shyness…. I suppose none of us can help it, but we all lose something in war."

He gave a heavy sigh that made James return worried eyes to him.

"James, with all of these troubles, I am afraid that my people will lose something … perhaps they already have…. The loss that is part of any war."

Seeing tears forming in the old warrior's eyes, James said quickly, "Kasim, you and I are both still charming, aren't we?"

He put his arm around the old man, who replied with a genuine if weak smile, "Oh, yes. And we are modest as well."

They shared a chuckle, then James' face turned solemn. "I have friends; good friends that I've asked to help your people. I think Mitrofanov'll give up any ideas he has to take Karabakh right now." He sighed. "And when I get back to Washington, I'll keep working to keep his hands off."

James gave him a gentle, but reassuring shake with his arm and turned to leave.

"James."

James stopped walking and turned around. "Thank you … my good friend. My fellow warrior."

He tapped his breast pocket, the one that held the ring, and Kasim nodded and smiled while giving a farewell wave with his pipe.

* * *

"We've got him cold."

P.R.'s voice almost sounded vindictive to Charles Purvis, who'd known this man for many years, long before he became a UN ambassador, long before P.R. ever thought about heading the CIA.

"Your buddy Ivan laid out his STRONG agenda for your camera audience, then?" Chuck asked.

"Basically … yes."

"Sweet."

"Thanks for getting us pointed in the right direction, Chuck."

"Anytime partner. Any word on the oil sample?"

"Preliminary tests are promising, but we don't have a final read yet. That's all Denton would say, except that we're going to be, quote, *astonished*. Still can't conclusively pin down the root source of the oil."

"Let me know.…"

P.R. gave him a chuckle. "Believe me, you're quickly becoming the linchpin of our strategy on this. You'll hear as soon as I do."

"We've gotta move quick. The UN Assembly's meeting in two days."

"We're on a fast track. Don't worry. Taking down Ivan should be easy. As simple as the right word in the right ear at just the right time. Your job will be the tricky part, Mr. United Nations."

"And I *am* the master of trickery…"

This brought a bellowing laugh from P.R. "Well … one of us is."

* * *

James walked along the dirt road that led toward Lev's home. He could still smell the faint odor of smoke, but the morning mountain air was invigorating, and the sun was now beginning to burn off the fog. The quiet was in stark contrast to the day before, and he appreciated the moment, but his head was pounding again. Hell, it had still been sore from where he'd slammed it against the airplane. And now he had some real head wounds to get healed up.

He touched the rough bandage on the back of his head. It stung a bit, and some blood had leaked through, but it didn't feel serious. He reflected on the memory of a conversation he'd had with a member of the 10th Mountain Division during combat operations in Afghanistan, could almost hear the distinct tone in the man's voice while they discussed target objectives while live ordnance was flying around. He hadn't understood that tone, that *something* in the man's voice, until now. It was that universal *something*, uniquely common between men who'd been in combat, subtle, difficult to put one's finger on, but instantly observable to another combat veteran. He'd heard that in Kasim's voice … until Kasim handed him the ring. Then his tone changed, became … what? Bittersweet? Hopeful? No, both, he decided.

Something so valuable, he thought while he walked. *Probably one of the few things of value he owns. And he gave it to me. Why?*

As he neared Lev's farm, the smell of horses and fresh-cut grass wafted past him, and his attention was diverted to his right, to several horses frolicking in a large pasture.

"James, my friend, you look like hell!"

He twisted his aching neck left and blinked toward the lone figure approaching.

"Themieux! You look only a little better than I do. You didn't get hurt, but you still look like a bus hit you, buddy."

"I feel that way. Come, we'll get you cleaned up and fed."

"While I'm doing that, how about saddling up two good horses for us?"

Themieux stopped walking. "The hunting cabin?"

James' nod brought another wince. "Yes. The hunting cabin." *And Aria.*

Themieux measured him for a long moment, so long, James wondered if he would refuse.

Finally, his answer came. "Okay."

CHAPTER

38

"What kind of *astonishing conclusion*?"

The general spoke while keeping his eyes on Denton's face. Steve Roberts, the team's petroleum engineer, had a somewhat different response; he strode over to where Denton had left a rambling odyssey of complex calculations, one of which he'd completed after the pad of paper ran out. That one was finished on the back of the barbeque dinner's receipt.

Denton noticed both men's scrutiny, but rather than being offended or uncomfortable, this made him more eager to fill them in.

"Well, for starters, there *is* a cavernous deposit beneath the Caspian Sea, just as the preliminary testing suggests. And yes, it does provide a common hydrocarbon genetic signature for each of the samples in question."

The general nodded, pointed to a chair, and took the chair behind the CEO's desk. "Okay, I'm keeping up so far. Keep going."

Denton lowered himself into the visitor's chair, wincing. "You know, until now, I hadn't realized how long I'd been sitting in that chair you're in. At any rate, I did conclude there is similarity in the genetic signature among the samples. The thing I found curious was the weakness of the common thread."

Steve spoke up. "You mean the concentration of the common hydrocarbon?"

"Exactly." Denton pointed at the engineer, and his index finger bobbed as he carefully chose his words. "There should be more than what we can see...."

"Natural gas?" Steve asked.

"Precisely! What we are seeing are *signatory traces* of a natural gas deposit. The readout from the deep-penetrating radar confirmed the lack of density. And here comes the *real zinger*, General, as you say over here: Based on what I've put together here, this deposit is not economically viable."

"What do you mean by that?"

Steve answered. "The density of the natural gas in the chamber isn't there ... they won't produce enough natural gas to make sense to drill for it." He shook his head slowly, his eyes filled with incredulity. "Aside from that skim of oil, it's just a hole full of hot air."

The general crossed his arms, considered this. "Are you certain, Mr. Roberts?"

"We will be in a couple of hours," Steve replied. "You know, an ounce of common sense goes a long way alongside a big computer." He glanced at Denton, then back at the general. "I'll discuss this with the team, get back to you ASAP."

As soon as Steve left, Denton cleared his throat as he rose from the chair, wincing again, and leaned on the desk, hands flat. "General, simply put ... and I am certain of it ... aside from the dribble Commander Marshall found, and that *was indeed* a geological anomaly, *there is no oil* in that area."

* * *

Aria wore a broad smile as she ran down the steps of the cabin and heartily embraced Themieux, and then James. "I'm so glad to see you two!"

"Oh God, what a trip that was." James looked over her tousled hair at Lev, who joined them.

"From what I hear from my messenger who just left, you guys gave Mitrofanov's men a good whipping." He paused. "Sorry to hear about the loss of your men."

"We held our ground," James said, looking out at the horizon. "I was also sorry to hear about what happened to Sattar."

Aria drew a deep breath and looked at Lev.

"I was going to tell you, dear, but you already had so many worries.…" Lev struggled with his words as he watched tears well up in her eyes.

"Who else?" She now was looking at James.

"Guns and Spidey."

She put a hand over her mouth and turned and went inside. James started to move past Lev after her, but Lev grasped his arm to stop him.

"Let's give her some space, James. And … we have some things to talk about."

James leveled thoughtful eyes at him. "That we do."

* * *

Scalding water sluiced over Ivan Mitrofanov's back as he knelt on one knee, alone in his open, orgy-sized shower. His other foot was planted flat in front of him, and both arms were flexed and extended, ending in balled and trembling fists. His wildly dilated eyes stared intently at nothing while he panted in a feverish attempt to revive his badly hung-over system.

A bottle of amphetamines lay open on the bathroom floor next to the shower, the remnants of its contents scattered about the room. Ivan had ended the night before with, even by his standards, excessive drinking, his overindulgence spurred by the sketchy reports from the battlefield.

No, he admitted to himself. It was news of General Lu's death that had driven him fully into a stuporous binge.

"This is not happening to me!" His voice was a low primordial growl, but at least now, he could form words.

He'd been summoned to his headquarters by news of the impending visit by a Chinese envoy from Beijing, who would be landing in just a few hours. The Iranians would be there as well. Neither group was happy with the situation, or with him. Ivan was fast losing control, on the precipice of losing everything he had worked for, and his unbridled rage hounded the last vestiges of his sensibilities and pushed him farther out onto the fringes of sanity.

Heedless of the boiling needles assaulting the skin of his shoulders, his head flew back in rage. "This can't be happening!

Damn you all to hell! You fucking Americans! You and your CIA
… your Marine Corps …why must you meddle in the affairs of
others?"

Then his head fell forward, and he began thinking of how he
could possibly extract himself from this mess.

* * *

"You just do not grasp what I am saying, do you?"

"Probably better than you think I do." James had been looking
at the six burly men who had arrived on horseback that afternoon.
As he replied, he fixed his eyes on Lev with more of an attitude than
Lev probably expected.

"But … look, I can't go into all the details," he continued.
"You just have to believe me that Ivan Mitrofanov's going down.
Maybe not right away, but he will. He *won't* get another chance to
harm your people. And … you understand history, just like I do.
You *know* this kind of revenge never comes to any good—"

"James, *you* must understand…" Lev struggled for the right
words while one of his field commanders inspected the chamber of
an AK-47 assault rifle. The other five were seated around a rough-
cut wooden table on the other side of the room.

Frustrated, Lev tried again. "Here, we do not have a big
government that takes care of everything, unlike the United States.
We only have each other. After the attack on our village … it is time
to act."

James considered his reply with care, considering what he'd
just learned about the man. In the frenzy of events unfolding in
this part of the world, Lev was quickly becoming a covert central
figure in the quiet, grassroots struggle against Ivan Mitrofanov, who
was considered only a selfish upstart with foreign backing. The
attack on the village had brought Lev's movement to the verge of
something that James believed was a horrible mistake but that Lev
kept insisting was necessary, although infinitely sad.

While Lev busily continued discussing his plan to face the
remnants of the insurgent army, James recalled what Lev had told
him in their discussion, which had been heated at times. Up until
the recent fighting, Lev and his followers had been patiently waiting

for the right moment to make their move. This was the moment, Lev had insisted, while Mitrofanov's forces were weakened and off balance.

"James, you say you understand this," Lev continued, "but I fear it is difficult for someone who hasn't spent his life in this country to do. Especially for you—you come from a country that fiercely protects individual independence. The people of Karabakh are a united people ... with a *united Christian heart*."

He made a fist of his hand and pounded his chest to drive his point home. "When your country learns to appreciate that concept's existence in *other* countries, then perhaps it will truly be a great power." He looked over at Aria and Themieux, who had been listening quietly, then back at James. "It all begins with that simple understanding of the people themselves."

"Like the people of Iraq," James said after a moment's thought. "Our government didn't know much about the people there ... before we invaded."

"Ha! You almost screwed that one up," said the burly man cleaning the rifle, whose name was Gustav.

Themieux stood up and glared at Gustav, said, "Let him have his say," and then motioned to James to continue. The tension between the two men made James a bit uneasy, but he saw it as an advantage he might use later if Lev remained obstinate.

"Yes, we didn't know the people as well as we should have," he continued. "But I don't think that's the only reason things went sour over there. We got rid of a dangerous tyrant. What happened after that was largely the fault of Iraq's meddling neighbors, and a people who wouldn't unite. Hell, Iraq wasn't even a country until after World War I, and they're still not a united country. "

He looked away, then back at Lev. "What I'm trying to say— it's not always simple to figure out why a particular coup didn't go perfectly. But don't ever forget that there are people, good people, behind that big government most of the world is so fond of talking so poorly of. People like me."

James could sense Lev softening, and he continued. "I am an American. But let an understanding begin between us.... I am with you and your people in trying to get this Ivan Mitrofanov off your backs. He's no good, and he's only in it for himself. I'm just not sure an armed conflict's always the way to go about it.

"But there's something else, something *much* more serious. And something that won't go away, even if he does. He's got allies, Lev … *big, well-armed* allies. And you guys are just a small army."

Lev's field commanders continued to stuff loaded magazines and other supplies into bags, but their pace had slowed noticeably while they listened to James and Lev.

"You say you are with us, James?" Lev said. "You probably could not make a good brandy. And, I'll bet you cannot ride a horse, even as good as my wife…" Lev paused, sensing that his poor attempt at humor was going nowhere, and took a hard look at James, who stood in front of him with hastily bandaged shrapnel wounds. *Yes, my enemies are his enemies too*, he acknowledged with a sigh.

"Nonetheless, James," he continued with a grin, "in spite of your … inadequacies … I would call you brother."

Sighing again, he picked up the rifle in front of him. "You say I don't understand what we face. *This* is what *they* understand. They call us unclean—*infidels*. And they blow themselves up along with their enemies, rather than live with them."

One of the other field commanders glared at James and nodded repeatedly, as if to place emphasis on that point. "You have seen it on the news … all over the world. Wherever there is conflict, there are Muslims."

James decided it better to concede. "That's generally true … but it's only a small radical minority of Muslims in the world."

"So if you have one hundred, one is a killer. Would you live with that?" chimed in a third field commander.

James shook his head. "Christians can be killers too, Lev. Do you know what's going on in those refugee camps?"

Lev's face stilled. "That is not a concern of mine."

"I beg to differ with you, Lev. It has everything to do with you."

Lev shrugged but didn't reply.

"Lev, those camps are a breeding ground for radical Islam. Radical Islam flourishes where there is poverty and despair. Don't you see that? Can you name a *prosperous* country that promotes radical Islam?"

Lev leaned back in his chair and rested the weapon on his lap. "Radicals come from prosperous countries like the United States … Germany … France."

"Because they observe what they think is the oppression of Islamic people."

"Look … nobody, including the Saudis and other wealthy Muslim countries, wants to give more than a token amount of their money to people who are, as you say, *oppressed*. Why is *that*?"

James threw his hands into the air and glanced skyward. "Global poverty will not be resolved tonight, Lev."

Lev smiled. "I'm glad you said that, because you were beginning to sound like a rock star trying to save Africa from itself."

James leaned forward in his chair. "I'm only suggesting that you let *them* live … let them live. Over time, with dialogue, there can be peace. I'm not saying it'll happen tomorrow, but it will happen if you work at it."

Lev reflected for a moment. "Okay. So what do you want me to do? Invite them all to dinner?"

"How about taking the first step?"

"Like what?"

"Accepting them for what they are." James considered the risks of his next words for a final time, then plunged ahead. "You know how to get hold of your counterparts across the border, don't you?"

Lev gave him a dubious nod. "Yes."

"Would they meet with you, as a sign of good faith? Couldn't we get all of the people together for a peaceful rally? Just as a beginning."

"Beginning of what? *They* would not let it work." Lev's skepticism showed in both his words and his face.

"Who wouldn't let it work?" James challenged.

The acknowledgement came off Lev's tongue as ice crystals breaking from a long-frozen waterfall. "Those who continue to hate … both Christian *and* Muslim. Besides, the Armenian troops still control the border. I have no say of who crosses that border."

"Border control?" James grinned in Aria's direction. "Don't know if you've heard about it, but I'm great at figuring out ways to cross the uncrossable."

The smile left, and when his eyes once again met Lev's, they were grim. "Main point, we can deal with that. Don't try to kill them and end up killing countless innocents in the process. *Defy them.* Surprise the heck out of them by offering … reconciliation."

James shifted in his chair to get up close to Lev, and put a hand on his shoulder. "Would you let *them* define your country … the future of your children, and their children? Now is your opportunity to define *your* country. Not as a medieval kingdom, but as a peaceful and tolerant society."

A long moment later, Lev said, "You are right, of course. This … *peaceful solution* has been discussed by many before us. But it will not work, not here."

"Lev, if you don't try, then it will never happen. Take charge here. You're a leader. *Lead.* Only leaders like you can turn this around and put Karabakh back in the hands of *all* its people."

Gustav stood up slowly, drawing everyone's attention by this deliberate action. "But, Lev … if you bring more violence to Karabakh with this action—this … this so-called *peaceful rally*—you will be held accountable."

"I have lots of friends, Uncle, friends who would support this," Themieux said, his posture and voice resolute in response to Gustav's veiled threat. The other field commanders seemed to shrug off Gustav and wanted to hear more.

"As do I," Aria echoed. "I know many people who would attend such a rally. Good people. Brave people who only want peace."

"What are you talking about?" Lev looked at all three of them. "A rally? I give up. What?"

"We have an idea," James said. "A vigil for peace … Something that's often done where I come from. I'll explain …."

* * *

Later that evening, James walked out onto the porch of Lev's home. It was now dark outside, but the moon was still full and illuminated the mountains around him. The placid evening offered a welcome change from the past few days. The fatigue lingered, but at the same time, he was driven to finish this. He pulled out his satellite phone and dialed a number, the first of a great many calls to be made that evening. The entire group was making lots of phone calls that would continue well into the night.

Just over a hundred miles away, a green telephone hanging on the wall in a restaurant began to ring. After a while someone answered, and spoke in a raised voice over the din of the crowd. "*Salam.*"

"*Salam. Zaehmaet olmasa—Rasul.*" Not knowing the language any better than he did, it was the best James could manage to ask for Rasul.

There was a long silence on the other end. Only the diners could be heard in the small family restaurant where James had shared dinner, and a moment in life, with a man who begged for help for his refugee neighbors.

"*Salam?*" said an out-of-breath voice.

"Rasul, this is James Marshall. You said you've been waiting a long time for a certain phone call. Well … this is it …. Yes, really. But first, let's get one thing straight between us. I'm not really a journalist…"

CHAPTER

39

"What'ya say we give Iran, and everyone else in the whole damn world, just what they want?"

As he strode into the office of the Secretary General of the United Nations asking the question, Charles Purvis waved his hands in a generous gesture. The only response was a quiet quizzical look.

"I mean, could diplomacy actually work if everyone got what they wanted?" Purvis continued, without any response from Tran Nguin, who remained seated expectantly in the U.N. conference room that was reserved for the highest levels of dialogue. Purvis knew that Tran would be wondering why he'd hastily requested this late-hour meeting, a question that most likely had quietly reverberated amongst the staff in the Secretary General's office, too. Purvis' tie was a bit loose, and the five o'clock shadow was getting heavy as the clock ticked closer to nine p.m. Fatigue produced a certain amount of delirium, and Purvis liked that because it made him seem unpredictable.

He was unpredictable. But what he'd just said was designed to get the man's attention. No matter how he was acting, Purvis knew that Tran was listening for what he'd say next.

"So, let's say we do just that…." Purvis leaned over the other side of the table with both hands spread out on its shiny maple surface. "…just give everybody in the world what they want … and we still can't agree. Then we really shouldn't be here at all, should we, Tran?"

Tran folded his arms. "Get to your point, Mr. Purvis. I don't like to waste my time, and I fear that is what is happening here."

"Ah, Tran, I come seeking the obvious answer to the most direct question, and you prove once again that it does not exist … in this building. Ha!"

Purvis continued to pace the room. Tran's face now held a grin. "Please have a seat, Charles, make yourself comfortable."

"Okay, you win, I'll sit down … it's getting late anyway." Purvis looked over at Tran from the other side of the table, as if to say: *Okay, I gave you something, now you give me something…. Isn't that the way it works in diplomatic circles?* He folded his arms and waited.

"Ahem," Tran cleared his throat ceremoniously. "Undoubtedly, Karabakh tops your agenda this evening … yes?"

"Yes."

"A good start to our conversation … everyone getting what they want. So, why are we here tonight?"

"Okay. Let's talk about what's going on there."

"In two days, the people of Karabakh will be a sovereign people…"

"Led by Ivan Mitrofanov…."

"Led by Ivan Mitrofanov."

"But what about the Caspian Sea oil debate? What about the economy of Karabakh … they've got no money. What about all of those refugees?"

"One thing at a time, Charles. Independence is a significant first step…. Would you agree?"

"Yes, but would you not also agree it would be best to solve all of these problems at once?"

A moment passed, then Tran said, "Your proposition?"

Purvis raised his eyebrows and jigged his head around, pretending this idea had just occurred to him. When it appeared that Tran wasn't really buying it, he said, "For starters, Iran wants ten percent of the Caspian Sea oil … they get their ten percent. Here's the rest of the pie, and how it's cut."

Purvis pulled out a single-page pie chart with the littoral

Caspian states listed next to each slice. He smiled in anticipation while Tran glanced over the chart.

"It appears that several of the littoral states are forfeiting a share," Tran said as he maneuvered his bifocals. "Have you spoken with them about this?"

"Well …, yes. The United States looks at this as an exercise in give-and-take. We've given a little on other fronts to compensate."

"I see. So they are in agreement?"

"More or less… Yes."

"Mmmm…."

Purvis was waiting for the line "What's the catch?" But it never came—just deep thought from the man on the other side of the table. *Got him on the hook,* Purvis thought, hiding his glee. *Now, I've just gotta yank on the line just right!*

"You know Tran … the whole world is a mess, in relative degrees. Can we get *this* one right at least? I mean, can we come together and really make a difference here, instead of just backbiting each other and watching people suffer?"

Tran recoiled slightly. "We never idly watch people suffer …"

"Don't take this the wrong way, Tran … but we, and I say that collectively, we don't always take the bull by the horns. But look at all the refugees, all the tension around the oil dollars … the conflict along the Azeri border, smoldering, ready to blow up anytime…. We can fix all that by enough of us in the UN leaning together in the right direction."

"You reference China … and Iran … when you say *enough of us.*"

"That's right. Actually, everyone's onboard but them. Not to say they wouldn't be, but … we haven't approached them yet."

A long moment passed while Tran regarded the pie chart as he might an ancient prophesy. "How soon can you get me your proposal?"

"It will be on your desk when you get to work tomorrow morning."

Tran nodded silently, then spoke. "We have our differences, Charles. But, what you say, and this allocation of the oil profits, makes sense. We'll push this into the agenda with the Security Council."

"The United States is here to help make that difference, Tran. You let me know what else I need to do to make this work." *And I don't trust you either buddy. Not until this fish is in the net and flopping around on the bottom of the boat.*

But with the Secretary General a bit firmer on the hook, that was a lot more likely. Purvis left the office fighting the urge to whistle and click his heels in the air.

Being a Christian, Lev Wolf might not have approved of some of the events happening in the conference room sixty miles away, but he would have cheered at the effect those events would have on his people. Ivan Mitrofanov had been led into the offices of his party headquarters, his face showing nothing except determined but agitated resolve. Seated at the highly polished antique conference table were his so-called allies. Lee Chen, the Chinese envoy, spoke first, after Ivan had been seated at the end of the long table.

"There has been a change in plans.…" Chen stood and began to walk around the exquisitely furnished room, whose thick, silent air held great tension. "The Americans have made things difficult for us here. It appears that we may no longer have the support of the international community for which we once hoped .…"

Ivan sneered at Chen. "You cannot be dissuaded by the loss of some tanks and some men! They can all be replaced!"

"The American Marines surprised us, but the damage they did goes well beyond the men and equipment. The oil is known to them.…"

Chen sighed heavily and frowned as he looked at the polished wood floor. "If only we had been given more time to execute our plan."

"That doesn't change anything!" Ivan stood, clenching his hands to hide their beginning tremble.

"Sit down!" The otherwise-stoic Chen was clearly enraged; the men on either side of Ivan moved forward to push him back into the chair. They were stopped by a wave of Chen's hand.

"The Americans have outmaneuvered us diplomatically," Chen continued. "We might now have to withdraw all together, in order to save face."

He looked directly at Ivan for the first time. "We are finished here. You are finished here. You are not as strong as you think you are, Mr. Mitrofanov." He smiled. "Not *STRONG* at all."

They know! Ivan tried to speak, but choked.

The two Iranians at the table, who had been whispering to each other, now spoke in turn.

"Iran will never bow to the Americans," the first said.

The second Iranian's words were particularly stinging in Ivan's ears. "The Americans would never have done this to us if *we* had been in charge at the United Nations. China has failed. And you, Mr. Mitrofanov, have failed miserably to control the groups you assured us you could."

Chen glowered at the Iranians, and again directed his focus to Ivan. "You must announce that you are withdrawing from the political process in Nagorno–Karabakh … shall we say, for health reasons? There is considerable opposition being organized against you as we speak. And we," he nodded at the Iranians to include them, "we have a …. sudden disinterest in helping you to quell it."

He walked around the table to stand behind Ivan, and put his hand on Ivan's shoulder as he continued in a near whisper, "Your life is in danger if you insist on staying."

His eyes furtive, Ivan searched the room for a friend. But there were none to be found. He stood up slowly as the hand slipped from his shoulder. This time, the men nearby made no move to press him back into the chair.

He had nothing to say. But was there anything, really, to be said? They all knew of his plot to wrest complete control of Karabakh through STRONG, which would have edged out the people who, until this moment, he'd thought wanted to put him in power: the people who were staring daggers at him right now.

The silence strangling him, he turned and left the room, hoping that his leaving would be sufficient answer—that he wouldn't have to say the words. Outside in the hallway, several more security men stood around chatting, including Lucent, Ivan's bodyguard, who put out his cigarette and motioned to the bathroom as if asking for permission.

Ivan gave a weak nod. "I will meet you downstairs."

He continued toward the stairwell, still in a state of shock and disbelief. *I'm finished. How did they know?*

He leaned into the stairwell door and nearly bumped into two men who were mopping and sweeping the stairwell's floor. As the door closed behind him, the man on Ivan's right, who'd been bent over, rose up in a swift, fluid motion and struck Ivan's head with a long leather blackjack, sending him reeling into the second man's arms. Before Ivan's bewilderment could fully form, the second man's grip tightened around his chin and neck, turning his head to the left. Ivan's resistance to this was surprisingly robust as blood streamed into his eyes from where the blackjack had split his forehead.

He might as well have saved his efforts. The second man reversed the pressure on Ivan's chin to the right, breaking his neck, creating an audible and unmistakable snapping when his clavicle also severed from the extreme and sudden torque. The perpetually hate-filled expression slowly faded from Ivan's face and his feet went limp beneath him.

The first man grabbed Ivan by the lapels of his suit coat and thrust his body down the staircase headfirst, calling, "Watch your step, it's slippery!"

Ivan's forehead slapped hard against each marble stair until he reached the bottom, where his body rolled halfway over and lay like a crumpled rag doll, a small pool of blood collecting in front of his lifeless expression.

"Oops, tried to warn you," the first man chided as he passed Ivan's body. Chuckling quietly, the pair disappeared down the staircase.

CHAPTER

41

The sunrise had been spectacular, though neither Rasul nor his sister Anatola noticed. Anatola's one-year-old son looked around the car curiously from the comfort of her arms as Rasul made a rambling stop on the side of the road after nearly a hundred miles of traveling.

"This is it." Rasul put the car into park and got onto the road, pulling his small backpack over his shoulder as he checked around them nervously. "It's just over that hill. Are you ready?"

Anatola studied him for a moment before responding. "We'll do this together. Let's go."

They walked along the side of the road up a hill, Rasul casting occasional glances behind him, toward their abandoned vehicle. At the top, they could see the border checkpoint another one hundred meters down the hill, where several Armenian soldiers stood in idle conversation at the red-and-white-striped crossing arm, which was in the down position now. As they got closer, one of the soldiers noticed them, and they all turned to address their approach.

"*Cheik kangnee aystegh* (Stop here please)," said the man in Armenian. Rasul assumed the man was the sergeant of the guard for the group.

"We are going home, to the place of our birth in Karabakh," Rasul said as calmly as he could.

"May I see your passports, please?"

Rasul and Anatola complied, and the sentry immediately saw their covers were the wrong color. "Those are Azeri passports. Do you have another?"

"No."

"Then I am sorry. You cannot enter Karabakh."

"We will enter Karabakh."

The man shook his head. "Sorry. Go home."

"That is what we are doing."

The sergeant put both of his hands on the crossing bar and gripped it as he leaned forward. "What are those orange strips of cloth tied around your arms?"

"They are a symbol for peace in Karabakh."

"We *have* peace in Karabakh."

"Not a lasting one."

"You are an insolent fool. Go away."

"We are going to cross."

"You are not going to cross." The sergeant leaned forward even farther. "Causing me problems today could be hazardous to your health."

"You will have to kill us to stop us."

The sergeant stared at Rasul for an unflinching moment, until a malevolent smile began to creep onto his face. "*That* can be arranged."

Three of the other soldiers unslung their rifles from their shoulders and went to a ready position.

Rasul steadied himself. "But if you shoot, you will have to kill us all."

"Don't worry…" The sergeant looked at his laughing comrades. "We have enough bullets for all three of you, foolish man."

* * *

Charles Purvis sat uneasily in his office in the United Nations building. It was getting late in the evening. Earlier, as a matter of routine administration, Austin Chritton had privately delivered a set of recommendations on a measure that would have a huge impact on the fate of the people of Nagorno-

Karabakh. In just thirty-six hours, Charles would deliver them publicly and cast a vote in the General Assembly.

The thing that kept him on edge was that he didn't have the final, *final* direction on what, exactly, he was going to propose. He'd been asked to buy more time by the White House while the question of oil or no oil played out, and there was some vague language in the proposal Austin delivered that gave them some wiggle room. That question of oil would determine the strategy going forward … which, in either case, would put the power of governance into the hands of the people of Karabakh.

While he fidgeted in his office, agonizing over the deadline bearing down on him, he had time to think about what was going on all around him.

He'd been met by protestors outside, who'd tried to get to his car to rock it, shouting all manner of accusations about every instance of genocide that had ever occurred in the Karabakh region. China had its diplomacy in overdrive, and the French, who usually behaved like a jealous sibling when it came to the United States, were gobbling it up. With China asserting itself on the world stage in the U.N. Security Council, France was absolutely gleeful in its support of a country not at all friendly to the U.S.

Purvis leaned back in his chair. Nobody liked the number-one global power, whenever there was one, no matter who that power happened to be. He looked at the gift the President had given him on the day his appointment to the U.N. was confirmed; he'd hung it on his wall for inspiration. It was three excerpts from a translation of the Greek historian and philosopher Thucydides, who chronicled a 431 B.C. dialogue between the then-dominant Greek state of Athens and the weaker Melians.

"Right, as the world goes," the Athenians had said, "is only in question between equals in power, while the strong do what they can and the weak suffer what they must."

To which the Melians replied: "…your fall would be a signal for the heaviest vengeance and an example for the world to meditate upon."

Which was followed by this from the Athenians: "Of men, we

know, that by a necessary law of their nature, they rule wherever they can. And it is not as if we were the first to make this law, or to act upon it when made: We found it existing before us, and shall leave it to exist forever after us; all we do is make use of it, knowing that you and everybody else, having the same power as we have, would do the same as we do."

Purvis often thought that these words were the only thing that kept him sane in this job. It was the same today as it was for the Greeks thousands of years ago, and for everybody else who'd ever been top dog. At the U.N., he witnessed so much grandstanding, posturing, and doublespeak that he was constantly challenged to push back when members of that body attacked the United States at the podium. He saw facts selectively chosen and spun and woven masterfully to such a high degree that they presented up as down, black as white.

Boiled down to its essence, the United States was the global superpower, one that generated thirty percent of the world's total gross domestic product with only five percent of the world's population. The United States was number one, and the vast majority of the world seemed to approach its status with various blends of the same two responses: envy and contempt. *So does the United States do what is right?* Purvis shifted his weight in his chair as he contemplated the answer to his own question: *That would depend on who you asked…a Greek, or a Melian.*

He knew the President had long supported the territorial integrity of Azerbaijan. But this new encroachment on Karabakh by China and Iran was self-serving. Insidious, too. It took something away from the people: not just their oil, but their sovereignty.

He looked at the small television on the sideboard, kept on whenever he was in the office. It showed a replay of the press conference held by Lev Wolf a few hours earlier, sharing news that Ivan Mitrofanov had had a fatal accident.

"At least something's gone right," Purvis muttered. "One of Ivan's many enemies has taken step one of the two-step solution."

He wasn't sure exactly how the President's next steps would play out, but he would support him, because he believed in him. He just had to mentally brace himself for whatever came next now that Mitrofanov was gone, when China and the Middle Eastern countries began their next rounds of power plays.

He wanted to call P.R. again, but they'd just spoken a few hours ago, and were both waiting for the same results.

His secretary buzzed him and he authorized the visitor's entrance. The door to his office opened. It was the Undersecretary of State, who'd just flown up from the White House, where he and the Secretary of State had met with the National Security Council.

The Undersecretary didn't actually have to say a word to convey his news; his expression as he explained the results told Purvis what he needed to know: The testing showed conclusively that oil *did not*, in fact, represent the "mother lode of the Caspian Sea." But Purvis listened quietly, asking the occasional question to be polite.

The Undersecretary finished, then said, "Okay, here's the deal. We've got a game plan that will rock the world."

Purvis let out a deep exhale, and then offered up a hopeful and expectant smile. "Now it's in the hands of us politicians. God help us all."

* * *

Rasul took a deep breath as the soldiers gathered around him and Antonia, who held her son in her arms.

"Yes my foolish friend, your expedient demise can be arranged right here." The sergeant unholstered his pistol and slid the chamber back. Anatola put her free arm around Rasul's waist. His arm was already around her shoulder, and he pulled her close with his trembling arm.

"Ehh?"

At the call, the sergeant lowered his pistol and growled, *"Mek rop EH! (Just a minute!),"* then looked to where one of the other soldiers was pointing to the top of the hill, drawing the others' attention as well. The sun was behind the prominence, and the sergeant cupped his burly hand over his eyes to get a better look.

Dozens of people were walking over the top of the hill. Men young and old, women, children of all ages, and all of them wore orange strips of cloth around their right arm. They kept coming over the hill, and coming, until hundreds of them had topped the crest … and more kept coming.

The sergeant fired his pistol into the air as a warning, and several other soldiers came running out of a small building with their rifles. He lined his men up, but the people kept on coming, thousands of them now, and those in the front were now just twenty meters away.

He ordered his men to their firing positions, but the people continued on.

Even if his eyes hadn't been glued to the scene coming over the hill, what the sergeant couldn't have seen was the caravan of vehicles parked behind Rasul's car. Every bus, car, truck, rickety cart … anything that could move under its own power had been filled to the top with people on their single-minded, peaceful trek to Stepanakert.

Rasul cleared his dry throat. "We are all going home. You will have to kill all of us.…"

The soldiers looked at each other nervously, and then to the sergeant, who lowered his pistol and signaled for them to do the same while the crowd, weaponless but powerful in numbers, began to push past them.

* * *

Cara Carmichael was enjoying a cup of coffee after a light breakfast in her hotel's ground-floor restaurant. She was halfway through her morning ritual on the Internet, getting up to speed on global affairs, when her cell phone rang.

She stated her name, as always, and the more the caller said, the farther her chin dropped: *"Half of Azerbaijan's on the road to Stepanakert! Get your ass over there right now and find out why!"*

Cara recognized the voice of her boss' boss at CNN, and sat up straight in her chair. Her assignment of covering the Islamic militancy in Baku just moved to the back burner.

The hotel she was staying at was preferred by western journalists, and other cell phones were beginning to ring around the restaurant. She glanced around, saw amazed faces that matched her own, and barked into her phone, "I'm on it sir!"

* * *

The horses leaned back as they gingerly descended this, the steepest portion of the rocky trail back to Lev's home. Cool spring winds caressed the four of them as they led their splendid Karabakh mounts farther and farther down the steep mountainside. Conversation was difficult in single file, but Lev, who was out front, looked over his shoulder to speak to James, who followed close behind.

"This really is coming together, James. It's a lucky thing we had already planned an independence rally for tonight. Changing the program agenda a bit *is something that we can control.*"

"This is shaping up to be a big day for Karabakh, Lev. It'll be as big as the March on Washington back in the '60s was in my country. Trust me. You'll see."

Lev stopped on a level spot and turned to James, who quickly caught up. "I am worried about the reactions to this along the border, and in Stepanakert. James … people are probably going to die."

"They know the risks, Lev. Let's just hope for the best."

"Mitrofanov's men won't interfere, not after the licking they took by you and your Marine Corps. I have gotten word that their patrols have stopped. And the Armenians are not a factor now."

James smiled. "See? That leaves a bit of a vacuum, doesn't it?"

He smiled back. "It's a little scary, not knowing what will happen next. There is no roadmap for the next step."

"Trust your instincts, Lev…. Like I said, you're a leader. *Lead!*"

* * *

"Good evening everyone, this is Cara Carmichael in front of

the Parliament building in Stepanakert, Karabakh's capital city. We are on the eve of an important vote in the United Nations, and there are all sorts of rumors about the outcome. Who knows what they will decide, but here in Stepanakert, there is definitely electricity in the air. In just a few moments, thousands of people here will light up candles in support of reconciliation, unity, and an independent Karabakh."

The camera panned around the throng of people who were packed into the city square. A single flare burst high above the crowd, signaling the start, and one by one, a wave of candles were quickly lit until an ocean of light not only filled the square, but the hills in every direction around Stepanakert. There was a soft and spontaneous, but powerful and proud murmuring over the display. Aria grabbed James' hand, and they both looked over at Themieux, who held a lit candle. His eyebrows went up and down quickly, and he called to them, "I told you I had *a lot* of friends!"

* * *

"Oh my God! There must be a million people here tonight!" Cara said, forgetting for a moment that she had a live microphone, "Oh my God!"

She had seen it here and there in the markets, on the arms of cab drivers, street cleaners and panhandlers, but for some reason it had never really registered with her. She kicked herself for being so unobservant as a journalist; it was her damned job to be observant. She spoke into the mic now for herself as much as for the millions of viewers, waiting for news.

"For weeks, the people of this area, all over, have worn strips of orange cloth pinned to their shirts in support of a free Karabakh. You see it everywhere. Hold on …."

She waved a hand at the cameraman, directing him to pan to the stairs of the Parliament building, which had suddenly lit up. Standing there were two hundred children, arranged as a choir. On the left were one hundred Azeri Muslim children, on the right were one hundred Christian children from Karabakh. Behind them was a small orchestra, tuning up.

"This is truly amazing folks, just amazing," Cara said quickly, her words coming out in a staccato. All these children, come together …."

But now, she couldn't speak. The children had started off with a soft, sweet folksong that echoed across the square. Their voices rose with the familiar tune and were joined by the crowd watching them. The people swayed back and forth together and sang softly along. In between successive songs, leaders representing both interests spoke words of reconciliation.

"We have all had enough of this. Let us forge ahead, into the future, together …"

"There has been great injustice and suffering all the way around, let's learn to love instead of hate!"

"What future do we leave for our children, unless we make peace?"

The crowd roared with each speaker, signaling an unmistakable desire for unity.

"Folks, it's almost impossible to believe what I'm seeing here tonight, but it's real!" Cara wiped tears from her cheeks with her free hand. "Folks, this is a watershed event in this area, this is history in the making. The people have spoken! Maybe the rest of the world can catch up tomorrow at the United Nations!"

The choir started up the Azeri national anthem, and the crowd enthusiastically joined in. The Armenian anthem followed. When anthem's last notes played out and while the cheering ended, the next speaker, a boy of about fourteen, went to the microphone.

"My name is Alex," he said. "And I have written a song for Karabakh."

Seeing the young boy speak, James nodded at Lev, then gave the boy a beaming smile of encouragement. It wasn't said, but Alex had lost both of his parents in 1994 during the fighting. He never knew them; he was just a baby when they died. Yet he still had hope.

Alex looked nervously at the orchestra, and began. The orchestra followed, and the crowd recognized the melody and lyrics as a rewritten folk tune, but one that drew from both the

Azeri national anthem, written by Uzeir Hajibeyov who hailed
from Karabakh, and the Armenian national anthem. But now, the
words had lost some of their nationalistic fervor in some changes
that Alex had given them.

Blest is he who gives his life, to defend his nation's freedom
But when he's laid out to rest, who will stand beside me?

He looked from side to side as he stood there alone, and
continued as one million people stood in silence while this boy
poured out his heart in song. Behind him, the lights went up,
slowly, on the new flag of Nagorno–Karabakh. The flag had
three horizontal stripes, red over blue over orange.

We are free to love or to hate, and when I speak for love.
Who will stand beside me? Who will stand beside me?

When he finished, the crowd roared with sustained applause
and wild cheers. Then, everyone followed the lead of Lev Wolf,
who stood at the microphone and enthusiastically chanted
"Peace, for Karabakh! Peace, for Karabakh!

Everyone joined in, and the sound of a million people
chanting in unison echoed in a thunderous message that raced
across the land. At the end, there was a shrill whistle as a
spectacular fireworks display began. The booms and trilling of
the fireworks was almost in competition with the thunderous
applause.

James turned to Aria. She still held his hand, but was
looking up at the display. She felt his eyes on hers and slowly
turned to face him.

She looks so … happy, he thought. *No … she looks ecstatic.*
I've never seen her like this.

She smiled at him, and the fireworks, and the candles they
held made her face glow. For the first time since he'd come
to this country, he felt safe, cradled in joy, not acrimony.
He extinguished their candles, handed them to an exultant
Themieux, and drew her near to kiss her. For a single, peaceful
moment, he drove the rest of the world from his mind.

CHAPTER

42

Three Gorges. The name meant little to the average person around the world, but to Chairman Sun, it represented China's new industrial might. He stood admiringly atop the center of the 2,300-meter-long structure, the world's largest and most ambitious water control project, and basked in light mist that rose from the reservoir stretching over the horizon and six hundred kilometers beyond. The world's largest dam.

"This is the new China. Nearly eighty-five-billion kilowatts of electricity here," he muttered, and sighed contently. "And Westinghouse will build four nuclear reactors. Once that technology is transferred, we can build our own from then on ... the new China."

The loss of the prospect of oil in Karabakh was disappointing, but it was only a temporary setback. The Chairman's rivals would seize upon this setback to gain leverage on him, attempting to portray him as weak, one incapable of providing the strong leadership necessary to take China to its rightful place in the world. He knew who these nationalists were, and how they would challenge him. What they did not know was how he would respond. These were lesser issues to the one that now held his thinking.

China had bested the United States technologically. The Reaper drone proved no match for China's new version. A thin smile crept onto his face. For decades, China's youth had pursued advanced degrees in the United States, had gotten high-tech jobs that allowed them to bring home the dividends of their efforts.

Technology flowed out of the United States like water through a colander, for how could their silly customs regulations stop the transfer of knowledge? Front companies purchased key technology from both the United States and Europe, and those items which could not be bought, could be stolen.

Now, in many sectors, China was taking the lead. The United States not only had lost the lead-time advantage that it had enjoyed in weapons development, it was now playing catch-up.

Other powers in the region were now feeling China's emergence. Japan, still high and mighty in attitude, but no longer of consequence in military prowess, was reeling. It was too late for them now. To the north, Russia still behaved like a muscular youth, no cash and no discipline. India was quick to challenge Pakistan over Kashmir ... but did not dare to challenge China over the territories on the southwestern fringes of the Plateau of Tibet.

His smile widened. That one shot which took down the Reaper had been, to use a bit of American irony, *heard 'round the world*. And China, Tiennamen Square in the shadow of the Forbidden Palace in particular, was the center of the world.

He relished this moment, even more than he would delight in dealing with his rivals in the weeks to come.

CHAPTER

43

"Are you sure this is how you want it?" While he waited for an answer, James could hear P.R. puff on his cigar.

"I'm sure." Knowing the direction his former boss was headed, James changed the subject. "How are my buddies doing?" He rolled up the window so he could hear better as he continued along I-40 near Raleigh, North Carolina.

"Rip? We've got him chained up in our basement, and we throw him a piece of meat once in a while. Seriously though, he's got his choice on his next tour of duty. And Agaki told me this morning that when he drinks beer, he doesn't leak anymore. He'll be fine."

"That sounds about right. They're both pretty awesome guys."

"You got that right."

"Tell me something else. How *did* you pick up on Bill Schoffner?"

"Same way you did, the nose... Or maybe it was just my Irish fey."

James shook his head and swerved to miss a hubcap abandoned on the road. "The nose? I didn't pick it up. I just didn't trust the guy. He was a jerk. *Greasy.* Okay, one last question, then I gotta pay attention to the road.... What ended up happening at the U.N.?"

"China and Iran stepped all over themselves, it was a riot. They crowed and they bellowed and beat the drum loud as sponsors for Karabakh's independence. But when we suggested Karabakh's inclusion in the littoral consortium … meaning they'd become part of a group that would *share* the Caspian Sea's oil revenues … they balked, thinking they'd be signing away their newfound monopoly on that oilfield. They must've felt pretty stupid when they found out later they'd been fightin' over a dry hole."

"No kidding. But things were going great in Karabakh when I left. Only thing I regret, all that effort on getting that sample was for nothing."

"No, not for nothing," P.R. countered. "We didn't know which way this was going to go. What if there *had* been oil in there?"

"Yeah … I knew that. I was just venting. It's just that, well, nobody will ever know … no one will ever appreciate why those men died."

There was a long pause, and P.R. said, "Well, this one's definitely below the radar. And unfortunately, it'll have to stay that way. But you did start something good over there. It wasn't for nothing. And don't think their loss doesn't eat away at me. All of them, including your friend Steve."

James gripped the wheel tightly with one hand and negotiated a curve in the highway. "Don't let it. At least we got ol' *Rog* out of there in one piece. As soon as he's back in business, I bet he'll be sending you a *case* of the best cigars he can get hold of."

"Another thing…that incident with our Reaper…it set off alarm bells all over Washington. It's like Sputnik all over again, except this time all eyes are on China."

"I just hope it's not too late…"

There was another, longer pause, and P.R. changed the subject. "James … I've got a job in Jakarta … a juicy one."

James sighed. "Like I said. Thanks, but no thanks. I'll take a pass."

P.R. continued, "But let me ask you this. And this is a serious question: Will you be happy being around people who have no clue what it's really all about? You said it yourself."

James had dreaded making this call, and for exactly this reason. Fighting to keep his voice level, he replied, "My ego doesn't need it … not anymore …. Everything I wanted from the job, I've already got."

Knowing that wouldn't be enough, he added, "It's taken a piece of my soul, P.R. I want my life back."

"All right … but—"

"Thanks my friend. I know where to find you."

* * *

P.R. hung up on his end and pulled a small object from his pocket. He had found new strength and inspiration in this item, because of a deep sense of connection with men like Sattar and Kasim, not to mention Rip and James, and Agaki. The course of the world turned on the actions of men like those.

He held the medal in his palm, noticing that it now shone, rubbed clean by the frequent movements of his fingers—the uncertain but hopeful and sometimes daring fidgeting of a simple man, who believed in his heart in being a patriot.

* * *

James set his phone on the dashboard and rolled the window down again to take in the fresh air coming off the nearby mountains. "No oil. Damn." He knew that from the debriefing, but to hear it again hurt as much as the first time. His thoughts drifted to Guns and Spidey, and to the porter, and his grip on the steering wheel tightened again when he remembered Steve Kranzer.

But at least we did avenge you, Steve. I did that much … I saw it to the finish.

He cruised along the last couple of miles of I-40 before his exit. He'd resisted putting on the cruise control, wanting to feel the rises and falls of the beautiful mountainous landscape as he abandoned the high speed, high risk, and high stakes of the spy business, and, above all, the killing. He felt good about his service to his country: a quiet thing, something he wouldn't discuss. In the months ahead, he would mix with ranchers and farmers, talk about things like seasonal changes and the price of feed … and they'd never have any idea or notion of his prior life.

And that was okay. His greatest reward was in his gut. At the end of the day, any day, the one and only person who knew was the only one who needed to know. Sure, he would remember. But the demons of the world no longer haunted him. He had dealt with them, and reconciled with them to a point where he found peace in his heart.

He'd left the Interstate now, and was glad to be on the smaller, slower road that led to his family's ranch. The townhouse in Virginia had become too cloying his first day back in it, and he was glad to put it on the market and move on.

The scenery near Raleigh gained familiarity. He thought about his parents, who were waiting for him, and Blackie, his favorite horse, and the trout pond, the secret one, and he wondered if it still was home to fishing worthy of legend. Most of all, he wondered if remnants of the magic of his youth still lingered there, waiting for him to scoop them up. Didn't matter if they weren't. He was going home.

It was all a waste. The thought came unbidden, and his stomach tightened again as he remembered P.R.'s words: "*But what if there had been oil in there?*"

Just as quickly, he reconciled the hurt with the good. *The people of Karabakh won out over tyranny, and we helped them. You and me, Kranzer. Just like we promised each other.*

His distant thoughts were again interrupted by a break in the music on the radio, and the top-of-the-hour newsbreak was announced. He reached out to turn up the volume. Another, slenderer hand beat him to the knob and turned the radio off.

"Whoa! You're gonna blind me with that fancy wedding ring, Mrs. Marshall." He reached up to the visor, retrieved his sunglasses and slid them on, then held up a hand, as if blocking the ring's brilliant reflections. "Don't think Kasim intended for you to use it to damage my eyes when he gave it to me."

Aria gave him a playful scolding look, and then looked thoughtfully at the ring, admiring the tiny diamonds flanking the two pear-shaped diamonds. "You're cut off," she said. "No more news for you. Just us … at least for a while." She spoke softly, with the warm smile he was seeing more often now.

"But I like the news."

"No more. It'll make you crazier than you already are. So yes, no more news."

"Just like that?"

She smiled again. "Just like that."

END

About the Author

Mike Green is a Naval Academy graduate and an MBA who enjoyed dual careers – one in commercial banking where he was involved in financing commercial enterprises, the other as a Naval Reserve Intelligence officer traveling the world. After three command tours and several operational assignments in the Middle East, Mike has delivered this first installment of a trilogy of spy novels that he refers to as *The Peacemaker Series*. He lives in Florida and is now hard at work on his second book.